A Cowboy Under
My Christmas Tree

JANET DAILEY

A Cowboy Under My Christmas Tree

KENSINGTON BOOKS
http://www.kensingtonbooks.com

A Cowboy Under My Christmas Tree

Chapter 1

The towering Colorado blue spruce stood straight and true, unshaken by the man working inside it. Fragrant needles scratched the strong line of Sam Bennett's jaw when he finally climbed down through the branches. He jumped the last few feet to the ground and walked clear of the group of trees he was helping to install for a holiday display.

The park that surrounded them didn't seem big enough to be called one. It was no more than a patch of green right in the middle of a busy New York street, more like a median strip than a park.

But it did have benches—two, painted dark green—and an official city sign that said PLEASE DON'T FEED THE PIGEONS. Undaunted, a gray and white bird waddled over, hoping for a handout.

Sam shook his head. "Sorry, pal. Read the sign." The pigeon gave him a beady-eyed look and fluttered a few steps away, puffing out its feathers against the cold and settling under a bench.

He unclipped the safety rope from his harness and draped the free end inside the temporary scaffolding around the tree installation. His hard hat came off next.

Sam shivered as the nippy wind ruffled his brown hair. Stepping back to look up at his tree, he felt a flash of pride.

The blue spruce held its own, even surrounded by glass skyscrapers and older buildings of brick and stone. He was glad to see it upright again. The tree had made the trip from Colorado on a flatbed trailer along with several others from his family's ranch.

Tyrell Bennett, Sam's dad, had planted all of them back in the day. They'd done the cutting with a measure of regret, but the deal had been too good to pass up. The New York company paid top dollar and covered out-of-state shipping costs for fine, tall trees like these.

Sam took a moment to brush needles and bits of bark from his broad shoulders, then bent down and did the same to his jeans, straightening to his full six foot two when someone shouted to him from inside a different tree.

"Hey, you going for coffee? Bring me an extra large."

Sam knew the voice. Greg Tsianakas was his boss on this temporary gig and also his friend.

They'd met in college ten years ago, both freshmen at the University of Colorado, but as different as two people could be at the age of eighteen. Sam had grown up on a sprawling ranch at the foot of the Rockies, fifty miles outside of a tiny town called Velde. Greg was a New York native, from Astoria, who'd returned there after graduating. He couldn't ski and he didn't know one end of a horse from another, but they'd been best buds all the same and stayed in touch ever since.

Sam had never been to Astoria, but he understood that it was a neighborhood in Queens, which was a borough of New York City, east of Manhattan and, for all he knew, west of the moon.

"Okay," Sam shouted back. He already knew Greg wanted a splash of milk and two sugars—the guys on the Christmas crew took turns fetching coffee. "Anyone else?"

No answer. The others probably couldn't hear him. He glanced out through the wrought iron fence that protected the park from the noisy traffic whizzing by on both sides.

Yellow taxicabs dominated among the cars and trucks. They seemed to travel in herds, like the buses, but now and then one broke away to pick up a passenger. A woman in a red coat was opening the back door of a taxi near the curb, putting several holiday-themed shopping bags on the backseat before she got in herself.

She barely had the door shut when the taxi drove away. Everything happened a lot faster here. But Sam was getting used to the pace.

The December day was clear and cold, with a biting wind that whistled through the branches of the trees above and stiffened his fingers inside his work gloves. Sam pulled them off before he tackled the buckles on the safety harness strapped around his lower body and removed it. He tucked the gloves into the hard hat, and put it and the harness in the area reserved for the rigging crew's gear.

Felt like a blue norther had slammed into New York. Sam picked up his Stetson and put it on before his head got cold, even though the coffee shop was right across the street. They sold muffins and bagels too, but not sandwiches. It was only eleven, but he was already thinking about a corned beef on rye.

Sam took a little more time to study the tree he'd been working on, the largest of the group and the only spruce. The distinctive silver blue of its needles made it stand out even more against the dark green of the others. He'd attached a few extra branches here and there to make his tree symmetrical on all sides. It looked good. He was close to done.

Stringing the lights was next, a painstaking task that would keep them up in the trees until nightfall tomorrow. He couldn't complain. Greg had crews all over the boroughs doing seasonal work. Some of the installations were for the city and some were for businesses. December was Greg's busiest month and the pay was great.

Sam was never inclined to turn down work in winter. The dry years out West had caught up with everyone in their part of Colorado. The cattle the Bennetts had been able to keep were eating costly bought hay—the price of feed had gone through the roof. Speaking of that, the Bennett barn needed a new one. Maybe next spring.

He and his brother Zach had both taken seasonal jobs this December, leaving their parents to run the ranch. They hadn't expected to end up on opposite sides of the country, with Zach in Oregon and Sam in New York. But their younger sister Annie had stayed in Colorado. His folks would manage, even though money was tight. They had everything they needed on the ranch.

Here in New York, everything was expensive and hotels were astronomical. Sam had lucked into a relatively cheap sublet right up the street from the Christmas tree lot, but he wasn't living there yet. The tenant was a cruise ship performer who would be leaving for Bermuda in four or five days.

In the meantime, Sam was staying with Greg's uncle rent free in exchange for helping the old man with whatever needed doing until New Year's Eve. He didn't plan to blow his earnings, either.

There were a lot of great things to do in the city that didn't cost much or were even free: the electronic dazzle of Times Square, the skating rink at Rockefeller Center right under the famous tree, the panoramic view of New York harbor and the Manhattan skyline from the Brooklyn Bridge—he had a list.

His bank account would be in good shape when he got back to Colorado.

"What are you waiting for?" Twenty feet up in a dark

green pine, Greg pushed aside the branches that concealed him. His black hair was held back by a bandanna tied under his hard hat and his gaze had an annoyed spark. "Go, already. I'm freezing up here."

"Okay, okay." Sam laughed. He dug in the pocket of his flannel-lined denim jacket for regular gloves, pulling them on as he waited for a chance to cross the street, his breath lingering in the cold air.

A red light stopped the oncoming traffic, and he was on the other side in a few strides.

He entered the coffee shop and returned the counter-man's greeting, ordering quickly but happy to wait where it was warm. He paid and left the change in the tip jar before he exited with a lidded take-out cup in each hand.

When he recrossed the street, Greg was waiting for him behind the fence, down from his tree.

"Thanks, man."

"No problem," Sam said, handing him one of the cups. "And it's on me."

His buddy popped the lid and blew on the coffee to cool it. "I owe ya." He looked up at Sam's blue spruce. "That is one hell of a gorgeous tree. The city got a bargain."

"Glad you think so."

Greg took a big sip. "Looks like you're done."

"Almost. That part over there needs a few more branches."

Greg looked to where Sam was pointing. "Yeah, you're right. None left, though, not in that color. But the parks guy is coming by with more."

"Fine with me." Sam grinned. "I was thinking of grabbing an early lunch anyway."

"Try the sandwich place two blocks up. They make 'em thick. Half is a meal."

"I can eat a whole one," Sam vowed.

Greg laughed and went back to his tree, studying it from several angles.

Sam finished his coffee, turning his collar up against the wind. Then he crumpled the cup and tossed it into a wire-mesh can that looked like it had lost a few battles with a garbage truck. He was one step ahead of the changing light as he crossed in the opposite direction, glancing downtown at the tall buildings looming over the sidewalks. The cold sun glittered off steel and glass, shooting rays through unexpected openings. Whoever had coined the phrase "the canyons of Manhattan" knew what they were talking about.

He spotted the new awning over the sandwich shop from the corner, walking fast to get there, wishing he had a scarf. The door was trimmed with bright tinsel and a bright-eyed paper elf advertising the special: *Sandwich and soda! Six bucks!*

A deli case loaded with cold cuts and a whole roast turkey got his full attention. Sam ordered from a man in a white cap, who lifted the slab of corned beef and took it to a slicer.

"Pickle or coleslaw? For here or to go?" he asked as he sliced and expertly assembled the sandwich.

"Neither. For here. Thanks." Sam had his eye on a spot at a high counter in front of the window. Perfect for people-watching.

"That's some hat." The counterman admired it as he worked. "Where ya from? That is, if ya don't mind my asking," he added. "Ya have an accent."

Sam had fielded the question before. New Yorkers seemed to think other people talked funny.

"Colorado."

"That's far," the counterman said.

Sam nodded. "Eighteen hundred miles."

"Ya miss the wild west?"

"I haven't been here long enough." Sam laughed.

In less than a minute, the man in the white cap slid over an enormous sandwich speared with frilly toothpicks and garnished with packets of mustard. Sam took the plate to the cashier and added a can of soda from a cooler by the register. He grabbed a couple of napkins and headed to the window seat where he could watch the world go by, putting his Stetson by him on the counter.

Entertained by the amazing variety of people on the street in front of him, he ate slowly, enjoying the flavorful corned beef. No one looked at him. He polished off the entire sandwich before he popped the tab on the soda and took a sip.

The flow of pedestrians thinned out for a few minutes, and he looked idly at the stores across the street, focusing on an expensive-looking boutique. Its display windows were covered by large shades printed with hats and dresses and shoes.

Sam squinted. A handwritten placard that he couldn't read from this distance had been taped to the outside of the glass. He glanced up when a neon sign over the entrance blinked on, spelling out a single word.

NOW.

If that was the name of the boutique, he'd never heard of it. But then he knew zip about fashion. However, he needed to pick up a gift for his younger sister, who did. The wilder, the better—she would love something from a New York store. Annie always went for something short, tight, and bright, he knew that much. She lived in Vail, went to a lot of parties. If the boutique sold anything that wasn't black, he was in luck.

Sam looked at his watch. Not even twelve. He had time to take a look, if they were open. The door was ajar. The sign kept blinking.

NOW. NOW. NOW.

He knew a hint from the universe when he saw one.

Sam left the sandwich shop and waited at the intersection, watching a college kid in skinny jeans and skateboarder sneakers come out of the boutique and wait on the sidewalk. A lumber company van screeched to a halt and double-parked. The driver stayed at the wheel, pressing a button to unlatch the sliding side door.

Awkwardly, as if he'd never picked up anything heavier than a pencil in his life, the kid hoisted long two-by-fours out of the van and settled them onto his shoulder. He turned around, whacking the taped placard off the window as he carried the lumber into the boutique, by some miracle not doing any more damage.

The light changed and Sam crossed, well behind several people who hadn't waited. Jaywalking seemed to be a very popular New York sport.

When he was in front of the boutique, he picked up the placard and read it. *Please come in and don't mind the sawdust . . . Now is getting ready for Christmas!*

Sam heard the familiar whine of a circular saw and caught a pleasant whiff of just-cut wood. He was curious about the carpentry in progress behind the shades but somewhat hesitant, now that he was there, about actually going in and buying something.

He didn't know Annie's exact size and she wouldn't be able to return something that didn't fit. Back home, he knew every clerk at the few-and-far-between stores in his thinly populated rural county and some who worked at the malls closer to the larger towns and Denver. And it seemed like they all knew his sister.

Gruff voices came from one of the covered windows, and he looked over at it, noticing that the printed shade hadn't been drawn down all the way. The shade itself was a giant version of the roller type that snapped up—a plastic ring dangled from it, resting on the floor. He could see workboots coming and going in the gap at the bottom.

They didn't have much room to move around, and the

job wasn't going well. Their low comments made that clear enough.

Then a woman's voice with a sultry note to it intervened. She was probably the owner of the boutique, since she seemed to be giving the orders, though she wasn't barking them out.

Sam glanced at the placard he held, wondering if he should bring it inside. It was a plausible excuse for a quick look around. He could hand it over and leave if he didn't spot anything he thought Annie would like.

Then the skateboarder sneakers came over to the window and stepped on the ring, drawing the shade taut to the floor.

Sam smiled to himself. He didn't think the kid meant to be so clumsy, but he had a feeling a minor disaster was imminent.

He heard the female voice say something. The sneaker lifted as the kid took a step.

The roller shade flew up.

Both sneakers were suddenly airborne. There was a loud thump, then a groan.

Sam saw four guys in the background of the window recess, putting down tools to go to the kid, who was getting up off the floor, red in the face. Then the owner of the female voice walked right in front of the window without looking out.

Wow.

Sam was riveted to the sidewalk.

He couldn't help but stare. Glossy, very dark hair was pulled back from her face in a practical ponytail that did something wonderful for her delicate features and full lips. Her arms were akimbo, hands on her hips.

Twenty-five, twenty-six. Around there. Younger than he was but not by much. Sam took in what she was wearing.

On top, a plain shirt, sleeves rolled up. Beneath that were not-exactly-baggy shorts over dark tights.

Nice curves. Amazing legs.

Her ribbed socks rolled down into small-size workboots. A narrow leather pouch on her belt held a multiuse tool, the real kind. He had one just like it.

He looked up again. Without thinking, he tipped the brim of the Stetson to her. She seemed puzzled by the gesture.

Sam gazed into her eyes.

They were hazel, flecked with chocolate, framed by dark, thick lashes. Her finely arched brows drew together. She glared at him.

He ventured a smile.

With a swift downward motion, she yanked the ring and covered the window again.

It seemed unfair. After all, he hadn't made the shade fly up. But obviously she had work to do, someone on her crew had just taken a spill, and she didn't like being gawked at.

Sam heard the people inside the window move around. Someone bumped against it, and the shade flew up again.

This time she was nowhere in sight. Disappointed, he glanced at the framework under construction in the confined space, not able to figure out what it was going to be. The carpenters ignored him.

The college kid was climbing a ladder positioned between the framework and a hanging backdrop painted with a snow scene that hung from a rod.

Sam shook his head. One sneaker had come untied.

Three steps up, he tripped on the shoelace and fell sideways off the ladder, clutching wildly at the paper backdrop. The light dowel it hung from detached from the rigging, and the torn backdrop rippled down over his head as he thudded to the floor. A stream of swear words issued from under the paper as the kid fought free.

The woman in shorts scrambled back into the window space and tried to help the kid before one of the burly guys intervened to lift him. An elderly lady stopped to see what Sam was looking at.

"Oh, my," she said in a reedy voice, peering through the glass. "I think that poor boy sprained his ankle, don't you? He can't put his weight on it."

"Ah—I really don't know, ma'am."

Sam moved to one side, not wanting to get caught staring a second time, and the elderly lady moved on.

A few minutes later, the burly carpenter assisted the kid out the door, holding onto the skinny arm around his shoulders. "Take it easy, Josh. Go slow," the man advised.

The kid leaned on him and hopped on one foot. They made it to the curb, where Josh looked anxiously at the oncoming traffic.

"Close enough. Mom oughta be here soon," he muttered, then cursed loudly. "I never knew a sprain could hurt so much."

"Get an X-ray," the carpenter advised.

Josh nodded, then winced in pain. "Just my luck. Nicole was nice enough to hire me and now this."

Sam made a mental note of the name, assuming that it belonged to the dark-haired goddess in shorts and workboots. The kid cursed again, distracting him.

"The ladder went over just like that," he groaned. "Now you guys are gonna be shorthanded."

"I think we can manage without you," the carpenter said dryly. A car pulled over and honked. "That your mom?"

"Yeah."

The two of them walked and hopped, respectively, off the curb as a motherly woman got out and opened the passenger side door, fussing over her son until he was settled and they drove away.

The burly carpenter went back into the boutique. The door was still open. Sam looked at his watch. He still had time.

Inside, a discussion quickly escalated into an argument when another female voice took over, shrill and tense. He caught some of it.

Four-week selling season. No time to waste. She could be sued. Whose idea was it to hire an inexperienced kid? And so on.

That had to be the boutique owner. She could be the woman Josh had mentioned, but Sam doubted it. She didn't sound nice enough to hire an inexperienced kid, for one thing. He could hear the one he thought was Nicole reply when she could get a word in, and the deeper voices of the men.

He got the gist of the argument and picked up a few additional details. Nicole was an independent contractor, and she paid her men out of her own pocket. The Christmas job would go to another crew if they couldn't get it done by Saturday. She needed all-around help, someone who could fix or rig just about anything.

That would be me, he thought.

A few seconds later, a very thin woman wrapped up in a ruffled thing stormed out, pulling a monogrammed suitcase behind her.

He checked. No letter N. Definitely not Nicole.

Her high heels clicked on the pavement as she blasted past Sam without seeing him, teetering on the curb and waving.

"Taxi!" she screamed, attracting a few stares. "Taxi!"

One swerved in her direction, ignoring the honks of other cars, and pulled up.

She jammed the handle of the rolling suitcase down and jerked the door open, slamming it shut when she and the suitcase were squared away.

"JFK," he heard her snap at the driver. "Get going. I have a flight to catch."

Off they went. Sam breathed in relief.

He saw movement in the boutique window again out of the corner of his eye and knew Nicole was back on the job by the sound of her voice and the indistinct replies from the crew.

There had to be something he could do. He thought it over. He only needed a couple more hours to attach the remaining branches to his tree, and another day, tops, to get the lights on. Greg had said there would be more work, but he hadn't been specific. No reason Sam couldn't take on a one-day gig after the tree installation was completed.

Sam flipped over the placard in his hand and took a pen from the inside pocket of his jacket. He jotted down a question on the blank side, then walked in front of the window.

It took a few seconds to catch Nicole's eye—she was close to the glass but studying what they had built so far, her back to Sam. One of the carpenters pointed his way and she turned around, exasperation in her beautiful hazel eyes.

He held up the placard before she could yank down the shade again. Nothing ventured, nothing gained. She read the scribbled question.

Help Wanted?

Nicole looked him over. Sam had the feeling she was measuring the size of his shoulders. He squared them and stood tall, smiling at her.

She frowned.

What was he thinking? Sam set the placard on the sidewalk and reached for his wallet. He pulled out his Colorado driver's license and the folded letter that confirmed his employment for seasonal work in New York, signed by Greg and stamped by a municipal official. He unfolded it and spread out his fingers to hold up the license and the letter against the window.

She looked around at her crew and back at him. She peered at his ID and read the letter. Slowly. Then she gestured to the burly man who'd helped Josh into his mother's car. He came over and checked everything a second time, then tapped the letter from his side of the glass.

"I know Greg really well. Did a job with him two weeks ago, in fact," Sam heard him say. "He has a crew rigging the Christmas display in that pocket park down the street."

"I'm working with them today—I mean, we're almost done. I'm on lunch break," Sam said.

The carpenter glanced at him, then exchanged a look with Nicole. "If you want, I can have Greg vouch for this guy right now."

She hesitated for a second, then nodded. The carpenter took a cell phone out of his pocket.

"Thanks," Sam said, making sure his voice was loud enough to be heard through the glass. "And hey, ask Greg if he wants me to bring back a sandwich."

Nicole gestured to him to come inside.

Not quite believing his good luck, Sam went in through the open door. The boutique was open for business. A chatty salesclerk was ringing up a customer to his left. He caught a glimpse of himself in a counter mirror and took off his Stetson. Sam quickly ran a hand over his hair. It wouldn't cooperate.

He sighed and turned right. The burly guy put his cell phone in his shirt pocket as Nicole jumped down out of the window.

"Hi," she said, looking Sam over again as she dusted off her hands. "I'm Nicole Young, he's Bob Eady." She pointed to the other three men. "Keith. Russ. Hank."

No last names for those three. Probably hired for the day, Sam thought. There were nods of acknowledgment.

"I'm Sam Bennett," he said to one and all, but his gaze stayed on Nicole.

Bob got right to the point. "We need to finish this job by Saturday—can you sign on?"

"Not a problem," Sam replied. "Only for a day, right?"

Bob nodded. "Greg says you know your stuff and he says he can spare you by the day after tomorrow. And he wants you to call him about the sandwich," he added.

"Yes to everything," Sam said, wondering if that was why his boss had been so cooperative.

Nicole reached for a rolled-up sheet of graph paper and handed it to him. "Here ya go." She sighed. "Josh's copy of my design with all the specs. Study it. See you Friday."

She turned and stepped back up into the window, crumpling up the ruined backdrop and stuffing it into a garbage bag.

"You're the designer?" Sam asked. "Not the lady in ruffles?" He realized his mistake when Nicole shot him an annoyed look and added quickly, "Just making sure."

"That's Darci Powers. She owns the boutique. You won't have to deal with her. Besides, she's on her way to Aspen for a week."

One of the guys muttered in gratitude.

"Oh," Sam replied. "Nice place to be this time of year."

"Is it? I wouldn't know. Anyway, to answer your question, I am most definitely the designer—and the crew boss," Nicole said briskly. "You're working for me and I pay cash. A hundred dollars a day."

"Okay. Great." He hoped he didn't sound ridiculously eager. Not about the money—about working with her, for her. Now that was something to get excited about.

Nicole picked up the fallen dowel and ran a hand over it. "Shoot. This is cracked." She snapped it over her thigh and tossed the halves into a corner. "Westside Lumber won't deliver an order under fifty bucks. Keith, take the A train down to Canal Street and get two more dowels, same length. And pick up more backdrop paper at Pearl Paint while you're there."

Sam absorbed the information. It was going to be interesting to work a job where materials arrived via subway.

Hank and Russ joined her in the window and tested the frame thing while Nicole maneuvered underneath it to look for other cracks. Bob, the biggest man on the crew, went up next, while Sam watched, trying to figure out how they all stayed out of each other's way.

Nicole crawled out from under the frame on hands and knees. "Have you ever worked in a store window?" she asked him.

"Um, no."

"It helps to be flexible." She smiled at him for the first time as she sat back on her haunches.

What a smile. One dimple. Almost perfect teeth. He was dazzled.

"I'll do my best," Sam replied. "Greg hired me as a rigger, but I've done just about every kind of carpentry there is. I grew up on a ranch. I don't suppose you have any fences that need mending."

She shot him a baffled look that eased into a smile. "No."

He wanted to say something funny, keep her smiling, but she was looking back at one of the guys, who asked her a question. She twisted her lithe body around to show them how she wanted the framework positioned.

Looking at her, the last thing he wanted to do was leave, but Sam realized that he had to get back.

"Hey, thanks again for the job," he said when she returned her attention to him. He held up the rolled graph paper. "And this. I'll look at it tonight, but I have to get back to the park. See you soon."

"Not so fast." Nicole took her cell phone out of her shorts pocket. "Give me your number."

He rattled it off and watched her enter it. *Tap tap tap.* She had pretty hands.

"Got it," she said, and smiled again.

What with one thing and another, Sam and the rest of the crew stayed at the little park until long after sunset. Greg hung caged lightbulbs from the scaffolding so they could get a jump on installing the twinklers. The guys ran power cords up the trunks of the trees, saving the detail work for tomorrow.

It would take hours to get lights on every branch and twig. But the result would be worth it. Sam enjoyed watching rosy-cheeked kids peer up into the trees and ask their moms and dads and babysitters what was going on. In his lofty perch he was as good as invisible.

Greg called a halt and got everyone down on the ground. Sam pulled off work gloves that were sticky with resin. He would have to buy a new pair tomorrow. One after another, all five of the guys slung their gear into a big yellow locker, too weary to tell jokes. Greg shot the bolt and padlocked the hasp.

"Good work," he told the crew. "Early start tomorrow. Seven a.m."

There was a chorus of groans.

"Like I care, ladies. Go home and get your beauty sleep." Greg herded them outside the wrought iron fence and padlocked that too. The men headed off to the subway and buses.

Greg tipped his Yankees ball cap to Sam. "Give Uncle Theo my regards."

"Will do."

Sam was grateful that his temporary accommodations

weren't far away. He liked the subway, but there was no point in riding it when the walk home was only about ten blocks.

He headed south, glancing in a few shop windows along the way but not stopping anywhere. The street he walked down was in an older area, with funky neon signs from decades ago and newer, vinyl awnings over small store-fronts. The colorful fruit and vegetable stands that also sold flowers brightened up venerable facades of red brick.

There were touches of Christmas everywhere he looked. Shimmering garlands decked apartment building doors—hung on the inside of locked glass doors, of course, where they wouldn't get swiped. This *was* New York.

The fire escapes that formed zigzags on the older build-ings were draped with outdoor lights here and there. Some people added illuminated figures that weren't any different from the ones decorating Colorado ranch yards and lawns in the small towns and suburbs. Reindeer. Carolers. An-gels, glowing white.

Outside the small grocery stores, live miniature pines in pots wrapped with crimson foil stood in rows next to flo-ral Santas made from red and white carnations. He'd al-ready bought one of each to decorate his sleeping quarters. Sam couldn't wait to hit the sack.

The following day, they were up in the trees until late in the afternoon. But yesterday's head start and Greg's en-couragement helped them finish by five.

Weary but feeling pretty good otherwise, Sam waited with the other three riggers to hand his gear to Greg to stow in the open locker. Dusk had fallen and the trees sparkled brightly above the end-of-the-day rush, adorned with thousands of tiny lights, down to the smallest twig. The men had drawn straws for the flip of the switch, and the honor had gone to Sam a half hour ago.

He'd waited until he saw plenty of children on the sidewalks on the other side of the street.

The riggers cheered, but it was the oohs and ahs and bright eyes on the kids that really did it for Sam.

After that, it seemed only right to be last in line to sign out and go on home. He watched Greg get the locker in order and padlock it, ready to be picked up by a city truck for some other job.

His cell phone rang in his pocket. He could barely feel the vibration above the constant humming of the city itself, from the subway trains underground to the buzz of signs and streetlights. Sam reached for it, not recognizing the number on the screen. Area code 212.

Excellent. That meant Manhattan. Could be Nicole. He answered the call, keeping the phone very close to his ear.

"Hello?"

"Hey, Sam. This is Nicole."

"Nice to hear from you." More than nice. He now had her cell number in his memory chip. "What's up?"

"I was wondering if you had a chance to look at the design yet."

"No. We just swung down out of the trees."

Greg shot him a quizzical look. "Say what, Tarzan? Who are you talking to?"

Sam put a palm over the phone. "Shut up."

He put the phone back to his ear to hear Nicole's laugh.

"Um, I was thinking—do you want to meet me at The Auld Alehouse in about an hour?" she asked.

He hadn't been expecting that.

"It's a bar, not too far from the park where you are," she explained. "They have booths and pretty good burgers. We could, you know, eat."

She sounded as nervous as he felt. Sam was surprised.

"Sure. I'll bring the design—um, I have to go get it.

And, uh, take a shower and change. How about an hour and a half?"

"That works for me," she chirped. "See you there."

Sam knew he had a goofy grin on his face when he said good-bye, even before Greg started laughing at him.

"You wouldn't happen to know where The Auld Alehouse is, would you? She wants to meet me there."

"Five blocks north of here. You can't miss it." Greg slapped Sam on the back. "Who is she? Where'd you meet her?"

"Her name is Nicole. She's designing the holiday windows at Now. It's a boutique. I was going to—"

"Aha. And I thought it was Bob Eady who wanted to hire you. You're too much, man. First time in New York and you got here, what, five days ago?"

"Seven."

"And you have a girlfriend. What's your ancient Chinese secret? I want to know."

"Huh?"

"I'm kidding. That's an ad for something. I forget what. Maybe a love potion." Greg walked with him to the gate, locking it.

"Oh. Well, Nicole's not my girlfriend. She's my boss."

"I see."

They crossed the street, fast, jaywalking.

Chapter 2

Without his seeing her, Nicole watched Sam Bennett enter the alehouse. So did several other women.

Their interest was understandable. He wasn't faking the well-worn denim or the Stetson. The moment she'd seen him for the first time through the shop window and he'd tipped it to her, she'd had the immediate feeling that he was a good guy.

If she happened to encounter any desperadoes, she was in luck. Sam definitely had that direct gaze and Western walk—slow and easy, with a touch of cowboy swagger. And his height and muscular strength made for a potent combination that really got noticed in New York. He just had a look you didn't see too often in a big city. That I-drank-my-milk-and-grew-up-tall-and-strong look.

The hostess was awfully friendly to him until he mentioned that he was meeting someone, and she pointed to the back booth. She brought him to Nicole, gave her a thin smile, snapped down two laminated menus, and stalked away.

"Hi," Nicole said happily. "You found the place, I see."

He set the rolled-up design on the table. "Greg gave me directions. On my own, it might not have been so easy."

"Oh, pshaw."

He laughed and slid into the opposite side of the booth, taking off the wide-brimmed hat. "Pshaw? Can you spell that for me?"

His skin glowed, freshly shaved, his strong cheekbones ruddy from the cold night air. His brown hair was a bit darker from the shower. He slid out of the lined denim jacket she remembered him in, tugging at the cuffs of a different shirt with nice, neat fold marks down its front and sleeves. She wondered who'd done the folding and hoped it had been laundry ladies.

Sam settled back against the maroon vinyl and folded his arms, giving her a shy grin. Yowza. Those were arms that could—he's going to be working for you, she reminded herself.

Showered or not, there was still a faint whiff of pine about him that she really liked. So outdoorsy. He smelled like clean, lightly chilled man—more intoxicating than chilled champagne, in her opinion.

He unfolded his arms and rubbed his big hands as if they were still cold, looking around the bar.

She took the chance to look at him, jumping a bit when he turned his attention back to her. Nicole realized he was waiting for an answer to a question he seemed to have asked a week ago.

"Pshaw," she repeated thoughtfully. "Um, I'm not sure how it's spelled. My grandma used to say it just to be funny. Want me to call her and ask?"

Sam shook his head. "No, that's okay. Does she live in New York?"

"Yes. In Skaneateles."

Sam seemed puzzled. "Is that anywhere near Astoria?"

"No," she laughed. "It's upstate."

"Did you grow up there?"

"Nope. In Manhattan, believe it or not."

Sometimes people from out of town seemed to think

that no one in their right mind would raise kids in the city. He seemed fine with it. "Ah," he said. "You're a native, like Greg. He knows everything about New York City. I'd bet anything he had a subway map printed on his baby blanket."

Nicole was charmed. Sam had a sense of humor in addition to being great-looking. The crinkles around his smoky blue eyes were getting to her. "That's a good idea. Mind if I steal it?"

"Not at all," Sam said. "Do you design baby blankets too?"

"Not yet."

Nicole had to smile. Five more minutes and he might just ask her to marry him. She kept the wry but interesting notion to herself. At least a Western man could mention the word "baby" without getting nervous.

There was no faster way to scare a New York man than to say that loaded word. Not that she was even thinking about a commitment or marriage at this point in her life, let alone a baby. But the last date she'd been on with a New York guy, he had been so absorbed in criticizing the fancy offerings on the menu, he hadn't even noticed when she bailed on him. Nicole remembered that had been the last date she'd been on, period.

She looked at Sam. He'd only been making conversation. And this wasn't a date. "So," she said casually. "Tell me about your other job."

He filled her in on his long-standing friendship with Greg, and the deal for the trees, and a few particulars about the installation. "You should walk down from Now and check out the trees," he added. "They look great, especially at night."

"Will do. That's so cool that one of them came from your ranch. Where in Colorado are you from exactly?"

She knew where Denver was, and that was it.

"Near the Front Range."

Nicole had not one clue as to where or what that was. He picked up on her momentary confusion.

"As in the front of the Rocky Mountains, northwest of Colorado Springs, give or take fifty miles. I grew up on a ranch, not too far from Velde—well, you wouldn't know it. Nice little town. Quiet." He took out his phone and tapped at it, then handed it to her. "I took this picture the day before I left. That's the main street right around rush hour."

Nicole studied the small screen and smiled. Not a single car. There were a few trucks parked in front of Victorian-era buildings with brick or clapboard facades and a few people out walking. Men with cowboy hats and jackets like Sam's. Women in shearling or knits and jeans.

She used the zoom function to look at the details and read the old-timey signs. Grizzly Bar & Grill. Albert's Mercantile. Jelly Jam's Pie and Cakes. Even though the photo had been taken at the end of the day, the shops looked freshly painted and prosperous, the windows bright and cheerful against the deep purple shadows of twilight.

"Can you e-mail this to me?" she asked. "I'd like to add it to my idea folder. It's a really nice image."

She raised her voice enough to be heard.

"Sure."

The alehouse had gotten noisy, packed with people now, talking a mile a minute into cell phones and occasionally to each other over the clatter of plates and commotion in the kitchen. The portholed doors swung open repeatedly as orders were brought out on trays. A passing waiter accidentally kicked the side of the huge tote she'd stashed under the table.

"Sorry," he said over his shoulder, rushing away.

"Not a problem. My fault," Nicole replied to the air.

She set down the phone to pull the tote to safety on the empty part of the booth.

"What's in the bag?" Sam asked.

"Art supplies and craft stuff and some things I found. I'm going to sort it all out once I get home."

The hubbub increased. Outside a fire engine wailed and honked its way through the traffic. Usually the city's racket didn't bother her, but right now she found it irritating. She picked up the phone again, thinking how nice it would be to visit a place like Velde right now. It looked so peaceful, nestled inside drifts of pure white snow.

"There's more where that came from. Scroll through the gallery."

Nicole did, looking intently at each one. "I've never been to Colorado. Everything looks like a postcard."

Sam nodded in agreement. "I couldn't imagine living anywhere else."

Nicole's expression turned a little wistful. "Must be nice to feel that way." She stopped on a photo of a white ranch house set behind a split-rail fence in the foreground. Flowers bloomed in front of the fence and lined the winding drive. The house nestled in the center of the surrounding land, which rolled in green waves to the mountains in the distance. She looked again and noticed other structures, half hidden by the dips in the terrain.

"Is this your ranch? Must be summer." She turned the phone so he could see the screen again. "How big is it?"

"About a thousand acres." Sam straightened in his seat and leaned forward to point out things. "That's the main house, and over there is the corral and the horse barn. The pastures are in back."

"Is that a bunkhouse?"

"That's right. Used to be a bigger operation. We had a couple of hands living on the place and cowboys coming in for roundups. Then my folks had to sell off some land and a lot of the cattle when the price of beef dropped—we're wintering over about a hundred head now."

Nicole blinked. Her beef came prepackaged and wrapped in plastic. She'd never really thought about where it came from.

"Anyway, my brother Zach and I took over the bunkhouse and fixed it up last year. He has his side, and I have mine. Works out fine."

His lighthearted tone told Nicole a lot. "You're lucky. I'm an only child. I always wanted a sister."

"I have one of those too," he informed her.

"Younger or older?"

"Younger. She got away with everything, unlike me and Zach." He chuckled.

"I heard that can happen." Nicole laughed.

"Well, it all worked out. Family is everything."

She was touched. "I know what you mean."

"Us Bennetts stick together, and we do all right. Most years we don't have to buy much."

He folded his hands on the table—rugged hands, with strong, calloused fingers. Intuitively, Nicole understood what he seemed disinclined to explain.

"But a ranch is hard work, no matter what," Sam went on. "My dad always said you have to be born to it."

"Sounds like you love it." Nicole couldn't help saying it. The conversation had taken an unexpectedly personal turn.

"It's what I know and who I am," he said simply.

She scrolled back to the first photo of Velde, noticing the background this time. Behind the single street rose a tree-clad slope, a dark, looming mass parted by a wide snow trail.

Nicole squinted to make sure she wasn't seeing things. "Is that a ski run? Right at the end of Main Street?"

"Yup. Not the biggest or the best, but I learned to ski there. So did Annie and Zach."

He took the phone back and touched the screen to pull up a photo of a laughing girl in ski wear, goggles pushed up on her head, her dark hair whipped by the wind. "That's her," he said proudly.

"What does she do?"

"She's a ski instructor in Vail."

"I'm impressed." Nicole laughed. "My downhill racing experience is pretty limited. I did set a speed record once, in a cardboard box on a slope in Central Park. I think I was five."

"Good for you. Gotta start somewhere." His smile warmed her.

"I think Colorado is a better bet for winter sports," she replied honestly.

He nodded in agreement. "Haven't seen any snow in New York yet. How much do you get here?"

"Depends. Sometimes we only get a few inches total for the whole winter. But they're predicting a lot of snow this year."

Sam raised his eyebrows. "Now that would be a sight to see."

Nicole sighed. "I wouldn't mind, so long as I can complete all my jobs and get paid. A really good snowstorm can shut down the city for a whole day."

He chuckled. "Only a day? The roads can close for a week or two out where we are. Sometimes more. But if you're prepared, you manage. Out our way, we all help each other."

"That's great." For a second or so, Nicole imagined herself out on the range, or wherever his ranch was, hanging out with Annie and his mom and dad and golden retriever.

Wait. Wrong dog, she told herself. Cowboys had—what was the name of that breed?—it came to her. Blue heelers.

If he had one, she'd bet anything the dog followed him everywhere.

She realized the waitress was impatiently looking their way and picked up the menu.

"I'm starving," she announced. "Let's order."

"Me too. Good idea."

The waitress came over before either of them even signaled and took their order for two cheddar burgers, then disappeared.

Sam's hand moved toward the design he'd set on the table, but Nicole stopped him before he could unroll it.

"Thanks for bringing it," she said, "but I thought up a new design. Bob and the guys are jigsawing it at his workshop tonight."

He acknowledged the update with a smile. "That was fast."

"Gotta get it done. By the way, I forgot to ask if you can do more than basic carpentry."

"Some. Although I'm no expert," Sam admitted. "I picked up what I know from my dad. He restored the interior of our ranch house, got it back to how it looked at the turn of the century."

"That's amazing."

Sam nodded. "The original house made it through more than a hundred Colorado winters. Built to last."

So are you, Nicole thought. He was leaning back in his chair, his arms folded over his broad chest. She liked the thoughtfulness in his tone and the warmth in his dark blue eyes.

"It was like going back in time when he was done," Sam said. "Huge beams, log walls. He uncovered the original fireplace too—native rock."

"Wow," Nicole said, distracted again. "I can just imagine it." A roaring fire, going strong. Sam, getting comfortable on a long cowhide sofa in front of it. The alehouse seemed a lot warmer all of a sudden.

Sam nodded. "Once the snow's up to the eaves and the back roads get blocked, a cord of wood goes pretty fast."

"I bet. There are some Manhattan apartments with fire-places—not mine, though. I live in a fifth-floor walk-up. But I probably wouldn't use it much even if I had one. I get so busy this time of year." Nicole shook her head. "Holidays in the city are just crazy."

More customers had come in, waiting in line, taking off coats and craning their necks to see if there were any open tables. Some headed for the bar. Piped-in music began to play over the din.

"That's New York, I guess." He smiled. "I have to say I'm enjoying it so far."

Nicole was glad to hear it. "You mean you don't miss Colorado snow?" she teased.

"Nope. Not yet."

"Well, if we get any, Manhattan streets usually get plowed pretty quickly. Around here snow isn't what you would call scenic after the first day. So, um, how long are you staying?" Nicole meant the question to sound businesslike, but she wasn't sure it did.

"Until New Year's."

She wanted to ask him who'd put him up, but she couldn't bring herself to be so nosy. The thought that he would be leaving in less than a month was unsettling. It wasn't like she could hire him for the next job, not when her goal was to join the staff of a large store—

Sam tapped on the table to get her attention.

"Hey, that reminds me—you ever go to Times Square on the big night and watch the ball drop?"

"No. It's too crowded and I'm too short to see any-thing." She couldn't help looking at his big shoulders. He was more than strong enough to carry her on them. Nicole imagined ringing in a brand-new year with Sam Bennett instead of sitting at home in her bathrobe watching the revelry on TV with her cat. Whiskeroo just was not a party animal.

"If you change your mind—" Sam ventured.

"Thanks, but I doubt it," she said quickly. They would probably have a great time. And he'd be gone the very next day. Not how she wanted to start the new year. She reminded herself once more that he was going to be working for her. And that she didn't date out of state.

"Then I guess I'll go alone."

There was a pause. Nicole suppressed a smile. "You'll have a blast. It's New York's biggest party. Now, getting back to the new design—"

He was suddenly all business. "Right. I had a question about that. Don't you have to get approval before we start?"

Nicole shrugged. "After I did the windows for Now last Christmas, Darci doubled her sales. I can always scan the drawings and e-mail them to her."

"Okay."

He didn't add anything to that one quiet word, but she felt compelled to ask if he'd witnessed Darci's tantrum. "Were you outside when she stormed out?"

"Yes. I was hoping she wasn't you. I mean, I knew there was a Nicole inside, but I hadn't quite figured out who was who."

"Aha. How long were you lurking outside the window?"

He knew she was teasing him, and he grinned at her. "Not very long. I was having a sandwich at the place across the street and I saw the shop and thought I'd pick up a gift."

Now sold only clothes and accessories, in sizes and styles

that targeted a young, female demographic with outrageous taste. Nicole debated whether to ask whom he had been shopping for, though by now she could guess.

He took the initiative. "For my younger sister, Annie. In case you were wondering."

"Of course not." Nicole beamed at him. "But I can help you out with that. Darci gives me a ten percent discount."

Sam seemed a little puzzled. "Even when she's mad at you?"

Nicole waved his concern away. "She's always mad at someone. We happened to be in the line of fire that day."

"Oh. Say, how's the kid who fell? I forgot to ask."

"Josh is better," she said. "Nothing broke. But he did sprain his ankle."

"Bummer. Especially before Christmas."

Nicole nodded. "I paid him anyway. Falling off ladders is one of the hazards of the profession, unfortunately. Window dressers work practically around the clock during December. You get so tired, things like that just happen, and you keep right on going."

She didn't add that Josh got plenty of sleep on his mom's couch no matter what, according to her mother, who knew his mother from back in their sandbox days. It had been Nicole's decision to give him a chance.

"How long have you been a window designer?"

Nicole thought back. "Since my last year at the School of Visual Arts. I started as an assistant, then took my portfolio around to design directors at the big stores and got turned down at every single one. But New York has a lot of little boutiques like Now, so I got some gigs. Took me a couple of years to make a living at it and charge enough to pay a crew."

The burger platters arrived, heaped with fries. The alehouse was a zoo at this point, and the waitress didn't stay to ask if they needed anything else.

"That's great. Good for you." The warmth in his voice and the admiration in his eyes embarrassed her.

Nicole picked up round, thinly cut slices of pickle from the side of her platter and made a flower out of them on top of the melted cheddar. She studied it for a second and added a circular squiggle of ketchup in the middle.

"You don't ever stop, do you?" Sam asked, laughing. "Pass the ketchup, please. Unless you plan to paint a mural with it."

She handed over the squeeze bottle. "Don't give me ideas."

Sam decorated his fries with ketchup, not very artistically. They ate quickly—they'd both been working hard. She finished first, and wiped her fingers with a paper napkin, then pulled several more out of the dispenser, arranging them on the table and unclipping a black marker.

He let her do the talking. The cheddar burger was great. She started sketching on the napkins, then turned them around so he could see. Sam seemed to follow just fine, nodding now and then.

"Okay. We're still going for a snow scene, but I repainted the backdrop—you'll see it tomorrow. The scene is going to be a winter cityscape."

"Sounds good."

She looked up, giving the marker a triumphant little wave. "Did I tell you Darci gave me a photo of the street from the 1920s with her storefront right in the middle?"

"No."

"It didn't look that different from now. It was a haberdasher's back then. Anyway, I'm having the photo blown up large-scale and printed on vinyl for a fast installation. Then . . ."

She kept on drawing and explaining through the rest of the meal. But she wasn't totally oblivious to everything around them. When they declined dessert and the check arrived a minute later, he put a hand over it. A split second later her hand landed inadvertently on his.

"This is on me," he said with a wink, before she could protest.

She withdrew her hand, feeling a little awkward. But she didn't argue. He paid and they got ready to go, shrugging into their jackets, then collecting the rolled design and her tote. Nicole drew on her gloves. The warmth of his skin stayed with her.

"Thanks," she told him, walking toward the curb. "That was fun."

"My pleasure." He put on the Stetson and angled the brim just so. "What's next?"

"Oh, I'm heading home. Long day. You too, I guess."

"Yeah. I'm beat. Time to turn in."

Nicole looked down the street, squinting into the rows of headlights coming at her. With the tote slung over one arm, she waved the other, looking for a taxi.

Sam wasn't sure of the urban etiquette involved. Did guys whistle down taxis for girls, or was that something only doormen did? She seemed very much in charge.

A yellow cab flashed its lights and cut across oncoming traffic to reach her.

Nicole opened the back door and hoisted the huge tote bag into the backseat.

"Thanks again," she said. "See you Saturday."

"Bright and early."

"Where to?" the driver asked her.

She slid in but didn't quite close the door, reaching for the handle and rolling down the window instead, as she told the driver where she was going.

Sam had the address memorized before it occurred to him that she lived only a block or two from where he was staying now. Nicole slammed the door and waved as the cab sped off. He didn't have her apartment number or floor, but if he had to, he'd ring every bell on her block. It was one way to make friends and a few instant enemies in the city.

But not just yet. She had to give him some kind of sign that she was interested. He thought she might be, but he couldn't quite read her. They might be living around the corner from each other for the next few weeks, but when you got right down to it, they were worlds apart and he was a long way from home.

He flipped up his jacket collar against the cold, walking downtown.

Sam stopped only once, at a sidewalk vendor's table on the way back to the trailer. He looked over the knit caps, looking for one that wasn't too thick to wear under a hard hat. He picked a stretchy black one, handing it to the vendor.

"That'll be three fifty. But I can give you two for five bucks. It's a good deal, man. That way you have one if you lose one," the vendor said.

Sam chuckled. "Okay. The price is right. Can you take the tag off?" He handed over the cap he'd picked and selected a second, identical one.

"You bet."

Snip. Snip.

Sam put both caps in his pocket. "How much for a scarf?" They weren't tagged.

"Five bucks."

He found a ten and gave it to the man. Couldn't beat the shopping location for convenience. He seemed to be the last customer for the night.

The vendor started piling up his stock and moving it into the van parked behind him. Sam said good night and walked on, wrapping the scarf around his neck and pulling the Stetson down just a bit. He didn't mind the occasional look or comment when he wore it.

New Yorkers seemed to sport every kind of hat there was except Stetsons. Still, if it happened to snow, it would serve him well. The wide brim and thick felt protected like nothing else. His was an old friend, a little worn, but broken in right.

He stopped at a corner after a while. Nothing seemed familiar, though his glance at the green rectangular sign on the pole told him he'd reached the right street. He looked around. The Hudson River glimmered faintly on the other side of Eleventh Avenue, beyond the whizzing traffic. He would have to head in the opposite direction on long crosstown blocks to get to where the trailer was.

Sam turned his back on the traffic and the river and kept on. He didn't feel tired. Nicole's enthusiasm for the redesigned window was contagious. She wanted him at Now by eight Saturday morning, and he would be. He glimpsed Christmas tree lights a few blocks ahead and quickened his pace.

Uncle Theo waved to him from his folding chair on the sidewalk, so bundled up he could hardly move. The fake-fur trim around the hood of the old man's padded jacket was the same gray as his bristling mustache, which reminded Sam of a walrus. Theo's deep, rumbling voice clinched the resemblance.

Sam waved back without calling a hello. Theo couldn't hear too well inside the hood.

The old man was somewhat protected from the wind by Christmas trees lined up in rows against a high A-frame made of wood. A heavy-duty extension cord ran from the frame into the all-night newsstand and cigarette shop a few steps away, courtesy of the proprietor, who welcomed the extra business the tree-selling brought in.

Strings of big colored lights, the old-fashioned kind, cast a luminous, welcoming glow over the trailer where Theo and Sam and a rotating lineup of relatives helping out with the lot slept in shifts. Out in Astoria, according to Greg, the extended family numbered in the low hundreds.

It was a good thing that Theo was a night owl and didn't mind the cold. There was a microwave and coffeepot in the trailer if he needed a hot drink or soup and time to warm up. Sam knew a cousin was coming in from Queens on the N train to keep the old man company and guard the trees.

They never encountered any trouble. The cops on the beat drove by on a regular basis until dawn, when another relative showed.

Sam wouldn't be sharing the trailer much longer. His sublet, a first-floor apartment in an old building, was supposed to be ready for him to move into it by the weekend. Theo had told him about it in the first place. The tenant, Alex Walcott, had been a customer of his for years. Everyone in the neighborhood knew Theo.

He reached the folding chair and thumped the old man's thickly padded shoulder in greeting. "Hi, Theo. How's business?"

"Could be better. How are you? How is my nephew?"

"Greg is fine. He went home. I thought I wasn't tired, but it all just caught up with me."

Theo jerked a mittened thumb toward the trailer door. "You work too hard. Sleep."

Up on blocks, with battered siding and cloudy windows, the trailer looked like heaven. Sam was more than tired. He was exhausted.

He mounted the wooden stairs with his hands in his pockets, glancing toward the city permit pasted on its side that allowed the Tsianakas family to operate their lot on the street and park the thing at the curb. They'd been there every December for the last fifteen years. For a few days, it had been his home away from home in the big city, but he was looking forward to a little privacy.

Sam awoke to a loud noise that made the trailer jiggle. He rubbed his eyes and opened them, then realized it was Theo banging on the side.

"Hawt caw-fee!" the old man yelled.

It took Sam a few seconds to auto-translate the last two words. Hot coffee. That sounded good. Whichever cousin had the dawn shift had brought tall cups of takeout and a bakery box from a place in Astoria, owned by another relative. Sam hadn't met him yet.

"Rise and shine, Sam! You up?"

"Yeah," Sam yelled back. The banging stopped. He'd gotten off easy. Yesterday morning it had been a street repair crew with jackhammers getting an early start.

He sat up and swung his legs out of bed. Blearily, he peered at the small battery-powered clock. Five minutes to six. He was good.

Sam ran a hand over his chin, then scratched the stubble. He would take care of that at the deluxe gym a block away. Just in case the sublet fell through, he'd paid for a one-month membership, so he could shave and shower and even take a sauna now and then. They supplied the grooming products and the towels.

He stood and stretched, glancing at himself in the small mirror on the door and frowning. Same old smoky blue eyes, not exactly bright at the moment. His tangled hair looked like the definition of bed head. He turned away and shucked his thick flannel pajamas and athletic socks, trading them for clean work clothes for the day. Everything went into a drawstring bag.

Theo had introduced Sam to the nice ladies at the laundry place on the corner. All he had to do was hand over the bag and they took care of the washing, drying, and folding for him. It was a great system.

Dressed, he opened the trailer door and stepped outside. Theo was already sipping his coffee, standing next to a young guy.

"You haven't met Apollo. Fifth cousin, third uncle," Theo said.

Same family resemblance, Sam thought. Apollo was shorter, but he had hair as black as Greg's.

"Morning. Nice to meet you."

"Gonna be a cold one," Apollo replied with a grin. "The pastry is still warm. Help yourself."

Theo held up the open bakery box. "Cheese Danish? Baklava? Croissant?"

"Baklava, I guess." Sam helped himself to a bite-size piece and popped the whole thing in his mouth. Soaked with honey and rich with chopped nuts and butter, the flaky pastry was delicious.

Fortunately, he had swallowed before Theo slapped him on the back. "Good, huh?"

Sam coughed. "It really is. Thanks, guys." He accepted the cup of coffee that the younger man handed him.

A boy with light brown hair wearing a plaid jacket that was a little too big for him came toward the group, a school backpack hanging from one shoulder. He looked to be about ten, if Sam had to guess.

"Hi, Theo!"

The older man looked his way. "Hello, Douglas. Where's your mother?" he asked as the boy reached them.

"She's coming. Takes her a while to get my baby sister into her snowsuit. Amanda is only three, but she sure can fight."

That clicked with Sam. He remembered being enlisted to help zip a very reluctant Annie into hers from November through April. New York was cold, all right, but it had nothing on Colorado.

The boy glanced casually toward the trees. "How's business, guys?"

Sam was amused by his grown-up tone. He didn't look Sam's way, but moved to the A-frame.

"Oughta pick up by the weekend," Theo replied. "People aren't ready to buy the big ones yet."

"This one is perfect," the boy said. He had stopped in front of the tallest tree for sale, shielding his eyes from the morning sun to look up at it. "Except for that crooked little branch up at the top."

"What? I don't see anything crooked. That's the best tree on the lot," Theo told him.

Fumbling a little because of the gloves he wore, the boy examined a white tag attached to a low branch. "Hey, it has my name on it," he said, grinning at his own joke.

Sam looked at the tag, which was marked with a price he knew was negotiable and the type of tree. *Douglas Fir.*

"Very funny." Theo laughed. "Want us to save it for you?"

The boy shrugged and stepped back onto the sidewalk.

"Mom hasn't decided about getting a tree yet. She's been pretty busy."

"Well, you let me know when she does," the old man replied.

"I think she's going to let Amanda choose," the boy said resignedly. "I want a real tree, though."

A gleeful giggle interrupted them. A nicely dressed woman—in her thirties, by his guess—was pushing a lightweight stroller toward them. She was blond, her hair streaming over her shoulders, holding a knit cap with a pom-pom and a pair of gloves, as if she hadn't had time to put them on. The tailored lavender coat she was wearing flared open with her quick steps.

Sam pegged her as Douglas's mother—they looked alike, with the same light freckles on high cheekbones, though her son's hair was more brown than blond, and his green eyes were darker than hers.

The giggling little girl in the stroller was a variation on the same theme, with pale, silky bangs and a chubby face. Amanda reached out pink-mittened hands that matched her snowsuit to her big brother.

"Good morning, everybody," the woman said.

"You're up early." Theo looked curiously at her. He seemed to know everyone on the block and their routines, Sam thought.

"Yes. I have a job interview at eight. I have to get Amanda to my aunt and drop Dougie at school. He's having breakfast there." She ruffled her son's hair with her left hand. Sam didn't notice a wedding ring.

"Ma-a!" The protest was softened with a smile he didn't try to hide.

"A job interview! That's why you look so pretty," Theo said gallantly. The woman blushed and seemed embarrassed. "But you oughta put on those gloves."

"Okay." She laughed lightly and looked toward Sam as she stuck the knit hat in her coat pocket and drew on the gloves. A flicker of curiosity lit up her sage-green eyes. Theo rose to the occasion.

"Allow me," he said. "Maureen Fulton, this is Sam Bennett. Sam is my nephew's pal from Colorado. Greg hired him for one of his Christmas crews."

"Oh," she said, extending a gloved hand to him. "Well, welcome to New York. Is this your first time here?"

"Yeah. I love it. The energy is amazing."

Maureen looked down when her little girl squealed. Amanda was tugging needles off a thin branch.

"Honey, stop that." She moved the stroller away from

the Christmas tree, and the little girl let go. "We have to run. Nice to meet you, Sam."

"Same here. And best of luck on that interview."

"Thanks. I hope—" Whatever she was going to say was interrupted by a soft click that registered on her maternal radar. "Amanda, don't unbuckle yourself. And sit down." She bent over the stroller to find the loose ends of the belt.

Douglas waited, looking up at the tall fir.

His preoccupied mother got his sister buckled up again and said good-bye, and the trio headed down the street.

Sam noticed the way the boy held one curved handle of the stroller and kept pace with his mother. Douglas was watchful for his age. He grabbed her arm to stop her when a truck barreled down the street too close to the curb and she was looking the other way.

Young, but somehow the man of the family. Sam wondered what the story was.

December was a tough time of the year to be a single mom, but it looked like Maureen Fulton was managing. He shook the thought away, suddenly remembering where he was supposed to be.

"Hey, I gotta get going myself," he said to the two other men. "Thanks for the breakfast."

"No problem. Say hi to Greg." Apollo sat down in the folding chair, taking over for Theo, who clumped up the trailer stairs as Sam hastily finished his coffee.

He waved and walked fast, reaching the corner before the light changed. No time for the gym. The stubble would have to stay where it was until quitting time. He would treat himself to a shower and a sauna tonight.

At least he wouldn't be seeing Nicole today. Sam hurried along, thinking about her, until he glimpsed the time on a digital sign atop a towering office building and broke into a run.

Chapter 3

Just to test the number in his cell phone's memory, he called Nicole the next morning at quarter to eight. She answered after several rings.

"Hey, Sam." He heard her say something else, but he didn't catch it as her voice faded away.

"Where are you?" he asked. There was a fair amount of noise in the background on her side of the call, people sounds. Then a loud *bing-bong,* followed by a *whoosh* and a clatter of footsteps.

"On the uptown bus," she said. "What's up?"

There was another *whoosh* as air brakes released. She must be standing near the exit door.

"I was just thinking I could pick up coffee for you and the crew on my way. Five, right?"

"No. Russ and Keith can't make it. So get three black coffees plus a cup of milk and sugar packets. The guys can fix their own."

"Anything to eat?"

She laughed. "You're too much. I'll take a bagel with cream cheese. Thanks."

The rolldown shades were in place when he reached the boutique, and the door was closed. Sam shifted the take-out bag with the coffees and extra bagels in case anyone else was hungry to his left hand, and tried the knob. It turned, unlocked. He entered and looked around for Nicole.

She came toward him, not wearing shorts and tights today. Too bad. He really liked that getup. But the slim-fitting jeans she was sporting were nearly as cute. And the black turtle-neck over them showed her curves better than the plain shirt.

"Here's your breakfast." He held up the bag.

"Thanks. That really was nice of you. I thought you were calling to cancel at first."

"I wouldn't do that. What happened with the other two?"

"They stayed late at Bob's workshop, so their part of the construction is done. Then Russ got an emergency call from the owners of the Coney Island carousel."

"Runaway horses?"

"Hah. The calliope is on the fritz. He does repairs for church organs. Russ is a big fan of Bach and Handel."

Sam didn't remember Russ that well, but he was willing to believe it.

"Anyway, I told him that was fine with me. He might stop by later to pick up his pay."

"Keith?"

"He went to a party that ended when the sun came up. Dead to the world, according to Russ. Did I mention that they're roommates?"

"No." He wondered if she had one. The subject hadn't come up.

She fished out the paper-wrapped bagel and put it on a radiator, taking one of the coffees next.

Sam helped himself to another while she found a low-sided cardboard box. "Here's a tray."

He dosed his coffee with milk and sugar and replaced

the lid, walking over to the window, where he almost tripped over a pile of miscellaneous objects he hadn't seen.

"Careful," she cautioned him.

Sam looked down at what seemed to be a pile of junk, then up at Nicole.

She was smiling like a little kid on Christmas morning. "I got lucky at the thrift stores yesterday."

It was kind of hard to tell what everything was, but he spotted a vintage record turntable missing its needle arm and knobs, and a crazy-looking lamp with Chinese dragons painted on its paneled silk shade.

Nicole picked it up, spinning the shade. "Fabulous, isn't it? It revolves. I've been hunting for a lamp like this for ages."

Sam looked at it. Fabulous? Not quite. The finial was missing, and some old lady's cat must have hated dragons. There were claw marks all over the silk.

"You did get lucky." It was the only tactful thing he could think of to say. He had no idea how she could use the lamp in the new design. Or any design. Watch and learn, he told himself.

Nicole set the lamp down and removed the shade, ripping off the painted silk, laughing at his puzzled look.

"You'll see."

Bob arrived, the down jacket he wore adding to his physical bulk. Hank came in a few minutes later, parking his skinny body by the radiator.

"I'm freezing," Hank complained. "Can we turn up the heat?"

Munching on her bagel, Nicole shook her head and handed him the bag with the coffee. The younger man kept his jacket on while Bob shucked his.

"You need to eat more," Bob told him. "Keeps ya warm." He patted his substantial paunch and adjusted his suspenders.

"Did you find a spot for the van?" Nicole asked.

Hank launched into an explanation. "Me and Bob could hardly get the new framework into it. We wanted the van close in case we had trouble getting it out. It's double-parked on a busted hydrant around the corner."

"Busted or not, you're begging for a ticket," she told him.

"Nah. The car next to the hydrant will get ticketed. Double-parking isn't that big of a deal."

She looked hopefully at Sam.

"Can I lift the framework by myself?" Sam asked the older man. Bob and Hank were suddenly very interested in the free breakfast in the paper bag. They weren't about to budge from the warmth.

Bob dug in the pocket of his ample chinos and tossed him the keys. "Your grandmother could lift it. Thanks."

Throwing on his denim jacket and Stetson just in case he was out there long enough to get cold, Sam headed out. He found the van and opened the double back doors. The second framework didn't look too different from the first one.

He unhooked the bungee cords that kept it from rattling around in the back of the van and took a closer look. It *was* the first one, with a whole lot of new additions nailed and glued to it.

Bob wasn't wrong about its being light. It was just awkward.

Sam felt a tap on his shoulder. A parking officer fixed him with a stern look when he rested the framework on the rear floor of the van and turned around.

"You planning to move that van, cowboy?"

He held up his ticket printer in warning.

"I just have to take this thing to a shop around the corner. Give me a minute."

The officer made a big show of looking at his watch.

"You got exactly sixty seconds. Then you better giddyap on outta here." He chuckled at his own joke and continued on down the line of cars, stopping at the next double-parked vehicle.

"Understood."

"Fifty-nine," the officer called over his shoulder. "Fifty-eight."

"I hear you," Sam muttered.

He watched the officer write up a ticket on the gizmo and slap it on the windshield of the car in front of the van.

Sam hesitated, then took out his cell phone to call Nicole. He explained the situation. In another minute, Hank came around the corner, still huddled inside his jacket. He took the framework and went back.

After slamming the double doors and getting behind the wheel, Sam turned the key in the ignition and moved on, tapping the horn when he passed the parking officer.

Dodged that bullet. Now to find a legit space. How hard could it be?

He drove around the block. And around another block. And another. He saw cars that had been parked for so long, the asphalt under the tires was a different color. There was not a single free space anywhere in the immediate vicinity that was big enough for a van.

A while later, he called Nicole. "Tell Bob I had to put it in a parking garage. Twenty bucks plus tax for two hours and an extra charge for an oversize vehicle! Can you believe it?"

"That's cheap," she said. "He'll be thrilled."

Sam shook his head, tucking his cell phone into his shirt pocket as he exited the cavernous garage under a large apartment building. At least it was close to the boutique.

The other men and Nicole had gotten a head start on the first window in his absence. She was bending over a worktable they'd improvised with a sheet of plywood over two sawhorses, smoothing out a huge piece of very thin vinyl by lifting it.

Sam guessed it was the vintage photo, blown up to wall size.

Lettering she'd cut out backward to reverse in the window had been set aside to be applied to the glass.

The boutique was open for business. A salesclerk had cordoned off the part of the store they were working in with colorful scarves strung between two undressed female mannequins.

Sam averted his gaze from the mannequins' perky plaster bosoms and ducked under the scarves. He moved to the window, not wanting to distract Nicole, who was cutting into the vinyl with an angled craft knife, her brow furrowed with concentration.

She scarcely seemed aware that Sam was watching. When she was done, she straightened, rubbing her back.

"There. That's done." Nicole bent over the table again to check her notebook, and crossed out a few lines. "Now we put it all together."

"Just tell me what needs doing."

Nicole explained the next steps, and they got to work. Sam did his best to keep a gentlemanly distance. To wrangle the half-completed framework into the store window, they had to climb over it and each other, while Bob and Hank did the shoving.

Sam didn't dare to look at Nicole's curvy body, keeping his gaze on her face or the back of her head when he didn't need to look at the work he was doing. That wasn't as effective as he'd hoped. He held the framework in position, his arms extended and locked, while she tacked the vinyl in place, edging in front of him step by step.

"Don't let go," she said absently.

"I won't."

Then she turned within his outstretched arms, staple gun in hand to tack a projecting part of the framework. Sam could feel her breath on his neck. Hell, he could feel her eyelashes flutter.

Nicole seemed completely unconcerned. Might be all in a day's work for her, but his self-control was seriously tested. He tried not to think about the reasons for that.

She dodged under his arm and jumped down from the window. "You can let go now," she said.

Sam stepped to the side and rubbed his stiff biceps. Maybe he could volunteer for a solo task that the other two men didn't want. But no, there was no way around it. They were a team.

She was a good boss and she knew her stuff, calmly telling all three of the men exactly what she expected them to do and when. The slight nervousness that Sam had chalked up to city-girl attitude vanished when they were in the midst of working.

By late afternoon, the window was nearly complete. Sam was tickled at being able to make the connection between her sketches on the napkins and the winter cityscape as it took shape.

The backdrop was simpler now, a rich, shaded blue that evoked twilight and brought out the whiteness of the artificial snow that drifted over the painted sidewalk. The greatly enlarged photo of the original storefront on the street had changed in the printing, its gray tones translated into graphic black and white that enlivened the foreground.

The doors and windows of the street scene were what Nicole had cut out in the vinyl, becoming display niches when she used spray adhesive to attach the vinyl to the finished framework. Accessories were tucked in each niche: sparkling bracelets, coiled scarves in gleaming silk, belts with elaborate buckles. Here and there, delicate crystals were glued to fine details of the vintage photo to attract—and delight—the eye.

The old record player had been transformed into a skating rink with white paint and drifts of snow, complete with paper people in tiny metal skates and one little dog.

Nicole installed the lamp last of all, but not where anyone could see it from the street. The lampshade frame was now covered with heavy paper in which she'd made a number of cutouts. She switched it on, and it began to revolve from the warmth of the bulb.

"Let's go outside," she told Sam. "That should do it."

"Lead the way."

She went ahead of him, eager to see how it all looked. Neither of them stopped to put on a jacket.

From the sidewalk the full effect was breathtaking. The hidden lamp cast soft bits of light that looked exactly like falling snow on the deep blue backdrop. The cityscape was silhouetted against it, the niches glowing with light. The rink revolved, as charming as a music box. She had even added a young couple, also cut from paper, gazing in the window of the storefront as it had looked long ago, just as she and Sam were doing right now.

"What do you think?" she asked Sam.

"It's really beautiful. You're amazing."

"Did you notice the theme? I got the name of the boutique into it." She pointed to the corner of the window glass.

NOW . . . AND THEN. HAPPY HOLIDAYS!

Sam smiled. "Nice touch. The whole thing is fantastic. I don't know how you did it."

That she could make something so magical out of a heap of junk and lumber really did amaze him.

Nicole turned her face up to his. "You helped. Thanks," she said softly.

He hoped the sparkle in her eyes wasn't just a reflection from the window. The soft radiance in her expression made him feel a little weak. He had never wanted to kiss a woman more than he wanted to kiss her at that moment, that was for damn sure. But they weren't alone on the sidewalk. A few people had already stopped in front of them to gaze into the window.

She turned her face away. The moment passed. She went back inside, staying ahead of him.

Sam took a last look at what they'd created, then followed her. Nicole was talking to Bob and Hank.

"Good work, guys. Don't forget that we still have to do the window on the other side."

Hank was slinging tools into a diamond-patterned metal box. "When? Do you have a design?"

"I'll come up with something," she said briskly. "Give me a day or two. We all want to get paid. Sam, what's your schedule like?"

Her tone was matter-of-fact. He must have imagined the look in her eyes when they were outside. So much for magic.

"I don't know," he answered. "Let me check with Greg and get back to you."

"Okay. Thanks." She walked around the work area, switching off the aluminum-shaded lights and gathering materials. "Bob, can you bring the van around to the front? There's a lot of leftover stuff here. Would you mind if I stashed it in the back for now?"

"Won't be in my way. Go ahead," the burly man answered. "I could bring it by your building tomorrow."

"All right," she said absently.

Sam fished in his shirt pocket for the parking stub and handed it to Bob. His cell phone rang a second later. "Maybe that's Greg," he said to Nicole.

She nodded without interest.

He looked at the number, not recognizing it, and answered anyway. "Hello?"

"Sam Bennett, please," said a tenor voice.

"Who is this?"

"Your landlord."

"Huh?"

"You sublet my apartment, remember? I'm Alex Walcott. We met once."

The light dawned. "Oh, right. Sorry. Just wasn't thinking."

"I understand." Alex chuckled. "Christmas is just around the corner. Anyway, the cruise show came through. I'm going to be an elf."

That fit. Sam remembered that Alex was short. Really short.

"We sail at dawn. You'll need a key. Come by and I'll give you the official tour."

Sam hadn't actually seen the apartment. He'd followed Theo's advice to pounce on it once the old man had introduced them. *Sammy boy, you can trust Alex. I trust him. A customer for years. Cheap sublets don't grow on trees in New York. The trailer's getting crowded.*

The deal had been done right there at the Christmas tree lot, in cash. Half in advance, half to come when the key changed hands.

"When?"

"Doesn't matter," Alex said. "I'm going to be up all night packing."

Sam hung up. Nicole was still busy. He picked up whatever else was lying around and set it on the worktable, then reached for his jacket.

"You heading home?" Bob asked. Nicole straightened up with a bag of scrap lumber and turned to look at Sam.

"In that general direction," Sam said cheerfully. "Anything else you guys need a hand with here?"

"No," Nicole said. "Thanks again."

"All right. I'll check in with you about the other window when I get a chance," Sam replied.

He turned onto Theo's block—he'd thought of it that way from the first, never mind the street sign. But he was on the opposite end from the Christmas tree lot.

The sublet couldn't be more convenient. He went up the worn sandstone stairs and rang the bell for 1-A, under a tattered slip of paper that said *WALCOTT*.

The outer door buzzed and he heard the lock release. Sam pushed the door in and stopped at the inside door, waiting for a second buzz.

Absently, he looked down at the entryway floor, realizing that he'd seen versions of it all over New York. In hallways. In bathrooms. The tiles were tiny white octagons with a decorative border. In an old building like this, some of the tiles were chipped, but someone kept them clean.

That would be the super. He reminded himself to ask for the guy's name, in case anything needed fixing.

He tried the inside door. Still locked. Alex Walcott seemed to have forgotten to press the second buzzer. Sam went outside and pressed the apartment bell again.

Simultaneously, the buzzer rang and an apartment door in the narrow hallway opened with a bang.

Alex waved to him. Sam didn't remember his hair being green. "Sorry! I was looking for my tap shoes!" He dashed back in.

"Not a problem." Sam walked to 1-A and went to the door his landlord had left open.

"Come on in," Alex said. "Did the green hair scare you? Job requirement. I don't even want to look in a mirror." His voice was muffled. Sam heard hangers being scraped along a rod. "Make yourself at home." Thumps and scrabbling sounds came from the depths of the single closet, and a box flew out.

Sam paused on the sill. Five more steps and he would reach the opposite wall of the single room. The furniture was sized to fit, he noticed. Elf-size.

Whatever. He would manage. The place looked clean and comfortable. If he shoved the coffee table to one end of the miniature couch, he could even stretch out enough to sleep. He didn't see a bed.

"Welcome to my humble abode," Alex said. He came out from the closet, tap shoes in hand. "Sit down, please. Would you like a drink? Soda, wine, beer?"

"I'll have a beer, sure."

Sam sat down on the sofa as Alex bagged the shoes and tossed them into an unzipped suitcase already bulging with clothes.

"The show provides costumes, but I have to have my lucky shoes," he explained.

In a couple of steps, Alex was in the alcove that served as a kitchen. Even the refrigerator was small. But it looked new and so did the stove. Sam noticed a row of pots and pans, neatly hung. He could do his own cooking, if he wanted to.

Alex returned with a couple of frosty bottles and handed one over. He unfolded a chair and positioned it on the other side of the coffee table, sitting down himself and taking a long swallow.

"Ah. I needed that," he said with satisfaction.

"Looks like you're almost ready to go," Sam said conversationally.

"Yeah. The suitcase is full. But I have to go over to my girlfriend's apartment and help her pack. I got her into the pixie chorus as an understudy."

Sam laughed and took a sip of beer, shaking his head.

"Never, ever volunteer to help a woman pack. You will always do it wrong."

Alex raised his bottle to that. "You're right. But if I help her, she will actually be ready on time, no tears, no craziness, no going back. Bermuda, here we come."

The phone rang, and Alex reached toward a side table to answer it. Sam guessed he was talking to his girlfriend. He looked around the apartment while he drank his beer, trying to figure out where the bathroom was.

A narrow door near the corner was shut. That had to be it. The only other interior door belonged to the closet that Alex had been rifling through.

"See you in about half an hour, okay? Love you too." Alex hung up. "Okay. Let's get started. Here's a set of keys."

He extracted them from his sweatpants and put them down on the table.

"Thanks." Sam slid a hand into his inside jacket pocket. "Here's the rest of the advance."

Alex didn't bother to count it. The bills went right into his wallet.

"You know how the door works. There's the buzzer." He pointed to a metal square with plastic buttons by the door. "No intercom, by the way. But you can see who rang if you stick your head out the front window. Careful of the bars."

He gestured toward it, and Sam turned around. He could just make out the wrought iron that protected the glass.

"The couch you're sitting on folds out," Alex continued. "Sheets in the closet, extra pillows in the coffee table, electric blanket with dual controls."

"I'll keep that in mind," Sam said.

For an elf, Alex seemed like a regular guy. He didn't ask any questions about Sam having company.

"And don't worry about kicking up the thermostat if you do open a window. We have steam heat."

Alex patted the radiator next to him, like it was a good old dog. Sam was getting the idea. If you sat right in the middle of the apartment, you could pretty much reach everything you needed.

"That means you can't control the temperature. The super does. But he's pretty good about keeping the boiler going. I saw it once. It's ancient. A real monster."

"That reminds me. I meant to ask you for his name."

Alex grabbed a piece of paper and jotted it down.

"Norm Krajek. He lives in the basement apartment with his wife. Big guy, middle-aged, bald, broken nose. You'll see him around."

"Okay. Thanks."

"If anything gets busted, don't ask him to fix it. He shows up with a can of wood putty and slaps it on the problem. Besides the boiler, he doesn't have a clue."

"Got it."

Alex tipped his head back and finished off his beer. Sam did the same. "You don't have to check the mailbox. I put a hold on it for the rest of the month. They won't deliver. Any other questions?" Alex asked.

"That about covers it." Sam rose, trying not to bump into the coffee table. "Nice place, by the way. I'll take good care of it."

Alex got up to shake his hand. "Thanks. You can move in tomorrow morning." He slapped Sam on the back. "I'll walk you to the door," he joked.

That took a grand total of three steps.

Sam went back the way he'd come to pick up takeout, deciding on pad Thai. The spicy noodles would take the chill off the night. If he walked fast, they'd stay hot all the way back to the trailer.

The thought that he had only one more night to sleep there restored his good mood, and he'd enjoyed the meeting with his landlord. He got to the Thai place and gave the counterman his order, then sat down at a banquette to wait.

An array of china statues and twisted bamboo in low vases at the cash register caught his eye. He guessed they were there for good luck. Right now, he was feeling like he had his share of that. Except maybe with Nicole.

An old lady in a silk jacket brought over a cup of fragrant hot tea he hadn't ordered, bowing slightly when he thanked her and shuffling away. He took off his gloves and held the cup until it cooled a little, thinking about Nicole and her standoffishness after they had gone outside to look at the window.

He figured he'd blown it by not kissing her. But not permanently. Maybe they were both nervous. He could be overestimating her city-girl confidence.

Sam pondered the matter. She could have just been through a bad breakup; he didn't know. Nicole definitely didn't seem like the type who regaled a guy with the details of things like that. Or maybe she just wasn't interested in fooling around with someone who was only passing through.

Which he was. Sam was getting a huge kick out of New York so far, but he didn't belong here.

Still and all, he'd never met anyone like Nicole. Maybe he'd just ticked her off temporarily. Hmm. There were tried-and-true ways to deal with that.

The counterman brought his order, and Sam eased out of the banquette. He paid at the register, where the old lady was perched on a stool. He put the change into a small dish full of other coins that was set in front of the statues.

She broke into a smile. "You have happiness now. Take care."

He smiled back and turned toward the door. "Thanks. You too. Good night."

Chapter 4

Only a few people were out, hurrying home, like him. No eye contact, no hellos, but Sam was getting used to that. Not paying too much attention, he passed the right street and had to backtrack.

Turning the corner, he saw a mother with a couple of kids coming toward him. Bundled up, but they looked familiar. Several more long strides and he was close enough to recognize the Fultons. They were going up the stairs—the stoop, he reminded himself—of an old apartment building up the street from the Christmas tree lot.

He did a double take. As of tomorrow, that was his apartment building. Theo hadn't mentioned that Maureen and her two kids would be his neighbors when he'd introduced them, but they had all been in a hurry that day.

Step by step, Maureen was half pulling, half lifting the stroller in which a cherubic Amanda slept. Douglas held grocery bags in both hands.

Sam closed the remaining distance in running strides, gripping the take-out bag to keep it from swinging.

"Hold up," he called.

Maureen turned her head to peer anxiously down the shadowy street. Her son had the same wary look.

Sam stopped at the stoop and tipped his Stetson to her.

"It's me. Sorry. Didn't mean to startle you. Just wanted to give you a hand. We met the other day at Theo's lot. I'm Sam."

"Oh," Maureen said, sounding relieved. "Yes, I remember you."

She bent over to check on Amanda, and he tucked the takeout into a broken part of the railing. If someone swiped it, what the hell. He could go back and get more.

Sam bounded up the worn stone stairs and reached for the stroller when she was ready to let go, handling it carefully so as not to disturb the sleeping child. Maureen took a moment to catch her breath, holding on to the wrought iron banister at the side.

"I have the key," Douglas said. He went around Sam and set down the bags he was carrying at the top of the stairs, digging in the pocket of the plaid jacket and retrieving several keys on a shoelace.

Sam waited for him to unlock the exterior door and went inside with the stroller while Douglas held the door open for his mother, then gathered up the grocery bags in one hand and clicked the door shut with the other.

"You're pretty strong," Sam said encouragingly. "That looks like a couple days' worth of groceries."

"More like a week." But Doug seemed pleased and he wasn't complaining. Again Sam had the impression that he was a capable kid for his age.

The vestibule was crowded with all four of them in it, and he barely managed to set the stroller down. Amanda might be only three but she was no lightweight. Maybe it was all the winter bundling. He didn't remember her having that heavy blanket thing over her the other day.

Maureen opened the inner door with her own key and gestured him and her son inside. "Thanks so much," she murmured. "I really appreciate it."

Sam could have done the opening. He had the same

keys in his pocket. "Glad to help. We're going to be neighbors. Sort of." He gestured toward 1-A. "I'm subletting that apartment for December."

"Oh." Maureen seemed surprised. "Do you know Alex?"

"Theo introduced us. He got a job as an elf on a cruise ship show."

Maureen smiled. "Now that you mention it, he told me once he was a song-and-dance man. Well, I'm glad he has work."

"He seemed happy about it," Sam said.

An unsubtle sigh issued from Douglas, who looked tired of listening to adults talk. "All right," his mother said. "Up we go."

Not one sound came from the first-floor apartment as they passed the door. Sam guessed Alex had gone off to round up his girlfriend.

"What floor do you live on?" Sam asked.

He glanced toward the narrow interior stairs set back in the hall, made of marble that had hollowed in the center from generations of trudging feet.

She hesitated. "The third. She usually doesn't fall asleep like this. I don't want to wake her up."

A little girl like Amanda still wouldn't go very fast up that many stairs. "Of course not. Lead the way," he said, hoisting the stroller again.

"We can manage. Believe me, we've done it before."

"I hold the foot part and Mom holds the handles," her son chimed in.

Sam smiled and shook his head. "Nothing doing. Glad I came along in time." He went up the stairs after Douglas, who followed his mother.

The grocery bags swung in the kid's hands, bumping into the iron spirals of the staircase railing. Douglas pulled the bags closer to him, looking into one. "Christmas cookies," he announced. "Awesome, Mom."

Maureen stopped to turn around and take that particular bag from him. "Those are for after you do your homework."

And on they went, up another flight of stairs. Maureen stayed in the lead.

Another week in New York and Sam thought he could climb a mountain, easy. He heard a slight sound from the stroller and glanced down to see round blue eyes staring back at him. "Hello," he said softly to the little girl. "Remember me?"

Amanda's lower lip began to tremble and she scrunched up her face. Apparently she didn't.

The sharp sound of her indrawn breath as she prepared to wail got her brother's attention. He set down the grocery bags on the second-floor landing. "Amanda, don't cry. That's Sam. He's helping Mom."

The boy took her hand when Sam got to the landing. Douglas distracted his little sister long enough for all of them to reach the third floor and the door that Maureen had unlocked with her own key.

She waited inside, holding it open. "Well, look who woke up," she said, laughing. "Amanda, I hope you're not planning to stay up late after a nap like that."

Douglas took the bags a few more steps into a tiny kitchenette as his mother unbuckled his sister, and Sam looked around.

The apartment was small, but welcoming, painted in warm yellow with prints and posters decorating the walls. He noticed lots of books and a wide-screen TV. Cozy was the word for it.

Freed from her snowsuit, Amanda went straight for a set of shelves at her level. "Buster!" she cried, grabbing a one-eyed, three-legged stuffed thing that looked something like a bear. It had been mended several times until the mender, who Sam suspected was Maureen, had finally given up.

Amanda flopped on the sofa, hugging her beloved toy and murmuring to it.

"I'd ask you to stay but . . ." Maureen began, slipping off her coat and taking her son's plaid jacket from him. She looked through the crowded but neat front closet for hangers as she finished the sentence. "Douglas has a ton of homework and I have housework." She gestured vaguely toward the immaculate kitchenette.

"Hey, I understand," Sam hastened to assure her.

She smiled, straightening the lilac sweater she wore over neat black pants. He noticed that the sweater matched the coat she'd just hung up and remembered that she had worn the same outfit on her way to an interview yesterday. Maybe she'd gone on another today.

Maureen pushed at the jackets and coats, closing the closet door with a firm click. She turned to him. There was something just as closed in her expression. He decided against asking how her job search was going.

"Thank you again for helping," she said, looking toward Amanda. "Honey, do you want to say good-bye to Sam?"

"No," said the little girl. "I don't know him."

Sam chuckled at Maureen's mock glare in Amanda's direction.

"He's going to be our neighbor," she chided her daughter. Amanda ignored him. "Be polite."

"It's okay," Sam said with a smile. The little girl was hugging the toy even harder. A clump of stuffing came out. Love was tough on everyone.

He nodded to Douglas, who was pulling out schoolbooks from underneath the coffee table. "Have a good night, everyone."

He exchanged good-byes with Maureen, stopping on the mat outside it for a moment when she closed the door. He reached in his pocket for the gloves he'd stuffed on top of the thin caps he'd bought, holding onto the gloves when a cap fell out. Just like the vendor had said when he'd bought 'em: one to wear, one to lose. Sam bent to retrieve it, then put on his gloves.

"Did you get either of those jobs, Mom?" he heard Douglas ask through the door.

"No," she answered. "They needed a person who could work nights and I can't, not with you and Amanda. But I'll find something. Don't worry."

Sam held the cap in one hand, not bothering to put it back on. It was only a short walk to the lot once he was outside. He headed for the stairs, looking thoughtful.

He was back in the trailer before he realized he'd forgotten the take-out order he'd stuck inside the broken railing. Sam settled for a pop-top can of ravioli, served cold.

Chapter 5

Nicole was curled up on the love seat in front of the window of her studio apartment, looking out. She was barely aware that icy raindrops were chasing each other down the glass.

What an incredible distraction Sam Bennett was turning out to be—and right when she was busiest. She made more money in December than in the other eleven months of the year combined.

Which worked out okay when prices weren't so high. She was going to have to scramble to get some decent freelance gigs come January. Creating displays covered up with big red signs saying EVERYTHING MUST GO was a little depressing.

It was a good thing that Sam was only in New York for one month, and working as hard as she was. Although completing the first of the two boutique windows with him had been an experience.

He knew how to get close without ever touching her. But after a while, his presence had rattled her—especially the way he combined strength and skill. That had never been a concern with the guys on her crew, who were actually more experienced carpenters but were awkward or unattractive or both.

And by the time they'd gone outside to inspect the finished window—and she caught that look in his eyes when she turned around to discuss it—for just a second, she'd thought he was going to kiss her.

Sam had just stood there. Whatever she'd seen in his eyes had vanished. Or she'd imagined it.

Nicole pulled a pillow into her arms and hugged it, watching open umbrellas, bright circles of color from her vantage point, moving up and down the street.

Someone dodged the umbrellas and dashed through the rain to go up the stairs to her building, moving too quickly for her to see anything more.

That was it for excitement today.

She picked up her bills for this and that, and leafed through them for something to do. No matter how hard she worked, she never had enough to pay everything all at once. Her good old hometown was getting incredibly expensive to live in. The rent for her little place was going up. Much as she loved New York and Manhattan in particular, the hassle of living there sometimes didn't seem worth it.

An ear-shattering scraping sound rose from the street. Nicole looked out the window again. Two trucks had jammed together in the street and the drivers were screaming at each other, disputing the width of the street and disparaging each other's ability to eyeball the space they'd misjudged. Only they weren't using words like "dispute" and "disparage."

A cop came along and joined in, threatening loudly to arrest them both and impound the trucks. The stopped cars caught behind the jam began to honk.

It was a real New York symphony. She was getting tired of that too. Fairly quickly, the cop got everyone sorted out and the trucks went on their way.

Several minutes later the bell from the intercom panel outside rang in her apartment.

Nicole tossed the pillow to one side and went to answer it, though she wasn't expecting anyone. It couldn't be Sam. He'd checked in as promised, told her he would be doing another installation with Greg's crew outside the city. She didn't remember the particulars. But she'd given herself and the guys the day off. Darci was still in Aspen.

"Who is it?" she asked after she pressed the button.

"Hey. It's me. Sam."

She felt a flush of foolish pleasure at the sound of his voice and squelched it immediately, trying to think how he'd gotten her address. Then she remembered: she'd told the taxi driver where she was going that first night. He must have overheard and remembered it.

The bell rang again. "Nicole?"

"Yes, I'm here. I thought you were supposed to be out on Long Island or something. Are you playing hooky?"

"Guilty with an explanation," came the cheerful reply. "Got a moment?"

Nicole hesitated, then buzzed him through the door at street level. She glanced at herself in the mirror and frowned, then yanked open her closet. Her apartment was on the fifth floor. Even if he galloped up all those stairs she still had time to change.

It was late in the afternoon, but she still hadn't bothered to dress, and the vintage kimono she wore over her favorite owl-print pajamas was a little too bedroom-y. Not that she had an actual bedroom. The love seat folded out.

Fortunately, she'd folded it up—creaking and groaning—after lunch. She ran back to it and punched the decorative pillows into shape, flinging them against the arms of the love seat. *Whump whump.* So much for that.

Startled by the sudden activity, Whiskeroo disappeared into a compartment of his carpeted tower.

The last she saw of her cat was his striped tail as she undressed. Nicole pulled on jeans and a purple sweater, dragging a brush through her hair. What with the humidity, it fluffed up nicely. No time for her usual ponytail.

Nicole gave herself a spinach-search smile in the mirror. All clear on the teeth. There was a knock on the door. No time for lip gloss. She bit them instead.

She glanced at him through the peephole. Even with the fish-eye distortion, Sam looked tall. He didn't seem to be aware she was looking at him, because he was inspecting the bouquet he held, adjusting a few petals. His Stetson was pushed back on his head, so wet the color seemed more black than brown. His denim jacket was wet too.

The bouquet was over the top . . . but she couldn't remember the last time a man had brought her flowers.

Nicole unlocked the dead bolt and the chain latch. "Hi," she said, keeping her tone friendly but just a little cool. "This is a surprise."

"I guess I should have called first," Sam said. "Hope you're not busy."

"I was just about to start sketching some ideas for the second window."

That was a lie, but she wasn't going to get caught. Scribbled-up paper and sketchpads were everywhere, as usual.

"So I see." Sam had his hands full, what with the bouquet. He took off the hat. "Got a place for this?" he asked.

Nicole took the Stetson from him, noticing that it was dry inside. The rain didn't seem to have gotten through the thick felt. She put it and his wet jacket on a hook by the door.

She wasn't going to ask if the flowers were for her.

He straightened. "Gloomy day, huh? I was, um, walking by the flower stand and just thought you might like these."

Shocking pink and brilliant orange pinwheels peeked out of the paper funnel he handed to her. Gerbera daisies. Her favorite. He didn't have to know that.

The hot colors were a jazzy note against the dull green of the hallway wall. She still wasn't sure why he'd bothered, but she could feel her resolve soften. "Come on in," she said.

Sam followed her inside and moved aside to let her shut the door. "Nice and bright, whatever they are."

"Did you get them at the place around the corner?"

"Yes, as a matter of fact."

"Are you staying near there? I never did ask. But you seem to have remembered my address."

He looked a little sheepish and pretty much dodged the question. "Two blocks south. I was staying with some friends, but I just got the keys to my sublet. I'm moving in today."

"I see," she said casually. She wondered why he wasn't more direct, but it really wasn't any of her business. "Well, thanks for the flowers. But how did you know I'd be here?"

"I didn't. Just thought I'd try. I had the flower shop lady stick the stems in foam so they wouldn't wilt. I was planning to stop by later if you didn't answer. Anyway, I rang every bell for the fifth floor.

Nicole sort of remembered telling him that she lived on the top floor of a walk-up. Her bad mood was ebbing away. She decided to give him a break. It was even possible that she had a good bottle of wine somewhere. Left by some forgettable date.

There was no real reason to continue the cool-chick routine. Sam was nice. "Did anyone buzz back?"

"Just you."

He looked at her holding the flowers, his dark eyes warm with—*stop it,* she told herself.

"And now my neighbors hate you," she pointed out.

"I don't doubt it." He didn't seem to care. New York must be rubbing off on him.

"Well, have a seat while I find a vase." She motioned toward the love seat in front of the window. "And let's hear the explanation for your day off," she said over her shoulder.

Sam launched into it. "Greg said the visual marketing director is snowbound in the Chicago airport. That's where the company headquarters are—they own malls all over the U.S. Apparently no one is allowed to make a move until she arrives. So here I am."

Nicole unwrapped the paper from the flowers and let them rest in the sink. "That's how corporate design works."

"Thought so." He ventured a few steps farther into the one room in which she did all her living. "Freelancers probably have a lot more fun."

"Depends on what level you're at," she responded, sticking to business.

"How so?"

"A lot of corporate designers are freelance, but they work online. Once you have a name, it doesn't even matter where you live. Unlike me, they don't have to drag a portfolio around to little stores like Now."

"You'll get there."

"Yes. But I'll never get rich. Though I'm not sure I want to be. I'd settle for enough to live on, plus ten percent for emergencies. And a bigger place than this."

He heard her opening cabinet doors. "What do you consider an emergency?"

"At the moment, not being able to find a corkscrew when

you find a bottle of wine is an emergency. I guess I have nothing to complain about, do I?"

"I'd help you look, but I don't know where anything is," Sam said.

Help her look? In a kitchen no bigger than a shoebox? No. Noooooo. She yanked open a cluttered drawer and saw it on top. "Found it. Would you like a glass of wine?"

"Sure." He took the opportunity to look around. Her place was bigger than his sublet but basically still one room.

Two high, old-fashioned windows framed a view of the building right across the street. It was almost identical to hers, with an ornamental cornice that seemed too heavy for it, squeezed in between others built around the same time, more than a hundred years ago, judging by the Victorian style.

Sam moved closer to the window. When he looked straight down, he could see the front steps of Nicole's building. The vertical perspective emphasized the narrowness of the front room.

There weren't any side windows, but there was a lot of natural light this time of day. And none at all otherwise, by his guess.

He couldn't shake the feeling of being boxed in. Give him a nice plain house on the ground any day. With windows all around, a view of open land and rugged mountains, and more than one door to go in and out of.

Funny how he'd always taken all that for granted. Not to mention furniture a man could stretch out on.

By the look of it, hers folded up or out into whatever she needed. She'd arranged other pieces ingeniously to fit the limited space and hung colorful framed artwork he was sure was hers. Tucked under a drafting table were wire-basket carts holding everything from pens to fabric.

She'd even stacked big books on their sides to prop up a shelf that held other books.

There was one substantial club chair that would do for him. But Sam still couldn't take a step without bumping into something. There was barely enough room to swing a cat, he thought.

He moved backward and caught his elbow in a tower thing covered with nubbly carpet. A faint hiss came from inside it, and he caught a glimpse of green eyes glaring at him as he righted the structure.

"I didn't mean you," he said to the unseen animal.

"What?" Nicole asked, coming back without the flowers.

"Oh—I was just talking to your cat. That is a cat in there, right?"

She peered into the dark compartment. "Sure is. Whiskeroo isn't used to company."

A paw poked out and quickly went back in when she turned away. The cat stayed hidden.

"You know how it is," she said to Sam. "Sleep, eat, work, repeat. I don't entertain at all."

He was secretly pleased to hear that. "Oh," he said, gathering his thoughts. "But you could. This is a really nice place." He moved away from the tower just in case the cat decided to sneak a swipe at him. "I like the collages. You did those, right?"

"Yes."

"All those bits and pieces add up to something amazing. You have a lot of interesting stuff."

"And no room for it," she replied, going back into the kitchen area.

He didn't argue with that, but he didn't agree with her either. "Looks great. Everything you need is right where you can find it."

"True enough." Nicole came back in with the bouquet

arranged in a vase. Sam was sitting in the leather club chair, his hands draped over the studded arms.

"This is a classic," he said approvingly. "Where did you get it?"

"The super gave it to me."

Sam lifted a quizzical eyebrow.

Nicole set the vase down on an end table and went back into the kitchen.

"Winfield is one of the good guys," she said. "Some former tenants left that chair behind when they vacated. Win and a buddy lugged it upstairs for me. One of the legs was broken, so he repaired it for me."

"Nice of him. I understand the super at my place can't fix a thing."

"That's typical. But you're only going to be there a month, right?"

"Right."

There was a clinking sound that had to be wineglasses and the squeak of a cork being pulled.

She came back in with the bottle and the glasses and sat down on the love seat. "Sorry. I don't have any cheese and crackers."

"You weren't expecting company." Sam leaned forward to look at the label. "This is a really good wine."

"Someone gave it to me last Christmas." She poured and handed him a glass, then poured one for herself, lifting it. "Cheers. Welcome to the neighborhood."

"So far it seems . . . pretty neighborly. I even know some people in my building. Small world."

"New York is, sometimes. But I couldn't say I know all my neighbors, even though you can hear everything in the halls."

"So I noticed," he laughed. "On my way up I heard a quarrel over how long to cook fresh ravioli, jazz music, and an old lady talking to her cat."

"I know her. Mrs. Green lives right below me. That cat's been dead for years."

Sam seemed very comfortable in the massive chair. He was the first person to sit in it who hadn't seemed swallowed by its size. And, with one long leg slung over the other, he was masculine as all get-out. Trade the work clothes for a tuxedo and smooth down his hair with brilliantine, and he'd look like a 1930s ad for very expensive scotch.

Nicole studied him for an extra few seconds. Actually, a man like Sam would look most at home in a log cabin with antler lamps and cowhide decor. She set down her glass of wine. It wasn't helping. She told herself to stop styling him.

"So," he said, breaking the silence, "I thought I saw a couple of snowflakes on the way over."

"Wishful thinking." She gestured toward the freezing rain on the window. "December is usually just gray. But that could change. Sometimes it does snow right around Christmas. Not very much, though."

"Got it." Sam seemed a little disappointed. "I just talked to my folks in Colorado. The snow's already drifted halfway up the house."

"It must be pretty."

He nodded. "Yes. But I get the feeling they'd like to live somewhere else in winter, now that they're retired."

"My mom and dad say the same thing. But if I mention Florida or Arizona, they start finding reasons to stay where they are."

Sam laughed. "I know what you mean."

Nicole jumped when she heard her cell phone ring. She leaned over to look at the number on the screen. "Yikes. I have to answer that. Sorry."

"Not a problem. Go ahead."

"Could be work. I won't be long." She picked up the phone and took the call. "Hi, Finn. What's up?"

Sam looked casually around the room, admiring her artwork again. Then he glanced out the window. It seemed to have stopped raining for the moment.

He couldn't help overhearing a rapid-fire stream of words from Finn, who seemed to be male. Nicole couldn't get a word in edgewise. For Sam's benefit, she rolled her eyes as the guy talked nonstop.

"Today?" she said when Finn paused to breathe.

Sam heard an impatient yes, loud and clear.

Nicole wrapped up the call, looking apologetically at Sam. "Okay. That was my friend Finn Leary from ENJ. Someone canceled and they need me for an all-nighter downtown. The first meeting is in an hour."

"Christmas windows?"

"Yup." She got up, seeming distracted. "Where did I put my sneakers?"

Sam spotted a pair with untied laces wedged under the love seat. He eased them out with the toe of his boot.

"Thanks," she said, sitting down again. She bent forward to wiggle her feet into them and tie the laces just so, her hair spilling over her face.

"What does ENJ stand for?" he asked.

"Take a guess," she mumbled.

"No idea. Tell me."

"The Emperor's New Jeans," she answered, looking up, her face flushed and laughing. "Yes, you heard right. That's the brand name and concept. Their jeans retail for seven hundred dollars."

Sam threw her a disbelieving look. "Seriously?"

"I'm not kidding."

"Why would anyone pay that much money for jeans?"

"I don't know." She rose from the love seat and he got

up out of the chair. "They look a lot like the ones I buy at the thrift store."

Sam took his jacket off the hook while she shrugged into hers. "There must be a difference."

"The word is distressed." Nicole found a warm scarf and hat but didn't put them on. "I understand they take new jeans into a back room and do terrible things to them."

She turned to rush back into the living room as if she'd forgotten something. "Don't let me forget—oh, there it is. Finn said to bring my portfolio. One job leads to another."

He looked disappointed, but he covered with an encouraging, "Of course. You're talented."

She picked up a black portfolio stashed next to her drafting table. "Oh, they just need a warm body who can operate power tools. Still and all, ENJ is the big time. It's a step up."

"Guess so." Sam sighed, sorry that the visit was over so soon.

The phone in her pocket rang again.

She moved away from Sam and looked at the number on the screen. "I'm on my way, Finn," she said with exasperation, not answering it.

Nicole rummaged through her kitchen cabinets and then under the sink, retrieving a big plastic bag to slip over the portfolio. She grabbed a tote and stuffed workclothes into it next. "Almost forgot those too," she said, pretty much to herself. "That'll do it. I'm ready."

"It stopped raining," Sam said.

"I don't trust this weather," she told him. "I'm going to make a mad dash, if you don't mind. I don't care if I get a little wet, but my portfolio shouldn't."

He understood that she couldn't turn down gigs, but she still seemed a little too eager to shoo him out. Sam let it go.

Nicole opened the door and waved him through with the hand that held the gloves and hat. "After you. Did you bring an umbrella?" Not that she remembered seeing one.

Into his jacket, he put on the Stetson and touched a finger to the brim. "This'll do it for me. How are you getting there?"

"Bus."

"I'll walk you to the stop."

She took his arm once they were out on the street. Sure enough, the rain began again, a light drizzle that soon intensified. She used her scarf to wipe her face.

Sam noticed. He took off his Stetson and put it on her head. Nicole was secretly delighted. It was too big, but she wasn't going to be wearing it long.

Sam grinned down at her. "You should buy one. You look damn cute in a cowboy hat. And get some boots to match."

"I have a pair somewhere. But that's neither here nor there," she protested, laughing. "You're going to get soaked." His thick hair was full of raindrops and his wet eyelashes seemed even darker.

Sam shrugged. "I don't care."

"Well, it's really nice of you to get wet to keep me dry."

They stayed close until they got to the corner. There was no one in the open shelter and the seat was drenched with splashes from passing traffic. They stood huddled together, looking down the congested avenue. Not a bus in sight. She chattered about the route she would take, and Sam listened patiently enough. The street noise reverberated in the shelter.

Nicole looked up at him. The cold air and driving rain had brought out a high color in his cheeks and his dark eyes gleamed. He wasn't even shivering. A bus shelter was about as outdoorsy as you could get in this part of New York, and he seemed totally . . . himself somehow.

Sam's gaze stayed on her face. She thought for a minute that he was reading her lips, and then realized that he was about to do what she didn't want to think about.

Before the bus finally lumbered across the intersection, it happened. Brief though it was, the kiss was anything but chaste. Her lips stayed parted when he raised his head. Nicole gazed up into dark brown eyes that regarded her with serious intensity.

The blue and white bus pulled up, the doors opened with a wet *whoosh,* and a lot of people got off in front, ignoring the driver's admonition to use the back door. Sam and Nicole waited until the last second.

"I'll call you tomorrow," Sam said softly. He brushed a stray lock of her hair away from her cheek.

She hesitated to answer but only because she didn't want to leave him.

"Yo, lovebirds," the bus driver called. "You two gettin' on or what?"

"Just me . . . Oh—here's your hat!" She took it off and handed it back quickly, fumbling for her MetroCard before she let Sam give her a hand up the bus stairs.

He remained in the shelter as the bus pulled away, giving her a gallant salute with the Stetson in his hand. Swaying in the center aisle, she waved back, even though she knew he couldn't see her.

Nicole got a seat after several minutes of standing. She rubbed the condensation from the bus window with a gloved hand, holding her portfolio and the tote on her lap as rush-hour passengers crowded on.

She couldn't think of the right word for how good that kiss felt. Sam Bennett was trouble. A poignant sigh escaped her, unheard on the packed bus.

She would be smart to quit while she was ahead and set a few boundaries. Especially since Sam was going to be leaving New York so soon. Whirlwind romances weren't worth the loneliness afterward.

But he's something different. Take a chance.

She ignored the inner voice that dared her and looked absently out the window.

The slow-moving traffic was a blur of taxi-yellow streaks punctuated with red lights as drivers hit the brakes on the slick streets. Most of the store windows and building entrances were already decorated for the holidays with colored tinsel garlands and gleaming balls.

She rubbed a clear spot into the foggy window to see better, thinking that she still hadn't picked out a Christmas tree. Nicole considered stopping by Theo's lot tomorrow. Last year he'd had one of his helpers deliver a tree for her. The guy had lugged it two blocks over and up five flights of stairs, and then refused a tip.

Nicole rested her head against the cool window. The window fogged over again.

Bundled up, she was overly warm inside her woolly cocoon. The weather had gone from bad to worse in less than an hour, with winds from the east turning sleet to accumulating slush on every corner.

The driver announced her stop and she rose, exiting with several tourists who were eager to start shopping on Fifth Avenue. They walked north, she headed south.

She rewound her scarf so that her mouth was covered and pulled her hat down to her eyebrows. She kept close to the buildings, trying to dodge the sleet and walking as quickly as she could on the slippery pavement. The icy freshness of the air didn't snap her out of her reverie.

Wouldn't it be nice, she thought wistfully, to be back with Sam under that bus shelter. There was something magical about the simple act of walking with him—she felt protected. He took the curb side, for one thing. And he kept her near him.

Talk about wanting what she couldn't have.

It wasn't like she could tell Sam to go away. Nicole fully intended to hire him again to do the unfinished window at Now before the boutique owner came back from vacation.

Her cell phone chimed with an incoming message. Nicole stepped into a doorway for shelter and found the phone. She looked at the sender: Darci Powers.

Hello fromm Aspen! Wish u war here!

Her boss had yet to master texting. Nicole opened the attached photo, taken on a ski lift. The rock-jawed blond guy whose lap Darci was sitting on had held the phone to snap it.

He had blindingly white teeth and wraparound goggles that reflected Darci's adoring gaze. Good luck, Nicole thought. See you around the ski lodge. Her boss's latest romance would gather speed and slam into a tree soon enough, at which point Darci would come home.

A longer text quickly followed. Nicole deciphered it. Darci was very happy with Lars. And she loved the completed window. Her accountant would make out a check for Nicole to pick up. *Adjö*. Swedish for good-bye. She was staying in Aspen for a second week.

Whew. That meant Nicole would be paid soon, which meant she could pay her crew before Christmas. She even had time to complete the second window. If she could come up with an idea as good as the first.

She texted back a thank-you, exclamation point, and tucked the phone back in her purse. Nicole picked up her portfolio and kept on going.

To round out her portfolio, Nicole had done a few sketches for the window that remained unfinished and added them to the photos she'd printed of the completed cityscape scene that captured every detail.

Finn wanted to see what she was up to. But the ENJ job didn't require thinking.

No improvising allowed. She knew every element in the windows had been designed and approved in advance, which was fine with her. Sometimes being creative was more work than she'd bargained for.

Nicole had done all-nighters before but not for a while. You got your orders and you did whatever it took to complete the windows before the store opened.

She thought back. Her first one, she'd been a few credits away from completing her degree in art and desperate for work to help pay the last of her tuition. She hadn't even minded having her armpit in the face of a complete stranger while they both drove nails into a splintery structure that really wanted to fall down on them.

Nicole stopped in front of her destination. The windows were already covered with huge sheets of white paper.

She moved to the enormous glass doors of the front entrance, remembering just in time to remove the plastic bag that covered her portfolio. She stuffed it into a pocket, squooshing out all the air to make it fit, then went through the doors, which swung inward at a touch.

She spotted Finn as soon as she walked in. Gangly and red-haired, he was hard to miss, especially on a ladder, where he was adding a few accessories to a high display.

His eyebrows, also red, went up when he saw her, and he broke into a gap-toothed grin. "Hi, Nicole!"

Shoppers, intent on hunting down bargains, moved aside as she went by. There weren't any out where you could see them in the pricey store, Nicole knew that. The clearance racks were down a short flight of stairs and in the back.

She walked his way, but not quickly, to get a feel for the visual displays that were already in place. The way the aisles were set up—narrow where management wanted people to slow down, wide in other spots to encourage flow to high-profit areas—guided customers without making them aware of it. Retail consultants did that: systems for every aspect of shopping boosted profits noticeably.

Jingle, jingle. A Christmas carol rocked out over the sound system. Subtly speeding up the music made people shop a little faster.

The holidays were crucial to the bottom line. A Fifth Avenue flagship store was a very big deal, and the daily take was closely tracked in December, sometimes by the hour.

She didn't envy the sales associates. They were under constant pressure to meet goals that got set higher every year. All she had to do was follow directions and stay awake.

Finn stepped off the ladder and folded it up. He held it in one hand and motioned for her to come over.

"I'm early," she said. "Sorry about that."

He gave her a friendly wink. "Not a problem. I'm glad we have time to talk before everyone else shows up."

Nicole followed him, eager to get behind the scenes so she could unwrap her scarf and take off her wet jacket and hat.

Finn stashed the ladder in a utility area behind the main display wall and unlocked a door with a key from the ring on his belt. "Welcome to my nightmare," he joked.

She walked into a room that was filled with bald mannequins and scattered with plaster arms and legs. Some mannequins were in halves, with legs stretching up to the ceiling and torsos resting on the floor. Shiny, artificial wigs for them were clipped to an improvised clothesline that stretched across a wall. One old wig had been turned into a freaky critter with googly eyes on springs and slung onto a featureless head.

Huge cardboard boxes were filled with items marked down or returned so often they were no longer for sale.

The staff got the pick of those. Other boxes held plastic hangers tossed in every which way. Nicole knew if she picked up one, all the others would come with it in a giant clump.

The ENJ design team had to eat on the run, she could see that. She noted a half-eaten hot dog in a bun in the palm of an extended plaster hand.

"Is that your lunch?" she asked Finn.

"Yes." He picked it up. "How did you know?"

"The extra mustard."

She and Finn had devoured way too many dirty-water dogs from street carts in their art school days. Nicole didn't think she could ever eat another.

Finn finished off his meager meal in a couple of big bites. "Late in the day, but better than nothing. They don't let us go out to eat just because it's noon, you know. By the way, the new visual manager is a real pain. His name is Xandro."

"Never heard of him."

Finn spelled it out. "No last name. Just Xandro. I think it means 'slave driver' on whatever planet he's from. Stay out of his way."

"Okay. As far as I'm concerned, you're the boss."

Finn made a wry face. "I wish. But I'm dying to see your portfolio. C'mon, we can sit over here." He pushed aside a heap of tagged tops and jeans that she guessed would go on the mannequins eventually. "Hang on a sec."

"Okay."

He reached into the tangled garments and pulled out a beautiful top in shimmering green. "Just wanted to set that aside for my beloved. Can't beat that forty percent employee discount. Janey looks fantastic in green."

Nicole was taken aback. They'd exchanged e-mails, but she hadn't actually seen much of Finn in the last couple of years even though they both lived in Manhattan. Somehow their infrequent conversations had never touched on their personal lives. "You're still with her?"

"Of course. We're going to get married in the spring."

Nicole felt a slight pang. Her various relationships hadn't lasted. But then . . . she hadn't wanted them to.

"How about you, Miss Busy? Found time for a boyfriend yet?"

Finn's offhand comment stung a little. She wasn't going to let it show.

"I just met a cowboy from Colorado," she answered quickly.

"You're kidding. A real cowboy?"

"He walks like one." Nicole blushed a bit when her friend shot her an amused look. "But maybe he's a rancher. I know there's a difference. I mean, he lives on a ranch—look, I didn't get all the details."

Flustered, she paused for a moment.

"That doesn't sound like you," Finn mused.

Nicole cleared her throat. "His name is Sam Bennett and he's in New York for the next four weeks, doing Christmas installations with a city crew. I needed some help, with a window, he happened to walk by, and, um, he volunteered."

"Sounds rooooomantic," Finn teased, trying to sabotage her quick recovery.

Nicole shrugged. Her old pal didn't need to know about a mere kiss, even if it had happened only an hour ago and left her tingling. That subject was slated for discussion with Sharon Levitt, her best friend.

They hadn't seen each other in way too long. Like her, Sharon worked on windows but as a team member, not solo. They liked to talk, eat, and stay in for rented DVD marathons, watching corny romantic movies one after another and laughing their heads off.

But both of them tended to get teary over the classics. However, Sharon could analyze an on-screen kiss and figure out how it would affect the plot in less time than it took to polish off a bottle of chardonnay between them. She was pretty good with real relationships too.

Nicole knew that meeting Sam in no way qualified as one of those. But she was going to call Sharon tonight.

"Don't be so juvenile" was Nicole's answer to Finn.

Setting the tote where she could find it later, she untied the strings on her portfolio and flipped to the sketches and photos of the Christmas windows. Finn sat down beside her, taking his time to study the details. "These are fantastic, Nicole. The now-and-then streetscape is great. Where is this place? I gotta walk by."

"Upper West Side." She told him the nearest cross street. "You don't think the concept is too sentimental?"

"Hell, no. Anything heartwarming is a big draw. And I love the moving elements—the snow, the rink. You get the kids to take a peek, you got the moms. And then the dads hear about a great window from the kids and go in to do last-minute shopping—you know how it works."

Nicole nodded. "The owner took off before I could show her the redesign, but she just texted me that she loved it."

"What inspired you?" Finn was looking at the first, preliminary drawings. "These are totally different. I mean, they're okay, but they don't grab me."

"I hired a new kid. He fell off a ladder and destroyed the backdrop. We had to start over, but I didn't mind. I never was all that happy with the first version."

"So you ended up doing twice the work for the same pay." He chuckled.

"Wouldn't you?"

"Yeah," he agreed. "I know where you're coming from

on that. I like to get it right." He leafed through the rest of the drawings. "Did any of these get built, or are they at the idea stage?"

Nicole shook her head to the first part of his question. "No. Just ideas. Strictly imaginary."

"The windows of New York need you, Nicole. You gotta start showing your stuff to more people," Finn said in a friendly way.

"Like who?"

He lifted his head as if he was listening to something. "Sounds like they're closing. Let's talk about this later." He set the portfolio on a high table and left it open.

"Is the meeting going to be in here?"

Finn shook his head. "Nope. In the shoe department. It's the only place with enough seating."

"How many freelancers did you hire?"

Finn did a rough count in his head. "Five windows, four people in each, so that's twenty—unless someone doesn't show."

She smiled wryly. "That can happen."

He picked up a piece of paper with a scribbled list of names that had been divided into columns. She saw her name at the top of one.

"I'm putting you in charge of three others into a window at the front. I'll decide which one after Xandro does his presentation."

The two big windows to either side of the front entrance were the most important. They weren't called focus windows for nothing.

"Thanks," Nicole said eagerly.

"Don't thank me yet," Finn answered with a shake of his head. "We have a long night ahead."

They exited the mannequin room and walked through the store. The sales associates helped the last customers finish shopping, and one unlocked the door as each left.

The CLOSED sign went up. A security guard took over the locking and unlocking, letting in the freelancers as they arrived.

The usual ragtag group of art students and design freaks, Nicole thought with an inward smile. Some of their outfits were pretty strange, but you didn't dress to kill, you dressed to survive. They would be working nonstop under hot lights, crawling over and around each other for hours in the papered-up windows.

"Okay, people, listen up. This is the concept," Xandro began. "I want to show the other side of Christmas. The bad side."

Nicole could imagine the stares the narrow-faced man was getting from the front rows, but no one said a word. Behind heavy, black-framed glasses, his eyes were hard to see. His long, dark hair was thinning on top, drawn back into a limp ponytail.

"The mood is disillusionment," Xandro went on. "Somber colors. Empty gift boxes. Unpaid bills. Ripped jeans that look tough enough to get our customer through the real holidays. I'm talking urban grit, not spun sugar . . ."

Nicole turned slightly to Finn, eyes wide. He was straddling a low bench with slanted mirrors built into the base, next to her in the back row. She hoped the visual manager couldn't hear her whisper, "Sounds grim. Is he for real?"

"Apparently," Finn muttered. "But I'd like to know how he got ENJ corporate to approve a concept like that."

Some sixth sense made him look up when Xandro pointed to him. "Excuse me, Finn. Is that you talking? Do you have questions?"

"No."

"Then let's move on. Here are the sketches."

His assistant set up one for each of the five windows on lightweight easels.

"Finn will assign people to teams with specific responsibilities for parts of the overall design. He and I will be checking to see that everyone stays on track and on time as the hours go by. Let's meet our goals, people."

Xandro snapped his fingers, and Finn rose with a sigh that only Nicole could hear. He moved in front of the freelancers.

"We're going to start by making oval frames for people outside to look through," Finn announced. "We're going for a shadowbox effect. Raise your hands if you have any questions."

No one did. They knew what he was talking about.

Finn pointed to several members of the group, including Nicole. "You, you, you, you, and you. Grab those cans of spray adhesive."

Nicole turned to look at the Plexiglas panels with large, peel-off ovals in their centers. The ovals would be removed when the "frame" part was sprayed on and the panels placed in front of the store's glass windows.

She lined up with the others and took a spray can from the table, plus gloves, a face mask, and goggles.

"Okay. You, you, and you"—Finn pointed to three guys—"follow her. Each window bay has a bucket of dust. When she's done spraying, throw dust in handfuls until the Plexiglas around the oval is covered with it. Do not, repeat, do not, throw dust at Nicole."

She smiled wanly at his joke. The guys were eyeing her already. They probably wouldn't act up—Finn wouldn't stand for it. But he couldn't be everywhere. Wouldn't it be nice, she thought, if Sam were here? He was good at following directions, for a cowboy.

Xandro clapped his hands. "The ovals do not come off until the frame is dusted," he warned. "And please note the pond liners already installed at the bottom of the window bays. We're going to fill them with more dust and grit. And some broken bricks," he added proudly.

Finn glanced at the drawings. "Then the mannequins go in. I need them dressed while the dust people are working." He pointed to a few more freelancers.

Nicole snapped on her paper mask and pressed the flexible edges to fit her face. She set her equipment by the window she would do and went back to her tote, finding a bandanna to wrap around her head and a worn workshirt to cover her clothes. It wouldn't be long before she was overheated and down to her tank top. This was the miserable part of making magic.

An hour or so later, she peeled off the large paper oval to reveal the clear space that people outside would look through, and carefully wiped away specks of dust with a squirt bottle of window cleaner. By now she had plastic grocery bags tied over her shoes so she wouldn't track the grit underfoot into the store. The frame was perfect. Finn gave it a thumbs-up.

Coughing, Nicole took off her improvised booties and gloves, and then the face mask, pitching everything into a huge trash can. The platforms that would hold the mannequins were in position. She'd put on fresh protective gear when they were installed.

She peeled off her workshirt and the sweater underneath. Tank top time. The only advantage to working under hot lights was sweating off a few pounds. She tucked the rib-knit top into her jeans, brushing them off and then washing her hands with a bottle of sanitizer.

Xandro had dragged Finn off to look at a window that wasn't as far along, and it was another minute before he came back to her.

"Think we should order the pizza now?" Finn asked. "We're going to need eight. Might take a while."

"Sure. I'll do it. Where's the phone?"

Finn moved behind the register counter and picked up an old-fashioned landline, setting it out with a thunk. He found a handful of take-out menus and fanned them out. "Here ya go. Make sure one pizza is vegetarian. Other than that, anything goes. And get nine six-packs of cola and one of ginger ale."

"Got it." Grease, salt, sugar, and caffeine. Freelancer fuel.

She picked the grubbiest menu, figuring it was the most popular. Then she placed the order and gave the street number.

"Hah? Say what? There ain't no apartment buildings at that address. You crank callers drive me crazy." The pizza guy hung up.

Nicole called the next one. Fortunately, the only question they asked was cash or credit.

"Cash," she replied, waving Finn over. He took out a roll of bills and whipped off four fifties.

About forty-five minutes later, someone thumped on the glass doors. Nicole nodded to the security guard, who turned the key left in the lock, opening the door with a flourish. "Do I get some?" he asked.

"Sure."

The delivery guy was so short that she couldn't see his face behind the stack of pizza boxes. Nicole took five off the top and set them aside. "How much?"

"A hundred forty with the soda." He went back outside to get drinks from the huge wire basket mounted on his bicycle. He must have balanced the insulated pizza carrier on top.

She handed him the cash. "Could I have a receipt, please? Take out twenty for yourself."

The deliveryman seemed happy with his generous tip.

One of the crew came running over to help, whooping as he took the boxes away.

The guy folded the money and stuffed it into his pocket, giving her the scrawled receipt and change in small bills. Then he tried to look over her shoulder when someone cranked the music to full-blast volume.

"You havin' a party in here?"

"No."

"Sounds like a party."

She glanced in the direction of his gaze. A female free-lancer was dancing with a slice of pizza in her mouth and a hammer in her hand, swinging it in time with the thumping beat.

"Looks like a party," the deliveryman said hopefully. He eyed her, and Nicole wished she still had her baggy workshirt on—or failing that, a garbage bag. Hard to believe anyone thought she was hot with no makeup and her hair under a dirty bandanna.

"It isn't. We're installing new windows. Good-bye." Nicole walked him backward toward the door and used it to move him out to the sidewalk. The security guard was chowing down on a slice and soda.

"*Mmf.* Sorry," he said when he came back, chewing. "Good pizza. Get some before it's all gone."

Nicole went over to the others, selecting a cheese slice and devouring it.

Xandro clapped his hands when they'd all eaten. "Wash up, people. Time to dress our boys and girls."

One of the freelancers had already taken apart the mannequins. A row of upturned legs awaited their ENJ jeans, socks, and shoes. The matching torsos would be stuck on and arms added, then dressed. Plaster heads, wigs on, were being artfully smudged with gray powder.

Nicole exchanged a look with Finn. They were probably thinking the same thing. The concept was depressing. Not a trace of red, no sparkle, not an iota of holiday cheer. But it was what they were getting paid to do.

Hours later, the installation was complete and the skinniest freelancer had squeezed between the Plexiglas and the store window to rip out the concealing paper. Not a soul was on the streets besides Xandro, videotaping the windows from the outside.

He came back in, shivering. "Stay where you are, everybody. I have to send videos of everything to Kevin Talley. Remember the name. He's the CEO of Emperor. Which is ENJ's parent company, in case you didn't know."

Xandro began to whistle as he plugged the video recorder into his laptop's USB port.

"He is going to love it, just love it," he enthused.

No one else seemed to share the visual manager's passion. But then Xandro wasn't totally exhausted and covered in dust.

The freelancers pulled off masks and gloves, filling up another huge trash barrel with that and the crumpled paper. Finn dragged out several vacuum cleaners from a utility closet and asked for volunteers.

The noise made Xandro look up from his laptop. "Can you keep it down?" he asked irritably. "Talley's looking at the videos right now. Says he'll get right back to me."

He stared into the laptop again, its glowing screen reflected in his black-framed glasses.

Slumped on a folding chair, Nicole amused herself by looking at the twin reflections in his lenses. She saw him frown and his eyes widen.

"Oh no. He hates it. Absolutely hates it," Xandro muttered. He typed quickly on the keyboard in response.

"Huh? Didn't he sign off the concept?" Finn asked.

"He saw the preliminary sketches." Xandro's eyes frantically scanned the laptop's screen as more e-mails arrived.

"I made a few changes after that. He says—oh, please—I don't believe this—"

The designer paused to read, then quoted aloud. "Talley says those are the ugliest windows he's ever seen—and that I—I went too far. He says to rip out the panels and leave the bays empty. And do it now."

A chorus of disbelieving groans went up.

Finn shrugged. "You heard him, everyone. Prepare to de-install. Vacuums, suck when ready. But take the mannequins out first. We can't get the clothes dirty."

A cold sun shot rays of light down the Manhattan street when they were nearly finished. Nicole was using goo remover and a paint scraper to get the last bit of dust off her Plexiglas when a long black car with a chauffeur at the wheel pulled up in front of the flagship store.

Without waiting for the chauffeur to open the back door, a man got out, barely glancing at her.

He was trim, walking quickly, with a mature face and close-cropped white hair. She noticed his black sweatshirt and distressed jeans were both ENJ styles as he pounded on the glass door. Nicole cast a glance over her shoulder at Finn, who looked at Xandro.

"That's Kevin Talley," the visual manager breathed. "Let him in."

The weary security guard unlocked the door and straightened to military uprightness as the CEO breezed past him.

Talley stopped and looked around. "Good morning," he said to the scattered freelancers. They stayed where they were, frozen, as if they were playing Statues among the dressed mannequins they had removed from the windows, which stood upright on round, heavy bases, staring blankly.

Finn helped Nicole down. The CEO stood where he was, rocking a little on his feet with his hands clasped in front of him.

"Guess you already know that we're starting over," he said. "Don't worry. You'll be paid the regular flat rate for the install and overtime for the extra hours. Someone will be in touch with each of you by tonight—I assume Mr. Leary has everyone's cell number."

He looked toward Finn, who nodded.

Talley's gaze moved to Xandro. "Of course, we have to find a new visual manager first. Someone who understands what a chain of command is."

The designer glared at him. The expression on the younger man's face made it clear that he knew what was coming. "Go to hell," Xandro snarled.

"You bet. Thanks for giving me one more reason to fire you," Talley said. "You can call human resources for the details," he added calmly. "I left a message with the department head. The office opens at nine."

Xandro closed his laptop and stalked off to get his coat. The only sound was the faint creaking of his highly polished shoes. He held his head high as he left. Nicole saw him stalk past the now-empty front windows and vanish around the corner.

All that work for nothing. But at least they would be paid, and then some.

Exhausted, she fell into bed after taking a shower. The morning sun moved across her pillow, but it didn't wake her. Nicole slept until two in the afternoon, when the ring of her cell phone finally jolted her into semiconsciousness.

"Hello?" she answered sleepily.

"Hiya!" Sam's voice was loud.

She held the phone away from her ear, frowning at it. She rubbed her eyes before she spoke. "Where are you?"

"Up in a tree. Downtown, looking uptown. Great view. I can see the Empire State Building."

"That's nice. Don't fall."

She heard faraway yells, probably from the crew he worked with.

"Sam?"

"Yeah. How'd it go with the windows last night?"

Nicole yawned. "Put 'em in, took 'em out. Lots of drama—I'll tell you later. The CEO hated the concept. He stopped by in person to fire the visual manager."

"He should hire you," Sam said loyally.

Nicole smiled to herself. "Not going to happen. Besides, Finn is next in line."

"Oh, okay. Hey, you have any plans for dinner tonight?"

She smiled and settled back down into the puffy warmth of her comforter. It was funny to hear Sam ask a question like that from inside a tree. "No."

"I'll swing by around eight. We'll figure something out."

"Absolutely not. I have to catch up on my sleep. Tomorrow night."

"We can order in. How about pizza?"

"Gah. No."

He laughed at the vehement reply. "You pick, then. I don't care."

"Let's go to—how about Chinatown? I know a little place with great dumplings."

"Sure," he said enthusiastically. "Hang on, I just turned around. Now I'm looking downtown. That must be Chinatown right there—that's the top of a pagoda."

She ran her fingers through her tangled hair and thought. He wasn't seeing things. There was a tall pagoda on Canal Street, five or six stories high. "I know that building."

"Is it a restaurant?"

"I don't think so." She yawned hugely. "Can we talk about this later?"

He didn't answer. She heard someone call his name. Sam came back on, sounding hurried. "Look, I gotta go.

Call me when you wake up all the way. I really want to see you."

"Okay. Bye." With a smile, Nicole rolled over and went back to sleep.

It was dark when she woke up again, but not very late. Sharon might even be able to come over tonight. Nicole got out of bed and checked her kitchen shelves for popcorn.

Several boxes in stock. She picked up her cell phone and hit a number on speed dial.

"Hello!"

Sharon was as bouncy as her voice.

"Hi. It's me, Nicole."

"Oh my! Haven't heard from you in a few weeks. Must be big news. I get three guesses."

"Not that big. But go for it."

"You're moving out of that glorified closet. A dream date stood you up. You took a nine-to-five job."

"None of the above. I met a cowboy."

Sharon giggled. "You're kidding, right? Did the rodeo come to Madison Square Garden?"

"No. That happens in spring."

"Does this buckaroo have a name?"

Nicole didn't answer the question, just extended an invitation. "Come by at seven. Hot popcorn, extra butter, free refills."

Sharon whooped. "Real life is better than a movie."

Nicole had the love seat, and Sharon was sitting cross-legged in the giant club chair. Her friend was lanky and liked to fold herself up into it. She fiddled with a curl of her brunette hair, fixing her green-eyed gaze on Nicole.

Sharon had calmed down some since they'd spoken on the phone, devouring most of a huge bowl of fresh popcorn while they caught up on every other subject but Sam.

Sharon set the empty bowl down for Nicole's cat to investigate, watching his whiskers brush delicately against the buttery sides. The cat found a split kernel and ran under the sofa with it in his mouth.

"Go, Whiskeroo. It's great popcorn." She leaned back in the club chair. "You really know how to microwave, Nicole."

"Ah, it's not that hard."

Sharon nodded vaguely. "So. Tell me about this cowboy."

Nicole hesitated for only a second. "His name is Sam Bennett, he comes from Colorado, and he installs Christmas trees."

"I could jump rope to that." Sharon rolled her eyes. "But let's get the facts out of the way. His eye color, height, build, personality?"

Nicole filled her in.

"Now for the good stuff," Sharon said eagerly. "Your thoughts and feelings. Where you want to go with this. Why you find him attractive—never mind. You told me what he looked like."

"I just hired him to help me finish the job at Now."

"Ohhh. You're the boss. Now, that is interesting. Does he let you make the decisions?"

"You are really annoying sometimes, Sharon, do you know that?"

"Moving right along," her friend replied cheerfully, "how about his prior relationships? I know all about yours, skip the recap." Sharon picked up a pillow and tucked it behind her neck, getting comfortable.

"I just met him!" Nicole wailed. "I don't know much about his background except that he grew up on a ranch."

"With a moo-moo here and a—"

"Shut *up*. He's incredibly nice. Way nicer than your average arrogant New York man."

Sharon adjusted the pillow and dangled her fuzzy-socked feet over the arm of the club chair. "None of them think they're average. That's why they're arrogant. So what does Sam do again?"

"Right now, he's doing Christmas installations for a friend's company."

"Oh. Not a designer, you mean. But good with his hands. That's a plus," Sharon said airily. "So when is he going back to Colorado?"

The question hung in the air between them. Sharon didn't mean everything she said to be a joke.

"Um, maybe New Year's Day. He did ask if I'd ever done the Times Square thing on New Year's Eve. I told him I hated crowds."

"So much for the date of a lifetime."

"I do hate crowds, Sharon. You know that."

Her friend sat up facing forward and crossed her legs again, putting the tips of her fingers together. "Nicole, there are eight million people in New York City. Divided in half, that's about four million males and four million females. Filter for availability and—"

Nicole made a wry face. "The number comes down to about forty."

"I wouldn't go that high. Not in the Verified Single category."

"Cynic," Nicole said.

"I'm a realist. But that doesn't mean you shouldn't enjoy this cowboy. Just have fun with him. How long has it been?"

"That"—Nicole pointed a finger at her best friend—"is a question I have no intention of answering."

Sharon held up her hands in mock surrender.

Chapter 6

Douglas sat at a card table, working on a school project. He traced three different-size circles on a sheet of white craft paper, then cut them out and taped them together to make a snowman.

"This is kid stuff," he grumbled.

His mother glanced his way. "Last time I looked, you were still a kid. What are those for?"

"Holiday decorations for the class window."

Amanda looked on admiringly. "Make me one," she begged.

"Your little sister is impressed."

That didn't quite mollify Douglas, but he didn't argue.

"Here. He needs a face." He handed over the snowman and started cutting out another for himself.

Amanda picked one of the crayons scattered on the table and began to draw, concentrating on the task. She was so quiet her big brother hardly noticed her, working on his own, until she held up her artwork for his approval.

He shook his head. "Amanda," he said patiently, "the small circle is for the face." He tapped it. "Here. The face always goes on top."

Amanda frowned as she studied her snowman. The smaller top and middle circles were blank. The bottom circle had four eyes, two above and two below a line for the mouth.

She peered at the snowman her brother had just finished. Then she rotated hers upside down to match it, more or less.

"Okay," she said with satisfaction. "He looks good now."

"Good enough." Douglas was trying not to laugh.

Amanda turned to her mother, who was making dinner in the apartment's tiny kitchen.

"Mommy!" she announced. "Look what I made!"

Maureen Fulton winked at Douglas and took the paper snowman from her daughter.

"That's very nice, honey. Let's put this up right now," she said. She used a magnet in the middle circle to affix Amanda's creation to the fridge.

"My snowman has a belly button," the little girl said happily. She plunked down the crayon and got out of her chair, heading to the low shelf that held her picture books and toys, scrambling up on the couch with a book and Buster.

Douglas looked up as his mother returned to the table. She set down an armful of cookbooks that she'd taken down from a cabinet over the refrigerator and slid into the chair that Amanda had just vacated.

"Are you going to bake?" he asked.

His mother nodded, opening the book on top of the stack. "Why not? Christmas is coming."

The boy gestured toward the big blue tin of store-bought cookies on the counter. "You don't have to, Mom. We have those."

"Uh-huh," Maureen said absently. "Finish that project and get started on your math worksheets."

"Later."

She held up a silencing hand. "No. Right now. And if

you really want to know, I was thinking of baking cakes to give away as presents."

Douglas thought that over while his mother stopped to study a recipe, tapping it with the eraser end of the pencil in her hand.

He read the title of it upside down. "Traditional Plum Pudding with Hard Sauce. How can sauce be hard?"

"It's just an expression," his mother explained. She turned the page, murmuring, "Too complicated. And too expensive."

A silence fell. The boy and his mother avoided each other's gaze. Douglas set aside the craft materials and got started on a math worksheet. He finished quickly, looking again at his mother.

"Wish I could get a job," he muttered.

"You have one," Maureen said quietly. "It's called home-work."

Douglas got started on another worksheet with story problems and little illustrations.

His mother continued turning pages and spoke again. "I'll find something. The man at the employment agency said new jobs are posted every day. And I'm applying on-line too."

He nodded, reading the first problem on the sheet aloud in a bored voice.

"If Billy charges three dollars an hour to mow a lawn with an area twenty feet by forty feet, how much will he earn if he mows a lawn five times larger? That's easy. Fifteen."

He jotted down the answer and drew a handlebar mustache on Billy.

Maureen smiled. "Your teacher might not appreciate the artwork."

With a scowl, Douglas flipped his pencil over to the eraser end and eliminated the mustache.

"Keep going," she said. "The first problem is always the easiest."

"Wish I was Billy," her son sighed. "There aren't any lawns to mow in New York City. Maybe I could shovel snow. If we get any." He raced through the next few problems.

Maureen pondered a recipe and took a minute to answer. "The super does that."

"Aw, Mom. What if we can't—"

"Christmas will come the way it always does," she interrupted him. "So don't you worry."

Amanda piped up. "Can we get a pink sparkle tree? Please?"

"We'll see, honey."

Douglas lowered his voice. "It's totally fake, Mom. No pine smell or anything."

"And no needles to sweep up. I have a coupon for the drugstore where she saw it. Thirty percent off entire purchase."

"Pink tree, pink tree." Amanda made up a little song for Buster, bouncing the toy on her lap. "Sparkle sparkle pink tree."

Douglas gave his mother his best disgusted look. She paid no attention. With a frown on his face, he returned to his homework, racing through the problems. The last one stumped him for a little while. He chewed his pencil and finished.

"I'm done. You can check it." He slid the worksheet on top of the open cookbook.

Without missing a beat, Maureen reviewed the math problems and his answers. "Very good. Everything's correct." She handed back the sheet and ruffled his hair. "Take the garbage to the chute, please. Then you can get ready for bed."

The boy skipped his usual protests, looking worriedly at his mother, who was absorbed in the next cookbook. "Okay," was all he said.

He went into the kitchenette and lifted the bag by its drawstrings, carrying it to the door. Douglas unlocked it and opened it, then shot the bolt so it would stay open for his trip down the hall to the chute.

It was several doors down. He dragged the bag, then hoisted it, pulling open the chute to shove it in and wrinkling his nose while he waited for it to fall.

An apartment door at the end of the hall opened and out came a neighbor in a hooded jacket with her fluffy white dog.

"Hey, Douglas," she called.

"Hi, Julie." He turned and walked back. "Can I pet Puff?"

"We're on our way out, but sure." The young woman with smooth dark hair and laughing eyes let go of the leash. Douglas kneeled, and the friendly little dog ran to him.

She stopped at the Fultons' door when Douglas's mother opened it to say hello. Amanda waved to her from the sofa.

"Hi, Maureen," Julie said. "I haven't seen you for a while. How's everything?"

"Oh, all right," Maureen replied. "How about you? Ready for Christmas?"

"I haven't even started shopping and I'm going to my folks' in Pennsylvania day after tomorrow," Julie sighed. She pushed the hood of her jacket back, looking a little flushed.

"Are you bringing Puff?" Douglas wanted to know.

"Yes, of course. My grandma loves her—she's knitting her a candy cane sweater."

Maureen didn't miss the disappointed look in the boy's eyes. The mother of two could read his mind.

"Doug, you can't take care of Puff for Julie," she said gently. "Dogs need to be walked at least twice a day, and I can't leave your sister alone to go with you. And bringing Amanda along is not an option. You know how much she hates to get into her snowsuit."

"Do I ever," he said with resignation. "I just want to earn some money for presents and stuff."

"I'm only going to be gone for a few days. Then Puff and I are coming right back," Julie responded quickly. "Tell you what. You could take care of my goldfish. I'd pay you a dollar a day."

"For how long?" Douglas asked.

"Oh, about a month. I'm going to be extra-busy until New Year's and I might forget to feed him. Goldfish don't bark, you know."

Douglas did the arithmetic in his head and seemed to come up short. "Maybe I could walk Puff right after school too. For two dollars."

"Doug." His mother's tone held a faint warning.

"Okay, make it two fifty and that way you're only paying half for the fish part."

Julie laughed outright, and Maureen pressed her lips together, fighting a smile.

"Please, Mom. It doesn't get dark until four. Me and Puff would just go down our street and back. Everyone on the block knows me, and Theo or somebody is always outside."

"Maybe."

"It would work," he insisted. "We have Julie's key and you're almost always home."

"That's true," Maureen replied. "But that could change."

Douglas scratched Puff's head, letting his mother think it over. "Julie, when did you get a goldfish?"

"Ah—I'm picking it up at the pet store tomorrow." Julie flipped back her hood, looking a little flushed.

Douglas didn't ask why. Julie looked hopefully at Maureen over his head.

His mother finally gave in, glancing down fondly at her son. "Oh, all right. Yes to both. For now."

"I won't ever forget to feed the fish, Julie," he said eagerly. "And I'll jog with Puff so she gets good exercise. Just on the sidewalk," he reassured his mother.

Julie extended a hand. "You got a deal. Two fifty a day until further notice."

They shook hands as the little dog wound her leash around Julie's legs.

"Mom, can I walk out with Julie and Puff right now?" Douglas wanted to know. "For practice."

Maureen hesitated for a second, then took his jacket and a knit hat from the front closet. "All right. You finished your homework. Here's some change. You can get a candy bar from the newsstand."

"Mom, you rock." It was his highest compliment. He handed the leash to Julie to slip on his jacket and held out a hand for the coins.

Unwound by her mistress, Puff scampered to the head of the stairs and zoomed down, with Julie and Douglas right behind her, both trying to catch hold of the leash.

Once out on the street, Julie made sure the boy was zipped up and got the knit hat on his head. She handed him the leash, and Puff trotted proudly between the two of them as they discussed the care and feeding of goldfish.

It wasn't long before they reached the newsstand and the Christmas tree lot right in front of it. There were fresh trees resting against the framework of two-by-fours, illuminated by several strings of colored lights.

Uncle Theo was sitting on a metal folding chair by the small trailer, sipping a cup of cocoa. He set it down to greet them with a wave. Douglas stopped, tugging on Julie's hand.

"Could I stay here with Theo? You can get me a chocolate bar," he said. "I don't care what kind. Puff wants to say hi, and I want to look at the Christmas trees."

The old man extended a thick-gloved hand to the little white dog trying to jump into his lap. "Hello, Julie. Douglas, you're out late."

"Candy run," he said.

Julie accepted the handful of change the boy gave her. "Be right back. Theo, do you want anything? A newspaper?"

"To sit on. Not to read. It's freezing out here."

She laughed and went into the newsstand. Douglas inspected the trees in a businesslike way before he found the fir with the crooked branch and checked the price without Theo seeing him.

Puff had made it to the old man's lap and was curled up inside his heavy jacket.

"Theo, can I set a tree aside?"

"I bet you mean the one you were looking at the other day. The Douglas fir."

Doug nodded. "Yeah. You have a good memory."

"Thank you," Theo rumbled. He peered at him from under shaggy eyebrows. "For how long?"

"I might have to owe you some of the money once I pick it up, but I can pay the whole amount by Christmas Eve for sure. I'm working for Julie—I'm going to walk Puff and feed her goldfish." Douglas hesitated. "I want the tree to be a surprise. For my mom."

"You know we close up the lot on Christmas Eve," Theo reminded him.

Douglas nodded, sticking his hands in his pockets. "I know."

"All right. We understand each other." Theo pulled off a thick glove and brought out a *SOLD* tag from an inside pocket. "Here you go. The tree can stay here until you're ready to bring it home. I won't say a word."

"Thanks!" Douglas hung the tag on a small branch and stepped back to admire the tall fir. "It's almost as big as the Rockefeller Center tree."

"It is a nice one," Theo agreed.

The boy looked at the old man as if he was about to say something else but didn't quite know how. Then his words came out in a rush. "Do you think I could work part-time for you too?"

Theo was startled by the question. "I don't know. What were you thinking of doing?"

Douglas scuffed the dropped pine needles and twigs with his winter boot. "I could sweep up the sidewalk after school. Make signs. Maybe help with bagging the trees. The smaller ones."

"Hmm," the old man said thoughtfully. "Did you talk to your mom about it?"

"No," Douglas said, abashed. "I just thought that maybe I could earn more."

"Ah." The old man considered the request. "Tell you what. You come by tomorrow with your mother and we can discuss it then."

Douglas thought that over. "She might have an interview or something."

"Then you can bring a note. Let's see what she says. I can't promise anything until then, but I won't tell her that you set aside a tree."

"Okay!" Douglas turned when he heard the door of the newsstand begin to open and saw Julie's gloved hand on the glass inside. He looked quickly back at Theo. "Don't tell her either. About the tree or about working for you."

"I won't."

The door swung all the way open and Julie came out with a newspaper and a couple of candy bars, letting Doug pick the one he wanted. "Looks like Puff made himself comfortable."

"Yes indeed." Theo lifted the fluffy white dog out of his jacket, tangled leash and all. "Time to go home, pooch."

"How about you?" Julie asked. She set Puff down on the sidewalk.

Theo jerked a thumb over his shoulder at the trailer. "I'll head inside when my nephew gets here. I'm too old for this kind of cold, let me tell you."

"Theo, you ought to let the younger generation take over," Julie said sympathetically.

He took the newspaper she handed him and shrugged. "Maybe so. Business is down."

"But—" Douglas began and shut up in the same second.

The old man patted his shoulder. "Of course you Fultons have always been my best customers. A tree, a wreath, fresh garlands—your mother likes to go all out."

Douglas hesitated a second before replying. "Well, this year, we might be getting just the tree. I don't think Mom has much time to decorate. But don't worry—Christmas isn't here yet."

He turned at the sound of squeals from a couple of kids, younger than he was. A family group was heading their way.

Theo rose stiffly from his folding chair so they would know the lot was open. "Customers. How about that. G'night, you two."

Julie handed Puff's leash to Doug when he'd put the candy bar in his pocket. She put on her gloves as they began to walk back. The energetic dog tugged him along, happy to be out in the fresh air again.

By the time they reached their building and climbed the stairs to their floor, they were both a little out of breath.

Julie's light knock brought his mother to the door with a finger to her lips. Maureen pointed to the alcove that served his little sister for a bedroom.

"Just got her to sleep," she whispered. "Thanks again, Julie."

"You bet. Talk to you tomorrow, Douglas," Julie whispered back. She went down the hall to her apartment, quietly unlocking and closing her door as Maureen brought her son inside.

He hung up his jacket and began to get ready for bed without argument. The little boy was in his pajamas and headed for the bathroom to brush his teeth when he stopped to look at his mother.

She was reading more recipes, working her way down the stack of cookbooks and making notes on a pad of paper.

"Past your bedtime," she said absently.

"You can't see the clock from there."

"Mom radar. We always know."

He went to her side and folded one arm to lean on her shoulder.

Maureen turned to kiss his cheek. "Guess you're getting too big to cuddle. You used to slide into my lap and stay there."

"Just wanted to see what you're doing." Douglas looked at the pad of paper, his gaze moving over the numbers. "Is that your math homework?" he teased.

"Just trying to figure out what it would cost to make some different cakes. Besides the ones for friends, I mean. And not from cookbooks."

Her son settled his chin on his folded arm, yawning. "Why?"

"Oh, it's fun to invent something new. Recipes are only a starting point once you know the basics."

Douglas thought that over. "I like the one we always have—the spice cake with white icing."

"And I always bake it," she reassured him. "Now go to bed."

"Okay. Love you."

"Love you too. Sleep well."

Douglas really was tired. Without a backward glance, he headed off to the small bedroom next to his sister's, going past the foldout couch where his mother slept.

Maureen watched him go, then closed the cookbook, thinking hard. She sighed, looking at a framed picture taken four years ago at the bakery, of all of them. Well, nearly all.

Amanda hadn't arrived yet. In the photo, Maureen was visibly pregnant, her white apron rounded out. Hank had his arm around her shoulders, smiling down at Douglas between them, munching on a chocolate cupcake.

After the car accident that had taken Hank's life—and shattered hers—she had kept going.

She'd had no choice.

A bewildered widow with no one to turn to and a baby on the way, she'd sold the business they'd started together, but not for much. The proceeds and the insurance Hank had insisted on buying had been enough to keep her and the kids since that dreadful time, but the money was running out.

Maureen had not anticipated that it would take so long to land a job now that she needed one. In her field—baking, catering, and food prep—night shifts were the rule, not the exception. Not something she could easily do with one child in grade school and one not ready for kindergarten.

She hated having to stall Douglas on the Christmas tree when she knew he wanted a big one—a real one. And now that Amanda was old enough to demand a pink sparkly tree, Maureen had to choose between them. They couldn't afford both.

She flipped over the page that Douglas had seen to the one below it, where she'd been balancing income with expenditures. Not fun, especially at this time of year. They were barely breaking even.

A scrawl at the bottom of the page circled some important names. Macy's Cellar. Bloomingdale's. Lord & Taylor. She still had contacts in the business, and she would just have to find more, see if she could get a buyer for a major department store interested in custom recipes.

It wasn't like she could bake a thousand cakes at home to sell. She needed an advance for supplies and to pay for the use of a professional refrigerator, and oven after hours, and a babysitter. None of which came cheap. Making a go of baking again was almost too much to imagine, but she had to try.

For now, they had a roof over their heads and everything they needed. She'd even managed to give them separate bedrooms—sort of. Maureen stared blankly ahead, half seeing her reflection in the window against the darkness outside.

The apartment hadn't seemed so small four years ago. She and Hank knew how to live on next to nothing, plowing their profits back into the bakery, happy just to be together, raising their little guy. The stairs that now seemed endless had been no big deal until her second pregnancy. Hank had done all the carrying, of course. Something else Douglas did without being asked, like a shadow of his father.

She needed the help, but it still hurt. Maureen bit back a sigh. She rose and put the cookbooks away.

About an hour before midnight, a truck pulled up with Greg at the wheel and Sam in the passenger seat. Greg put on his flashers and double-parked. Outside of the occasional pedestrian heading home, the side street was deserted.

Greg rolled down the window to talk to his uncle, who was on his feet, roping the trees to the framework. "How's business?"

"Picked up a bit tonight. Sold some nice trees."

"Which ones?"

"The biggest," Theo said proudly. "You know how it goes, the family comes looking for a medium and the kids get Mom and Pop to spring for a seven footer. They hail a taxi and bribe the guy to tie it on top. Ho-ho-ho."

"How many?"

"Four out the door, and one on layaway."

"What? We don't do layaways."

"Special customer—" Theo squinted into oncoming headlights, his wrinkled face suddenly white. "Hey, watch out!"

Greg looked into his rearview mirror and saw a large pickup that had just turned the corner. It raced toward them and swerved around the SUV, clipping the far corner of the A-frame. A tree fell forward with a thump, just missing Theo, who stumbled as he dodged it.

The old man swore loudly in Greek as his nephew and Sam scrambled out. Mohsan, the newsstand owner, looked through his window, concerned by the commotion.

"You all right?" Greg asked Theo.

"What does it look like? I'm on my feet, ain't I? Somebody pick up that tree."

Greg led his uncle to the folding chair. "In a minute. Who the hell were those guys?"

Sam saw the truck reach the other end of the block, zooming through the intersection several seconds after the light turned from yellow to red. A few cars honked. The streetlights gave him a glimpse of the truck's cab, filled with what looked like Christmas trees, tightly wrapped and tied down.

"Tree sellers, maybe. The cab was piled high with 'em."
He turned to Greg and Theo.

The old man grunted. "Sellers, hah. More like thugs.
Seen 'em before, but not for the last few years. No permit.
Dried-up trees. They sucker people with low prices and
muscle in on legit operations by parking around the corner
and siphoning off customers."

Sam listened as he walked around the frame, looking
for damage. Except for one broken brace, it was intact and
felt solid. He reappeared in the area where the sellers
waited for buyers and lifted the fallen tree, settling it back
into the frame.

The newsstand owner had come out. "They were driving
like maniacs! You could sit there and get killed! Theo, you
okay?"

"I'm fine."

"You want cocoa? Free."

"It's always free," Theo reminded him.

"Even so," the newsstand owner said. "It'd do you good."

"Thanks, Mohsan," Greg said. "Not right now, I guess."

He had a hand on his uncle's shoulder, staying close to
him. It was clear to Sam that Theo would never admit he
was shaken up, but his nephew wasn't taking any chances.

"Should we report it?" Sam asked.

Greg looked at him skeptically. "You see the plates?"

"No. The truck was moving too fast."

"Then there's nothing to report."

Theo rose, brushing off Greg's hand. "I'm tired. I oughta
turn in."

"Good idea," his nephew said. "I'll drive you home."

The old man didn't argue about staying in the trailer, for
a wonder. He stomped over to the passenger side of the
SUV and got in, staring straight ahead with fire in his eyes,
as if he could still see the vanished truck.

"Sam, can you cover the lot for an hour?" Greg asked.

"Sure."

Greg looked toward his vehicle. "I'll drop Theo at his house in Astoria, have some soup with him and Aunt Effie, make sure he's all right. Then I'll be back. It's time I took a shift."

"Fine with me. I doubt that truck will be back." Sam walked with Greg to the driver's side. "Take it easy, Theo," he said when the door was open.

The old man didn't look his way. "Fifteen years in this location and no trouble," he muttered. "I don't like it. I don't like it at all."

Greg gave Sam a what-can-you-do shrug and got in. They drove away.

A couple of people walked by after a while, but no one stopped to browse. Sam figured he might as well go inside the trailer and pack. He could leave the door open. It wouldn't take him long. Outside of the Stetson, everything he'd brought to New York could be thrown right back into his dad's old GI duffel and taken up the block.

Except for the Santa made of red and white carnations and the red-foil-wrapped miniature pine tree. He decided to leave those on the shelf over the trailer's messy bed.

He made sure he had his phone, stopping for a minute to look at the photos he'd taken of Nicole while they were working on the Now window. There were only a few. He wondered why she hadn't called him back.

Hard to believe she'd been asleep this long. She was probably out with friends, or someone from the ENJ crew. Still, she could have let him know. He was kind of ticked off about it.

He tossed the phone on the bed and started to fill the duffel. It took longer than he'd thought to fold the clean clothes and bag the dirty ones, and find all his socks.

Sam set the duffel by the trailer door and propped his

Stetson on top of it. Then he looked out, catching a glimpse of a customer in a puffy down jacket. Male or female, he couldn't tell. The hood was up and the person's back was to him.

He stepped outside. "Can I help you?" Maybe the person hadn't heard him, what with the hood. He waited another second.

"Oh, just looking," said a muffled female voice.

"Nicole?"

She whirled around. "Sam? What are you doing here?"

"Ah, I live here. Or I did. I was just packing." He pointed to the duffel bag.

"I like the Stetson," she murmured. "Not too new. It has character. I may have to borrow that for a window."

Sam shook his head. "Nope. Sorry. You can borrow anything but that."

"Oh. Excuse me. I didn't know it was that important."

The faint huffiness in her tone surprised him. What was that all about? Hormones, maybe. Hard work, making her cranky. He didn't really want to ask. "So how have you been? Greg's keeping me busy. I was about to move this morning and then he called."

"Into the sublet?"

He held up the key. "When he gets back, I'm going. It's right up the street. Can't wait."

She took in the trailer in all its battered glory. "You were this close to where I live all this time?"

"Yup." He smiled a little sheepishly. "Nothing to brag about." Sam gestured toward it. "Not exactly a palace, is it? I would invite you in, but there's nowhere to sit besides the bed."

"No, thanks." Nicole seemed to take the lack of space for granted. Or maybe she just didn't want to get close yet. "So you must know Theo."

"My friend Greg—I told you about him—is his nephew. I help out here sometimes."

Sam didn't want to explain about the truck that had just clipped the A-frame or what Theo had said about thugs muscling in on his business. He was just glad to see her. He'd been worried when she hadn't returned his call. He and Greg had gone to Long Island and back since he'd last spoken to her.

"Oh." She connected the dots. "Now I get it." She gave him a guarded look.

"I guess I should have told you, huh?"

"Too late now."

He just hadn't found the right time, that was all. He did understand why she was being prickly about it. If his sister Annie had told him about some guy she just met with no fixed address, he'd tell her better safe than sorry.

But Sam got the feeling there was now an X beside his name in an invisible black book. He hadn't done anything to deserve it.

He cleared his throat. "By the way, how come you didn't call me back? I thought we were going to go to Chinatown."

"I fell asleep again." She gave him a look that said she didn't think he was entitled to question her on the subject. "Off and on, anyway. Look, the ENJ gig was a bear and I still haven't recovered from that. And I, um, hung out with my girlfriend Sharon and talked all night. Besides, mornings just aren't the best time to call me."

Sam got it. He wondered if his name had come up. No use speculating. Girls liked to talk. He glanced down, feeling a bit awkward.

Cute. Underneath the puffy jacket were owl-print pajamas stuffed into her winter boots.

He looked up. The jacket hood didn't quite cover her

dark hair. She pushed wayward locks away from her face with a mittened hand.

She wasn't wearing makeup, but she didn't need it. The frigid night air had put roses in her cheeks and reddened her lips. She looked even prettier than when they'd waited at the bus stop. But her dark eyes flashed with annoyance.

She wasn't the only one who was tired. He worked long days that didn't stop at sundown. Sam wasn't feeling all that patient. Nicole was sauntering around, pretending to look at trees.

He counted to ten and back again. Then he proceeded to lose his temper. Quietly, but he lost it.

"Okay. I'm sorry I woke you up," he said. "I'm sorry I didn't tell you where I was living. I'm sorry I kissed you. I'm sorry for what I haven't done yet."

She lifted an eyebrow. He couldn't read her mind or her expression. Outrage? Indifference? She was good at looking haughty. Right now it was rubbing him the wrong way. But maybe he should take the third apology back. He suspected she wouldn't let him. He'd blown it again.

"And I'm really sorry I can't keep my mouth shut sometimes."

She glared at him. "Work on that."

Sam raked a hand through his hair. "Let's start over. I like you a lot, but I think I crossed a line with the romance stuff. The flowers, the kiss—I shouldn't have."

Nicole bit her lip, as if she was holding back some scornful comment. "You're right."

"So can we be friends?" Not what he wanted, but he wasn't giving up.

She had turned her back to him. "How much is this tree?"

Sam was glad she couldn't see his exasperation. He went over and stood next to her. The price tag was deep inside, wrapped around the trunk, but he found it.

"Seventy dollars. Theo would probably give it to you for half that."

"I don't want him to." She moved to the next one. "I'm not ready to buy. I really am just looking."

Maybe that applied to him too. She still hadn't answered his question. He changed the subject.

"I guess it's too late to go to Chinatown and that great little dumpling restaurant."

"It closes at eight. It's too late for anything much except going clubbing, and I hate clubs. All that earsplitting music and crazy showing off." She looked at him suspiciously. "I hope that's not on your list of things to do."

"You're not exactly dressed for it. Neither am I." Sam had to smile a little. She wasn't too bad at reading his mind, although she was wrong about the clubs. "How did you know I had a list?"

"Every New York tourist does."

He ignored her condescending tone. Sam reached into the pocket of his shirt and unfolded his. "Times Square. Rockefeller Center. Brooklyn Bridge. Empire State Building and/or Top of the Rock. Staten Island Ferry," he read. "Unless any of those are clubs, you're safe. I assume you've been to most of them."

She shot him an annoyed look. "Some but not all. If you actually grow up in New York, it's not a priority. Don't ask me why."

Sam held up both hands in mock surrender. "Okay. Whatever you say. Does anything on the list appeal to you?"

Nicole half wanted to get over her pique and half didn't. "What were the choices again?"

He skipped the whole list and went to what he wanted. "We could go skating at Rockefeller Center tomorrow."

"I don't know how."

"Does that mean yes?" Sam asked carefully.

Nicole stuck her hands in her pockets. The action made the hood fall away from her head. Released, her hair shone under the Christmas lights of the tree stand. She shook it back.

"It means I don't want to make a fool of myself by wobbling around the most famous ice rink in the world in rented skates."

"That will make two of us."

She wavered, then relented. "All right. But let's go in the afternoon. I'd better get some ideas down on paper for the second window at Now. Darci is coming back in another week. Meet me at four."

"Where?"

"I'll wait outside my building," she said after a moment.

"Want to walk or take a taxi?"

"A taxi takes forever in crosstown traffic. Rockefeller Center isn't all that far from here. It's about a fifteen-minute walk."

"Fine with me."

"All right. You're on." Nicole gave one last look around at the row of trees and the single strand of lights. "This place could use some better decorations."

"Yeah, maybe so. I understand business is down a bit this year."

"Spoken like a tree man."

The glare of headlights pulling up startled him. He got between her and the street, then realized that they belonged to Greg's SUV.

His pal was at the wheel. Greg killed the engine and the lights slowly dimmed. He got out.

"Hey, Sam. Thanks for staying." Greg looked curiously at Nicole. "You look really familiar, but I don't know your name. Do you live around here?"

"Two and a half blocks away. I buy a tree from Theo every year. I'm Nicole."

Greg was all smiles. "Pleased to meet you. I'm Greg. Theo's my uncle. So, you looking for a tree?"

"Just browsing."

"Oh, okay. We can set one aside for you if you want."

"Thanks. Not just yet," she said. "It's getting awfully late. I should be going. But I'll be back."

"I'll walk you home," Sam offered.

Greg looked at Sam and then back at Nicole. "I feel like I came in during the second act. Do you two know each other?"

"We're friends." Nicole smiled. "Just friends."

Chapter 7

The next day they headed east, under a sky already turning dark at half past four. The deep blue above set off the brilliance of the giant electronic signs covering the facades of Times Square. The ever-changing colors seemed heightened by the cold air. Sam could barely make out the buildings behind the shimmering displays.

Nicole walked briskly through the dazzling, ever-changing brilliance, too used to it to gawk. But she seemed to be enjoying it. Sam was glad to have a New York native with him. The street signs nearly vanished amidst the visual extravaganza in constant motion.

Part of Broadway, which cut diagonally through the area, had been turned into a pedestrian thoroughfare. Signs and traffic stanchions funneled cars away, sometimes to the loud complaints of drivers who weren't aware of the change in the world-famous square.

The river of people in the intersecting streets freely overflowed the curbs. It seemed to Sam like thousands upon thousands jostled for space, taking photos and videos while they walked, or just gazing up in wonder.

Couples and family groups headed for the red staircase that formed the roof of the TKTS booth to snap pictures. A few show-offs danced up and down its illuminated steps, singing, what else, show tunes. Kids clung to the railing, turning around at the top for the best view of the narrow building at the southern side.

"That's where they drop the ball on New Year's Eve," Nicole told him. "Can you see it? It's not lit up."

Sam stopped to stare. He didn't care if he looked like a tourist. It was all here. Fashion, theater, movies, music, candy, you name it—everything was advertised at colossal size and scale.

He looked to where she pointed. "Yes, I do. Wow."

Nicole laughed. "It's fun to come here with someone who's never seen Times Square before."

"Thanks for bringing me this way. It's something else. Almost overwhelming when you're in it."

"I know what you mean. Come on. Turn right. Eyes front."

He followed her, amazed all over again by the sudden quietness of the side street. There were no more gigantic signs and only a handful of tourists. He looked over his shoulder. The vast crowd of people behind him almost looked trapped in all the craziness, surging back and forth as if they couldn't find their way out. Made him think of cattle in a chute.

A little of Times Square went a long way.

The mind-numbing sensation ebbed as they walked at an easy pace crosstown. The people here seemed to be leaving work, wearing somber-colored coats and jackets over business clothes.

He hoped the rink wouldn't be too crowded this late in the day. But Nicole hadn't said anything about it one way or another.

"We're almost there," she said. "That's Sixth Avenue."

Sam looked down the street and made out the neon marquee of Radio City Music Hall. Atop it were a row of giant toy soldiers, which fell backward with mathematical precision when a large cannon boomed.

"That's the March of the Toy Soldiers from the Christmas Spectacular," she told him. "It's an annual show. That's the one thing that doesn't change from year to year."

"Starring the Rockettes, am I right?"

"Yes."

Sam watched the toy soldiers on the marquee stand up again. "I wish my father was here. He loves the Rockettes. Those brown velvet reindeer costumes and the little antler hats knock him out. He always wants to know how they do it."

"Do what?"

"The high kicks. What else?"

"Practice."

"It's like precision machinery," Sam went on. "With legs that go on and on—"

"Oh, shut up," she said, faintly nettled.

"Sorry."

Nicole was about to head for the other side of the street when a double-decker tour bus zoomed through the intersection. The people on top looked down at them curiously. Sam suddenly knew what a zoo animal felt like.

"Has your dad ever been to New York?"

"Never. But we watch the tree lighting every year," he admitted. "My folks wouldn't miss it for the world. My mother gets all misty-eyed and sings along with the Christmas carols."

They had finally crossed Sixth Avenue in front of an unbroken line of yellow taxis waiting for the light to change.

"Watching it on TV is a lot easier than actually being there," Nicole said. "If you think Times Square is overwhelming, try bucking the crowds at Rockefeller Center during that. You literally can't move forward or back."

"Really? They don't show that."

"Why would they?" Nicole asked wryly.

Sam noticed that the buff-colored buildings of Rockefeller Center were getting taller as they moved forward. Beams of white light rose to the heavens from an open space ahead of them. That had to be the rink. It wasn't visible from where they walked. Neither was the giant tree.

But the silver and gold flags that outlined the viewing areas were. There seemed to be hundreds, a soft contrast to the subdued buff of the buildings that surrounded them. The year-round trees, now bare of leaves, had been carefully strung with delicate white lights, down to the smallest twig.

Nicole turned right. Sam looked up.

Towering in majesty above them was the great tree, adorned with jewel-colored lights and nothing else. The white light that seemed to emanate from the rink below illuminated the high ramparts of the tallest building in Rockefeller Center. The sight was breathtaking.

She stopped. "What do you think?"

"No words."

Nicole laughed. "Look your fill. The Zamboni is on the rink right now."

She moved to the black railings that let visitors peer down into the rink. After a moment Sam realized she had gone. He rubbed his neck and went to find her. The ice-smoothing machine lumbered around in circles, its driver in no hurry high up in the cab.

"I love watching those things."

Sam leaned over the railing, looking down at the huge golden statue of a nearly nude male figure that presided over the rink. "Who is that guy?"

"Prometheus. Bringing fire to mankind."

"I'd rather have a cup of hot cocoa. How about you?"

"Sure," Nicole said. "We can get down to the lower concourse through one of these stores. You can see the rink from there too."

They went into an upscale clothing establishment, with Nicole pausing now and then to check out the displays. Then they found a staircase and exited at the bottom into the elegant concourse with other fine stores and a fancy café.

They ordered two cocoas to go and sat at a burnished metal table to drink them, looking out at the rink through glass walls. The Zamboni was moving off the ice and a line of skaters waited to get out on it.

The novices and the little kids clumped awkwardly over the rubber tiling and headed immediately for the red railing. The confident ones soared out. Some started out with steady laps around the rink, and a few made figures and practiced professional-looking maneuvers.

Nicole raised her cup in a toast. "Here's to the railing. I'm never letting go."

Sam grinned at her. "It's easier than you think."

Her eyes narrowed. "Is it, now. You led me to believe that you didn't know how to do this."

"I thought you'd never go if I told you I was a pretty good skater."

Nicole finished her cocoa. "I'm here. Let's do it."

They had to go up the stairs, through the store, outside and down again to the other side of the rink, where the skates were rented. It wasn't that crowded, but the small size of the available ice meant some waiting.

He made a point of looking in the other direction when she took off her coat. Nicole had decided on the shorts and thick tights combination. He seemed pleased to see it again when he turned back to her.

She slid her cell phone into one front pocket and a thin,

small wallet into the other, and put on her skates, struggling with the laces until he kneeled down to do them for her.

"Aren't you gallant," she teased him.

"There's a right way to do it and a wrong way. You want them comfortably tight." His deft hands took care of that. He gave her a light slap on one calf. "There you go. Now stand up."

Nicole made a face. "Do I have to?"

"Like you said, you're here. You want to."

"You stand up first."

Sam obeyed. He seemed to have grown at least a foot taller, even though Nicole knew that the skate blades only added a few inches. But they made his legs look fabulously long and strong. Like the rest of him.

He reached out and pulled her up.

Hanging onto Sam's hand for dear life, Nicole clumped across the black rubber tiles. He clumped too.

But when he reached the opening to the rink, he uncurled her fingers and rested her hand on the railing. Nicole clutched it and pressed herself against the see-through side.

Sam skated away, swinging his arms, moving effortlessly over the ice. She watched him, hypnotized. Until she felt a bump from behind.

A middle-aged woman in a polka-dot parka smiled tentatively at her.

"Isn't this fun? Mind if I get by? I don't want to let go either."

Nicole gulped. She let go and scraped her skates back and forth very quickly, reaching for the railing in back of the woman. She caught it just before she lost her balance.

The polka dots moved on. Sam caught up with her, doing a one-skate-in-back-of-the-other thing that had him balancing on one leg and coming to a stop that kicked up a nifty spray of ice.

"Good going," he said. "Want to try skating with me?"

"No. I really, really like this railing. It's my new best friend."

"You don't need it. Come on," he coaxed her.

His few turns around the rink had brought that high color into his face that she liked so much. His smoky blue eyes shone with amusement. She wanted to plunge her hands into his wind-ruffled hair just to . . . just to have something else to hang onto besides the railing.

Sam had lifted her hands away from it. He held them in his own and skated backward slowly, helping her move forward.

Without knowing how, Nicole realized that she was skating. Not too well, but not too badly.

"Keep going. Don't stop to think. You're a natural."

She beamed. "I am?"

"Yeah!"

"How about that—whoops!" Nicole was suddenly flat on her back on the ice. "I fell." She was astonished that it hadn't hurt. Sam looked taller than ever.

"Yes, you did. Now get up before you get shredded."

She sat up, looking anxiously at the oncoming skaters. They swung around her, keeping their momentum without a backward glance.

"I was kidding," Sam laughed. "This isn't a hockey game. No one's going to hurt you."

He helped her up and off they went again, Sam skating backward, Nicole moving forward to him. He held her hands more loosely this time, but every once in a while he let go, still keeping his hands where she could reach them if she wanted to. She had to bend forward a bit from the waist to do that.

"Bend your knees some."

It seemed to help.

"Use your thigh muscles."

That did too.

"Don't look down. Don't look back. Find your rhythm."

That seemed like excellent advice for living, not just skating. She kept going.

"You got it. You're skating."

Nicole didn't say a word. She really was.

She was aglow with triumph when it was time to leave the rink and return the skates. Her legs ached. Nicole put on her boots again and stood up, a little wobbly, but for a different reason.

"I feel so short," she said.

Sam seemed to have returned to his normal height as well. "You look the same to me." He chucked her under the chin. "Beautiful, that is. I mean that in a friendly way."

"Right." They went up the dark granite exterior stairs to street level, squeezing past a lot more people this time. Sam looked up. The sky was now a velvet black without a single star—at least not one that he could see. But the stars had to be up there somewhere.

"Want to go look at the Saks Fifth Avenue windows?" She pointed toward them. Through a double row of airy, sculpted angels blowing trumpets, Sam saw what she was talking about.

"Sure."

They made their way there and joined a slow-moving line to enjoy the windows in proper order. A story unfolded in each one, presented by fairy tale characters. Each window was lavishly draped at the sides, like a small theater, with a deep perspective that drew the viewer in. Kids and adults alike marveled in silence at the wonderful scenes and the artistry that had gone into creating them.

Sam felt Nicole very close to him. Of course, she had little choice. The people in line kept going, though this was nothing like the chaos of Times Square. She was absorbed in the scenes, pointing out tiny, delicious details he hadn't noticed at first. He saw much more when he was with her, he realized.

"Are these the same every year?" he asked.

"No. They always change. But the same companies design and build them. Windows like these, with animatronic figures, take a year to create."

"That's amazing."

They had reached the last window, a charming snow scene. Different moving figures, animal and human, waved good-bye to the viewers and wished them happy holidays. The music and voices were in perfect sync.

Nicole and Sam exited. She took his hand and tugged him back the way they'd come, but on the sidewalk. "There's another tree you should see. It's in the Saks window on the corner."

"Okay. Lead on."

There wasn't a line, but there was a crowd. Mostly kids. The parents stayed to the side. Sam had no problem seeing the main attraction, though the tree itself was essentially invisible. Hundreds of unique glass ornaments, each made by hand, completely covered it from bottom to top.

"Fantastic. Wow."

Nicole smiled up at him. "You keep saying that."

"I don't know what else to say," he answered honestly. "I'm wowed."

They were suddenly caught up in the flow of fresh crowds heading for Rockefeller Center, retracing their steps and walking north. Some people continued on, mounting the blockwide stairs of St. Patrick's Cathedral and going through the massive bronze doors to attend evening services. Sam stopped to look up at its stone spires, deeply carved, as light as lace.

Across the street from the cathedral was a massive bronze statue of Atlas holding up the world. The statue's face gazed down at the hurrying passersby, impassive and timeless.

Sam looked down at Nicole. She had slipped her hand around his arm. "What now?" he asked softly.

"I don't know. Are you hungry? We could go out to eat."

"That's an idea."

She led the way again, but this time they were connected by their linked arms. Nicole headed for a street off Fifth, stopping in front of a restaurant on Madison and looking in the highly polished, brass-framed window. The interior was decorated in deep red, with snowy damask tablecloths already set.

"There's the menu." They moved to the frame within the window that held it.

Sam read the offerings with puzzlement. One in particular caught his eye.

Slivers of raw sole enrobed in kelp-infused foam and finished with shaved alpine truffles, nestled in grappa-sauce risotto studded with organic pomegranate seeds.

"Does all that fit on one plate?" he asked.

"It probably fits on a saucer," she laughed.

"Oh. Then what is grappa?" he asked. "Have you ever eaten kelp?"

"Not that I know of. This place looks ridiculously pretentious. And much too expensive."

"Hey, price is no object," he protested.

"We're not eating here." She tugged him away in the direction of Park Avenue and they looked at a few more menus in other windows, not seeing anything that appealed to either of them.

"You know something," he said, feeling his stomach

begin to growl. "I bet I could cook you a better meal than any of these places. Do you like steak?"

"I love it."

"So tell me where I can buy the best steak in New York and we can go to my place and I'll cook it there."

"You're on." Nicole seemed pleased by the idea. She thought for a moment. "Okay. We're a block away from Lexington and an uptown train. We can go to Ottomanelli's for the steak."

She just about dragged him to the subway station, and they went quickly down the stairs as a train approached. She swiped a MetroCard through the turnstile and handed it back to him to do the same.

Sam saw the number 6 glowing red in a circle and stood back as the sleek, brushed-metal train streaked in. The doors *whooshed* open. People streamed off as he and Nicole stood to the side, and then they entered.

There was one open seat. Nicole swung into it as the doors closed and the train moved on. Sam grabbed a bar overhead and looked around, surprised by how new the train was. An electronic board at his eye level informed the riders of the stations coming up, and the announcer echoed it. No graffiti anywhere. The blue and gray of the sleek interior was soothing.

But it was crowded. The riders, standing and sitting, followed an unspoken etiquette, he noticed, and nobody got stepped on. You just had to move fast, that was all.

Nicole craned her neck to glance at the board. "We get off in two more stops."

Sam nodded. He swayed with the movement of the rushing train, studying the ad placards and the wacky MTA poster art. There was always something to look at in New York, no matter where you were.

The crowd thinned out at each stop. Nicole rose when the electronic board flashed for 81st Street. "This is it."

They exited and went up a square-tiled staircase to an East Side neighborhood that looked a lot like theirs. But here the streets were wider, and the brownstones and corniced brick buildings had been well maintained for decades. Some of the street trees had been strung with tiny lights as carefully as the ones in Rockefeller Center.

"Ottomanelli's is a block up and two blocks east on Second Avenue."

He nodded, matching his stride to hers.

"We lived there when I was a kid." She pointed to a tall, white-brick apartment building. "The neighborhood hasn't changed much."

He didn't want to argue. But he could see new residential buildings that towered over the white-brick ones, and made the old brownstones look small by comparison.

The butcher shop was a pleasantly old-fashioned place, immaculately clean. The glass meat case held an array of fine cuts, laid out in overlapping slabs.

Nicole and Sam waited to be served, listening to the butchers chat with neighborhood customers. The aproned staff greeted the regulars like family.

"Ready ta order?" a butcher asked them. "Specials on the board. How're ya today?" The growled patter was friendly.

"Doing fine. Yourself?" Sam stepped up.

"Can't complain. What'll ya have?"

"Give me a porterhouse and a couple of T-bones. That one and those two."

The butcher behind the glass counter winked at Nicole. "Your man knows his steak." He took out the cuts Sam had pointed to and wrapped them in traditional brown paper, then bagged and weighed them.

Sam put his hand over the digital display on the scale. "Don't look. On me," he said to Nicole.

She pretended to sigh. "All right."

Purchase made, they left and added a few items from a fruit-and-vegetable market. Sam spotted a liquor store and made her wait outside with the Ottomanelli's bag while he went in and bought two bottles of really good cabernet.

"Done," he said with satisfaction. "How do we get home from here?"

She rattled off an answer. He listened carefully. It involved taking the 6 downtown to Grand Central, jumping on the shuttle across midtown to 42nd Street, and switching to a C or an E going uptown one stop to their neighborhood.

"Nothing doing. I vote for a taxi." Sam stepped out into the street and whistled, seeing one in the near distance stopped at a light. The piercing sound made her cover her ears.

"Ouch!"

"Sorry. I usually use that for cattle dogs."

"Poor things."

The taxi veered in their direction when the light changed, crossing several lanes of traffic to reach their side of the street. He was even getting used to death-defying stunts like that.

"After you." He opened the back door for her and slid in when she was settled. Nicole told the driver where to go.

"Can I make the salad or anything?"

"Did that while you were checking your messages."

A small folding table was already set, with the salad on it in a wooden bowl.

"The potatoes are baking in the toaster oven. Guess I should say re-baking."

The market had had a great selection of prepared food to go. Sam saw no reason not to take advantage of it.

"Okay. I have nothing to do but sit here and enjoy this glass of wine."

Sam grinned. "That is the plan." He poured one for himself and adjusted the dishtowel he'd tucked behind his belt. He was going to rock this dinner, big-time. Alex Walcott apparently liked to cook too. Sam had found a well-seasoned cast-iron frying pan in a drawer of its own.

"Are you ready for cowboy steak, Colorado style?"

"Absolutely." She took a big sip of wine and looked his way. "I assume you don't want help."

Sam shook his head. "Nope."

Nicole settled herself on the tiny sofa. "Cute little place. How'd you find it?"

"The guy came by to look at Christmas trees and I overheard him telling Theo that he'd auditioned for a cruise ship show and was thinking about subletting if he got the gig."

"You really got lucky," Nicole said.

"For a big city, it sure seems like everybody knows each other."

"That's true," she admitted. "Sometimes."

"Anyway, long story short, he's an elf."

"That explains the size of the furniture." she laughed.

"I don't even want to think about how I'm going to sleep on that foldout thing you're sitting on."

Nicole had moved into a corner of the couch, tucking her tights-clad legs under her. She'd taken off her boots when she'd come in.

She seemed utterly content, her cheeks already rosy from the wine. Sam unwrapped the steaks.

"T-bones or porterhouse?"

"You pick."

He lifted the smaller T-bones out of the brown paper, putting them on a platter and rewrapping the porterhouse before he stuck it back in the refrigerator.

"So here's what you do." He poured a healthy dash of oil in the cast-iron skillet and turned on the gas.

"I'm watching."

"First get the oil good and hot but not smoking. You want to see the surface roll just a bit. Like a Colorado meadow. Then you season it. Nothing fancy."

He poured a healthy pinch of coarse salt into his hand and let it fall from between his fingers over the raw steaks.

"Like this. Let it float down like the first snow of a Colorado winter."

She giggled. "You're too much."

"Yikes. Almost forgot the fresh-ground pepper." He picked up a pepper grinder he'd set to the side of the stove and put it to good use.

Sam jabbed both steaks at once with a carving fork and got them into the pan.

"Listen to that sizzle," Nicole said encouragingly.

"Music to my ears."

The savory smell of good grilled T-bones filled the air. Sam hovered over the frying pan, long fork in hand, "Two or three minutes on each side. Until it smokes like a Colorado forest fire."

He took a step and opened the tiny kitchen window. It opened onto a brick wall. Sam grabbed a dishtowel and fanned out some of the smoke, coughing.

"Can't wait. Medium rare for me."

He flipped them over in time. "Remove to a hot platter when done." He had a clean one waiting on the back of the stove.

Served up and on the table, the steaks were incredibly tempting. Nicole and Sam didn't say a word as they ate, savoring each bite.

She leaned back in her folding chair as he cleared. "I don't think I ever had a steak that delicious."

"Told you. Forget the potatoes—they got dried out. And I guess we can have the salad for a second course. I didn't get around to putting dressing on it."

"Whatever. I'm too stuffed to think."

Nicole folded up her chair and headed back for the same corner. "Thank you. That was the perfect ending to a perfect day. I didn't think about work once," she added with a guilty smile.

Sam came back to put the table away. "Me neither."

They were both settled in, and a comfortable silence fell. He stretched out his long legs as far as he could.

Nicole's cell phone rang. She didn't get up to take it out of her bag. The call went to voice mail.

"Mind if I look? That could be Darci."

"Not at all."

She half rose, twisting to reach her bag and fished out the phone, looking at the screen. "Nope. Just a text from Finn." He watched her read it. Her eyes widened. She seemed slightly stunned. "Holy cow. I don't believe it."

"What's up?"

"He showed my portfolio to Kevin Talley. He's the CEO of ENJ."

"And?"

"Talley loved it. He wants to meet with me and Finn tomorrow at the company headquarters here in New York and brainstorm a new campaign."

"Really? That's fantastic."

"It's just a meeting. But I have to prepare. That means I need to get home."

"Not a problem. This is a big deal, right?" He was sincerely happy for her.

"Could be the chance of a lifetime. Or Talley could be picking my brains. I don't know, but oh, my gosh—" She was up and slipping on her work boots, tying the laces in double knots. "I'm so sorry to eat and run."

"Don't worry about it." Sam knew he was going to spend the rest of the evening watching some dumb movie on a teeny-tiny TV.

Couldn't be helped.

Nicole turned to pick up her wineglass. Sam took it from her.

"Leave it. I'll take care of the dishes later. Have everything you need? I'll see you home."

"Sam, no. I dragged you all over town, you shopped, you cooked—no way. I live only two blocks away and it's not even that late."

He got up and found her jacket, holding it out. "Doesn't matter. Where I come from, that's what a man does. Get used to it."

Chapter 8

Sam was stacking a delivery of fresh, intensely fragrant trees against the A-frame. It was Saturday morning, and they had sold nearly all of the first bunch by now.

"Put the biggest trees on the ends," Theo instructed him. "They're not as easy to swipe."

"People actually do that?" Sam asked.

"Every so often, yeah. Especially the dinky trees. It happens. We get busy, don't pay attention or we're inside the trailer—what can ya do? I'm not going to chase anyone. But we don't have to make it easy for tree-nappers."

He sounded fairly philosophical about it. Sam shook his head and went back to work. To fit in more trees, he tried to move a big fir with a *SOLD* tag, but he couldn't budge it. Sam stepped back to see if its branches were caught somehow and saw that the fir's trunk had been placed in a bucket of soggy peat moss.

"How come this one is getting the royal treatment?" he asked Theo.

"Just keeping it fresh. The customer is going to pick it up soon."

"Oh. Mind if I shove it out of the way?"

Theo was swinging his arms to warm up. "Go ahead.

The new stock is more important. Customers have been asking when we'd get a delivery. Are we ready?"

"Yes, we're ready," Sam replied by rote. He knew Theo's motivational routine by now.

The old man's deep voice boomed out of his hood. "Hey hey hey! Ho ho ho! All these trees have got to go!"

Sam finished for him. "Let's sell, sell, sell and make big dough."

Theo looked his way. "Very good. Greg never gets it right. Don't tell him I said that."

"I won't."

Theo came over to help Sam with the last of the trees. "The sun is out and so are the kids. Always a good sign."

Sam only nodded. He wasn't exactly in the best mood, but he kept a lid on it. He missed Nicole. She had checked in now and again but never talked for long. Putting together a presentation for her upcoming meeting with Kevin Talley wasn't just a matter of bringing in a portfolio, apparently.

"They bring the parents," Theo was saying. "And do you see what I see?"

"Nice-looking family."

A mother and father in a late-model SUV had just pulled over and were lifting identical twin girls out of their car seats.

Theo waved.

"I take it you know them."

The old man shook his head. "Never saw them in my life. But I treat every customer like a new friend."

He greeted the family once they reached the lot and chatted with them for a bit, then spun a little tree around on its stand to make the toddlers laugh.

"Oh, we want a bigger tree than that," the dad said to them. "Which one is the tallest?" he asked Theo.

With a salesman's flourish, Theo indicated it. Sam wandered away to the far corner of the lot, looking idly at the usual assortment of double-parked vans and cars blocking the vehicles on the other side of the street. Alternate parking days took getting used to. But the cops never bothered them about staying where they were, just waved and drove on.

Looking up the block, he saw Douglas come down the stoop of their building, half-pulled by a small white dog. Sam didn't remember the Fultons having a dog or cat the one time he'd stopped in. It wasn't long before the boy reached the tree lot.

"Hey, Douglas," he said. "When did you guys get a dog?"

"This is Puff," Douglas explained. "I'm walking her for a neighbor. Is Theo here today?"

Sam had been standing in a clump of tall trees as thick as a forest. He could see over, but Douglas couldn't.

"Yeah. But he's with a customer right now. Anything I can help you with?"

"No. I just wanted to say hi. Puff, quit it."

Sam felt eager paws scrabbling on his jeans. The little dog was straining on her leash and just about airborne in her own efforts to say hello. "Okay, okay. Down, girl. I'll pet you."

He squatted on his haunches and got his face licked for his trouble. Sam laughed and wiped off the canine kiss, getting up again when he heard Theo call his name.

"Be right there." He looked at Doug, who hesitated. "Come on. He probably needs me to bag the tree and get it on top of a car."

The boy followed. Sam's prediction was correct.

"Sam, can you take care of this while I finish the sale?"

"Sure."

The parents held their wide-eyed toddlers while Sam stepped forward to lift the huge tree from the A-frame, fighting the springy branches to get it into the bagging machine. Neatly contained by mesh, it was a lot easier to carry. He took it over to the sawhorse and trimmed the trunk with a portable electric saw.

"Beautiful tree," he said. "The best on the lot, in my opinion. Where do you want it?" he asked the dad.

"On top of that, please." The man indicated the parked SUV with his credit card and fluttering receipt, which Theo had just handed back to him.

Sam grabbed a coil of thin poly rope and hoisted the tree over one shoulder. It was quick work to get it secured to the SUV's roof rack.

"You're good to go, people."

"Thanks." The dad handed him a five. Sam tucked it in his pocket. Getting tipped didn't bother him. He passed them all on when he got a chance, slipping the bills and change into the charity bucket manned by the bell-ringing Santa on the other corner.

The family drove off, and he turned to see Douglas chatting with Theo, the dog's leash wound around his hand. Puff pulled toward Sam, begging for another pat.

"Nothing doing." Sam kept his distance. "Even if you are cute."

A honking war broke out on Eighth Avenue. "Back in a flash," he called to Theo. Sam strolled away from the lot to see what was going on.

As if he'd been waiting for his chance, Doug took a white envelope out of his pocket and gave it to Theo. "This is a note from my mom," he said. "She says it's okay if I work so long as it's just for an hour and during daylight."

Theo felt inside his jacket and took out a pair of reading glasses before he opened the envelope and unfolded the note. "Guess I don't need these," he said, putting the glasses away. "Nice of your mom to use big type."

"She wrote it on her laptop," Douglas said. "You can change the size of the letters to anything you want."

"Ah," said Theo. "I don't have a laptop." He read the note with a smile. "Well, we can use you," he said as he put it away inside his jacket. "These dry needles underfoot need sweeping up right now. And it's all right if the dog stays."

He sat on the folding chair, and Puff jumped up into his lap, content to be held.

"Hang on a sec. I have to check in with my mom. She gave me her old cell phone." He pulled it out of his pocket and speed-dialed her. "Hi, Mom. It's me."

Her clear voice asking a question hung in the air.

"I walked Puff down to the lot. Is it okay if I stay here for about an hour? Theo, say hi." Douglas held up the open phone.

"Hello, Maureen!" Theo boomed.

Douglas put the phone back to his ear. "I didn't forget my gloves and it's nice out," he said to his mother. "Okay, see you later." He hung up.

"She went to talk to some people about cakes," Douglas said. "Amanda is with Julie."

He didn't waste a minute. He'd spotted the broom and big dustpan with the handle for himself, and got to work.

By the time Sam came back with a take-out tray of hot drinks for all three of them, the boy had finished sweeping. He poured the needles into the tall can they kept handy for trimmed trunks and other tree debris.

"What next?" he asked.

Theo looked around. "You could arrange the small trees. Put the really little ones in front and the bigger ones in back."

"Like a class picture," Douglas said.

"Exactly."

Sam set down the take-out tray. "And you can have a

cup of cocoa when you come back. Theo, I got us a couple of hot ciders."

"Over there, Doug. Thanks, Sam." The old man set Puff down at his feet, holding onto the leash. Douglas ran to the group of small trees, studying them for a minute. Then he started to move them around as Theo had requested.

Sam smiled and turned his attention to Theo. "You putting the kid to work?"

"Why not? He wants to buy something for his mother, surprise her. He's growing up."

Sam took both lids off the ciders. Apple-scented steam wafted into the cold air. "Better let these cool." He glanced at Douglas, making sure he was far enough away. "What's the deal with his father?" he asked, too quietly for the boy to hear.

Theo's expression was suddenly tinged with sadness. "Hank Fulton died four years ago," he replied just as quietly. "An accident, so I understand. I don't see the family except for this time of year, but you get to know people in this job."

Sam looked over at Douglas again, absorbed in his task. Theo got up and tied Puff to the A-frame. "Customers."

"Go for it. I'm here if you need me." Sam stayed where he was, keeping an eye on Douglas. Theo's answer explained why the boy seemed so self-reliant. And why he was so protective of his mother and little sister.

He picked up his cider and drank it quickly. Sam turned to throw away the crumpled cup and spotted a pickup truck running the red light at the avenue. Instinct—and a good memory—put him on alert.

Sam craned his neck to look through a gap in the tree display. The truck had pulled over into a loading zone before a delivery van could claim it. Was it the same truck that had clipped the frame and sped away the other night?

He looked closer. The back was heaped with bagged Christmas trees, but it seemed to be a different vehicle entirely. The paint was faded red with blotches of rust. He was pretty sure the other truck had been dark gray.

The van driver leaned on his horn. The unseen truck driver rolled down his window and made a rude gesture. Then a different van pulled out farther up the street and the driver of the first gave up on the argument to take the spot.

That seemed to be the end of the confrontation.

Sam watched as a hulking man in a dirty jacket got out of the truck and pulled a folding sign out of the back. He put it right on the sidewalk, partially blocking it.

FRESH CUT TREES R BAGGED 2 GO!
NY'S LOWEST PRICES!

Then he dragged down a few trees and leaned them against the truck's fold-down door.

They covered the license plate, Sam noticed.

The man jammed a dark ball cap down over his forehead and added a red scarf for a touch of cheer. He talked to a few pedestrians and didn't seem bothered by the rebuffs. No one stopped to buy. He leaned against the truck and thrust his hands into his jacket pockets, looking around. One hand came out again, holding a metal flask. He unscrewed the cap and took a big swallow that made him cough.

The man waited.

If the prices were low enough, he would get takers sooner or later.

Plus he could move that truck every fifteen minutes if he wanted to, Sam thought angrily, and use it to make deliveries. Theo was right. Fly-by-night operators were bad for business.

He was inclined to go talk to the brazen SOB, but he knew better. It might end up in a good old-fashioned fist-fight, which wasn't good for business either. The cops had to be on the scene to do anything about an unlicensed seller, and a call to the precinct house in the busy holiday season wasn't going to be a high priority.

Besides, the hulking man hadn't broken the law yet.

"What are you looking at?" Douglas came over to him, brushing needles off his hands.

"Nothing. You ready for that cocoa?"

"Yeah. Thanks. I owe you."

Sam had to laugh. "I don't think so, kiddo. But you should drink it while it's still warm."

"Wait a sec." The boy took out his cell phone again.

"Checking in with your mom?"

"Uh-huh." He waited. "It went to voice mail. I'll send her a text."

Maureen sat at the side of a cluttered desk in the business office of Nash & Thomas, Gourmet Purveyors. They were on the fourteenth floor of an Upper East Side building with a great view that she wasn't looking at. She unwrapped three sample cakes and set them on a small disposable tray.

Fred Nash himself had stepped out of the office to see to something. She smoothed her hair, then looked in her purse for a compact, flipping it open. Her makeup was fine, but an anxious line had appeared between her eyebrows. She drew in a calming breath and willed the line to go away when she breathed out. It didn't work.

Her cell chimed in the bottom of her bag and she looked at it quickly, seeing a text from Douglas on the screen. **Going back to Julie apt w Puff. Sam says hi.** The brief message put her mind at ease. He had been out exactly an hour, and she would be home soon.

She heard Fred Nash returning and put the phone back, turning it off.

"Sorry about that, Maureen." His loud voice made her jump a little, but her first impression of him had been that he was a nice man.

"Not a problem. I appreciate your taking the time to see me, Mr. Nash, especially on a Saturday. This must be your busiest time of year."

"You got that right. I work seven days a week in December. And you can call me Fred." He passed in back of her and dropped into his swivel chair, throwing a pile of printouts on top of everything else.

Fred Nash was not that young and far from thin, but he crackled with energy and so did his shaggy gray hair. Behind black square-framed glasses, his blue eyes regarded her with interest.

"Okay, bring me up to speed before I taste." He looked down at the little cakes and then into a drawer filled with a jumble of plastic cutlery, taking out a fork.

"Starting from the left—your left, I mean—" Maureen paused for a second to compose her thoughts. "That's spice cake, chocolate babka, and a cinnamon-walnut bar."

"Okay." He jabbed the fork into the spice cake first and took a bite, finishing it fast. "I like this. Real flavor, just enough ginger and the allspice is nice. The nutmeg too."

He'd listed every spice in it accurately. She was impressed. "It's my son's favorite."

"He has good taste buds." Nash moved on to the babka, helping himself to a bigger bite of that. "Mmm," he mumbled. He reached back into the drawer for a paper napkin.

His expression was thoughtful. Maureen waited nervously for the verdict while he wiped his mouth.

"Love it," he said with a happy sigh. "Absolutely love

it. I'm a huge fan of babka, just so you know. My grand-mother was Russian. She used to make babka just for me."

Maureen smiled. She could see how he had acquired his girth.

Nash poked the cinnamon-walnut bar with the fork until a bit of it fell off. He ate it and thought some more. "Nice but maybe too crunchy. But again, good flavor."

Maureen let out the breath she hadn't realized she'd been holding.

"So," he said, setting the tray of cakes aside, "tell me something about yourself."

This was the part of being interviewed that she liked the least. "Well, I—I used to own and manage a bakery over on Ninth Avenue."

"I never go that far west in Manhattan. What was it called? How long did you have it?"

"Icing On The Cake."

His blue eyes crinkled with amusement. "Oh, yeah. I heard of it. Memorable name. Bet you got a lot of kids coming in."

Maureen smiled. "How did you know?"

Fred Nash leaned back in his swivel chair and chuckled. "Stands to reason. We run a family business too. My wife and I started this one. Twenty-five years and counting."

"That's great." She was beginning to relax a little. Just a little.

"We wouldn't let our kids in the company kitchens," he went on. "They went straight for anything that was iced and waiting to be boxed. And then they tried to sneak a spoon into the icing vats."

Maureen knew what he was talking about. "Exactly. Whenever I let my son have a cupcake, he would poke a finger in the icing and eat that first. So I invented a treat for him. I called it Poke-A-Dot Cupcakes. White icing, with one big colored dot in the middle. We sold an awful lot of those."

"I bet you did." Fred laughed. "How old is your son?"

Maureen brightened a bit. This wasn't one of those interviews where you didn't dare mention that you had children. Fred Nash was genuinely interested—and he was going out of his way to put her at ease.

"Douglas was six then. He's ten now. And he has a little sister who's three."

"So who came up with the bakery name?"

Maureen hesitated. "My late husband."

Fred Nash nodded without asking any questions on that subject. Maureen guessed he was shrewdly filling in a lot of blanks.

"Well, it sounds like you know the business. There's no substitute for that kind of experience," he said warmly. He tapped the tray with his fork. "These samples are excellent."

Maureen looked at him hopefully.

"But I have to tell you, we contracted for our Christmas orders months ago. You aren't looking to sell into the holiday market this late in the year, are you?"

She lifted her head high. "No. Of course not. These aren't specifically for Christmas. I was looking ahead to spring and summer."

"Good, good." He rocked forward again. "Now, we don't do our own baking anymore. I take it you're not working out of your apartment."

"N-no."

The slight catch in her voice went unnoticed. Deliberately or not, Maureen couldn't tell.

"With a background like yours, I'm sure you can rent work space and professional ovens. Can you deliver in quantity?"

"I have contacts and good friends in the business. I don't anticipate any problems on that score."

It had been so long since she'd thought of herself as a businesswoman, she was almost surprised to hear how confident she sounded. But her answer was the truth.

"All right. Tell you what. Let me give these samples to my partner and get his opinion. I'd introduce you to him, but he's down at our place in the Chelsea Market today. He's the other half of Nash & Thomas. That's him." He pointed to a framed photo on the wall. "Jonathan Thomas."

Maureen barely glanced at the photo. She just hoped her disappointment didn't show.

Maybe it did. Fred Nash gave her a reassuring smile. "It's possible we might be able to do a deal as early as January, depending on our Christmas sales. You know how it is."

"Oh, I do," she said quickly. "But I can give you some fresh cakes for Mr. Thomas." She reached into her bag and took out a box filled with wrapped samples, placing it on the desk.

"I was hoping you'd say that." Nash looked happy. "I hate sharing. These would go great with my afternoon coffee."

"I'm glad you like them. And thank you. It really has been a pleasure. Oh—here are a few business cards."

He rose when she did and took the cards, leaning over his desk to shake her hand. "The pleasure's all mine. Best of luck. Happy holidays."

Maureen wished him the same and made her way out, stepping carefully between other sample boxes. Fred Nash's office was stacked four and five deep with them in places. There was competition. She was going to have to take her chances like anyone else.

She thanked the receptionist in the front space and went

through the double glass doors to the elevator, looking for her gloves in the bag.

They were under the remaining sample boxes inside. This had been her first stop. Fred Nash had been more than nice, but he hadn't made any promises. Still, it was a start.

Maureen entered when the elevator arrived, absently watching the floor numbers on the panel display go down to 1. There was a faint chime and the doors opened.

She was already thinking about her next potential customer, too preoccupied to notice the tall, well-groomed man with a pepper-and-salt crew cut standing to one side as she exited.

But he looked at her with frank admiration as she went past him, taking in the details in a respectful way.

Classic profile, silky blond hair, coat not buttoned yet over a slender figure. And great legs.

Jonathan Thomas watched the lady in the lavender coat go through the revolving door. The elevator doors began to close automatically and he snapped out of it. He got in and pressed 14.

Chapter 9

Sitting down for what felt like the first time in days, Jon didn't get right to work. He watched random, preprogrammed graphics flow on the flat screen of his computer for a while, not wanting to touch a key and get going, needing a few minutes to decompress and actually think. He knew damn well there would be more than a hundred e-mails waiting to be read and dealt with, all marked URGENT. Very few were.

Someone from Accounts Payable had left a memo on his desk. He glanced at it as he loosened his tie. It was only a silent scream for everyone to get expense accounts in before the end of the year. That too could wait for a bit.

If you weren't careful, running a company could swallow your life. He'd done that for too many years, traveling constantly, drumming up business. It had paid off: Nash & Thomas was finally in the big-time.

They had several shops in Manhattan and would open two more in Brooklyn's trendy neighborhoods next year. N&T, their spin-off company, supplied cakes and sweets for over a hundred fine restaurants and three major department stores in the city, and was looking into franchising a line of products for a nationwide supermarket chain.

Clouds were rolling over the December sky. Not ominous, just depressing. Jon turned away from the window of his corner office. That particular perk didn't thrill him like it used to.

Fred Nash, the founder, had taken a larger but windowless space when they'd moved the company into this building—Fred didn't care about things like corner offices. Even though he'd founded the business, hiring Jon a year later, he didn't stand on ceremony. Anybody could walk into his office. Jon understood why. Once you shut the door, you were alone. He'd gotten in the habit of leaving his open.

Fred knocked on it as he breezed into Jon's office. "Hey. I wasn't expecting you to come back this late in the day."

"I have a lot of work to do. What's up?"

Fred smiled. "I left you a sample box. Did you open it?"

"No. Which one do you mean?"

The older man located Maureen's samples and set the small box precisely in the center of Jon's desk, tapping it with a stubby finger. "A nice young lady came this afternoon, brought these. Best goodies I've tasted since I was baking them myself."

"Really? That was a long time ago."

Fred nudged the box toward Jon. "I'm telling you, you need to check these out."

"All right, all right."

He took a fork from others in a container on his desk that had never held pens and pencils. The business had been founded on taste, after all.

Fred opened the box for him and hovered. Jon was used to it.

He started with what seemed to be a spice cake. "Hey, that one is good." He took another bite. "Upgrade that. It's fantastic. Just the right balance of spice flavors."

"Try the babka. A mouthful of heaven."

Jon sampled it. "You're right. It's phenomenal."

"And there's one more."

"Walnuts, huh?" Jon looked at the last piece. "The health option." He tasted it. "Pretty good. So who is this young lady?"

"She used to own a bakery. Icing On The Cake. Heard the name?"

"Yes, I think so. But you still haven't told me her name."

Fred paused for dramatic effect. Jon was used to that too.

"Maureen Fulton is the young lady. She's something special—I can tell." Fred was only warming up. "Gentle but strong. A hard worker but with a soul. Beautiful but . . . beautiful."

"Fred. I'm not looking for a date. Please."

"You're too old for dating, Jonathan."

"Thanks," the younger man answered acidly. "Jot that down on a sticky note and I'll put it on my shaving mirror. Who asked you?"

Fred didn't believe in shutting up. "I'm old enough that I don't care who asked me. I say what I think."

"Let's get it over with," Jon groaned. He folded his arms over his chest. "What did you tell her?"

"Nothing about you," Fred said indignantly. "We talked, she told me about herself—she knows the business, Jon. So I told her to come back in January and we'd take it from there. You two almost crossed paths. In fact, maybe you saw her going out. Lavender coat? Blond hair?"

Jonathan sat bolt upright. "I did see her. She went by me like a cool breeze. She made these?"

"Our holiday orders are already coming in. We can't buy more now."

"Too bad. We could sell the hell out of these all over town."

Fred raised a disapproving eyebrow. "Just so you know, Maureen Fulton does not look like the kind of woman who swears."

"Whatever. I'm not looking for an angel either," Jon shot back.

His partner raised his hands in an I-give-up gesture. Jon knew he wouldn't.

"Just call her in January. Is that too much to ask? Find out for yourself if I'm wrong about her." Fred tossed Maureen's business card on his partner's desk.

"I will," Jon said. Not because Fred was pressuring him to. Because he remembered her.

"Good. She's one in a million, in my opinion. And I didn't get rich by making a lot of mistakes. You neither."

Several blocks to the south on Third Avenue, Nicole had arrived at the glittering building that housed the North American headquarters of ENJ.

"I am so nervous," she said to Finn.

"Why?"

"Can't you guess? This is my first meeting with Kevin Talley!"

"He saw you the night of the flagship store fiasco, didn't he? So technically this is your second meeting."

She ignored his reassurance. "Flagship store fiasco," she muttered distractedly. "Sounds like one of those crazy bands you listen to. Didn't they play at McCarren Pool?"

"Ha. Calm down."

"I can't. Finn, he hardly looked at me that night. But don't remind him that I was there. Don't you remember that grubby tank I had on, and that filthy bandanna?"

"No. You always look fine to me. You look fine now."

"Spoken like a guy."

She was grateful to him for it. Nicole had agonized about what to wear, settling for a subdued gray fitted suit that didn't call any attention to her. It matched. It wasn't missing any buttons. She'd paired it with gray suede heels that were startlingly sexy because her plain pumps had seemed too shabby. Her dark hair had been brushed to glossy smoothness. She flipped it back over one shoulder.

"Anyway, this *is* the first meeting," she insisted.

"Have it your way, Nicole. All he really knows about you is what he saw in your portfolio. And he liked it a lot. Wait until he sees the new, improved one."

"He'll probably hate it," she said dolefully.

"I don't think so." Finn took the portfolio from her hand and opened the glass door. A cavernous, chilly marble lobby lay beyond, staffed by building security officers behind a sweep of teak.

They signed in and each received a stick-on tag, then passed through a gleaming electronic turnstile to get to the elevators.

Nicole smoothed hers onto her portfolio and took it back from Finn. Once they were in the elevator, he looked into the polished metal control panel and ran an indifferent hand over his red hair.

"You look fine too," she told him.

"Who cares? I'm not going to be the star of this show."

Nicole clutched the portfolio handles until her knuckles showed white.

"Relax." The bell rang for their floor. She flinched.

Finn gave her a grin Nicole didn't think was funny at all. "Come on. Showtime!"

"Stop saying things like that."

He patted her shoulder. "Turn right."

"You've been here before?"

"I never got as high as this floor." They waited outside a glass wall until the receptionist buzzed them through. Both of them looked around at the austere decor. Beige silk was stretched taut over the walls. No artwork. A niche held a sculpture consisting of a single, gigantic rusty nail, lit from above. Nicole wondered silently what it meant.

The matching beige carpet underfoot was so thick she could feel herself sinking in slightly.

The receptionist, who didn't introduce herself, spoke suddenly, breaking the hushed silence. "Mr. Talley and the visual team are waiting for you in the conference room."

It was kind of creepy that she seemed to know their names without their having said anything. That wasn't the only reason Nicole was uneasy. No one had said anything to her about meeting the visual team.

"Thank you," Finn said cheerily. Nicole hoisted her portfolio, wishing she'd had one last chance to look in a mirror.

The only other sound was a button being clicked on the phone. No doubt the receptionist was summoning a person to bring them there.

Good guess.

"Alonzo will show you the way," the receptionist said. "He's Mr. Talley's personal assistant."

In another minute, a young blond guy appeared, dressed all in black but wearing beige suede shoes that exactly matched the carpet. They gave him the appearance of being barefoot.

Not a bad idea. She wouldn't have minded kicking off her heels.

"Come with me, please," Alonzo murmured. He brought them to a glass-walled conference room that seemed to be filled with people, also dressed in black. Nicole did a hasty head count. Not quite filled. There were only seven of them, five women and two men.

Nicole lagged behind, forcing Finn to slow down so she could whisper to him.

"Finn, what's going on? You told me it was going to be just you and me and Talley."

Finn finally looked a little nervous himself. "That's

what Talley said last time he called. Obviously that's the visual team."

"They look more like the Alpha Centauri high command," she whispered.

Finn took a second look. "You have a point. I didn't know shoulder pads and spiky hair were back."

Each outfit was different. Each seemed calculated to intimidate in a different way. "Me neither," she whispered.

"Nicole, just ignore all that and wing it. Don't worry so much."

She was about to hiss at him when Finn opened the door. "Mr. Talley, this is Nicole Young."

She went in ahead of him.

Kevin Talley rose and shook her hand. "I'd like you all to meet a rising star," he told the team. He didn't bother to mention who they were. They were much too cool to wear name tags.

The assembled group looked daggers at her. Nicole quailed for a moment, then walked to a chair near Talley's at the head of the table.

The men were nearly as thin as the women. They seemed to have been at the conference table for a while—there were tall cups at each chair. Five were marked with blood-red lip prints. Fortunately, Nicole saw only coffee in the cups, blacker than the clothes they wore.

She reminded herself that every member of Talley's team had once been someone's sweet little baby. They'd never had enough to eat, that was all. There was nothing wrong with any of them that a fat hamburger wouldn't cure. She could use one herself after this was over.

Alonzo was listening very carefully to an almost inaudible request from Kevin Talley.

"Yes, sir. The usual? Double shot of extra-strong espresso in dark roast with a dash of soya skim? Right away, sir."

Flunkies that good were born, not made. But Nicole still felt sorry for him.

Something told Nicole that Alonzo didn't have to go out to the nearest fancy coffee place to get it. There was probably a sleek machine pumping it out for upper management in a room of its own.

She was right. Alonzo was back in less than a minute. He set the cup down at Talley's side. The CEO ignored it.

"Okay. Do we all have our favorite beverages?"

There was a murmured chorus of yeses.

"Then let's begin. Our holiday week-to-date numbers in all categories are pathetic. We need a new direction. When Finn—I take it you all know Finn Leary—happened to show me this girl's portfolio, I was thrilled."

Someone coughed.

"I brought Nicole Young in today to help us brainstorm. Now, Nicole, I know this is a bit of a surprise, and you may even feel like I'm throwing you to the wolves." He chuckled. "But that's not the case at all."

Seven pairs of unblinking eyes fastened on her. It was the case. Only Finn and Talley were on her side.

"So here's what we're going to do. I came up with a concept I thought was pretty good. I even ran it by the wife, and she gave it a thumbs-up. I'm just going to throw it out here and I want everyone, absolutely everyone, to give me a completely honest opinion."

A silence fell that made Nicole want to run and hide.

Kevin put a hand on a pile of spreadsheets and dragged it over to himself. "Just as background, you all should know that we have a ton of denim that isn't moving. Jeans don't seem to be what people are thinking of for Christmas gifts. So we need to change their minds. That brings me to my concept."

He cleared his throat and finally took a sip of his brew. "You ready?"

Kevin Talley was a ham, Nicole thought. He would be doing them all a favor by getting to the point.

The CEO slapped a button attached to a cable cord. A huge screen behind him came to life.

Denim and Then Some. The slogan was five inches high, flat white against navy blue. The first word that came to Nicole's mind was *boring*.

"Fantastic, Kev," said the woman next to Nicole, a little too quickly. "Really says what needs saying. Let's go with it."

"Very catchy," a man agreed.

The general consensus was much the same. Nicole dreaded the moment Kevin Talley would turn to her. Everyone agreed with him.

"What do you think, Nicole?"

She took a breath. "It is catchy," she began.

"Don't be an echo. Tell me what you really think," Talley ordered. "You, Nicole Young, are our target demographic. Give it to me straight."

"Denim and Then Some just is not—it's not magical. Someone looking in the window is going to see that you're selling denim, right? So you don't need to spell it out like that. What people want is magic."

Kevin Talley looked at her with disappointment. He managed a smile. "Thank you, Nicole."

Finn was jotting down notes in his sketchbook. His ever-so-slight nudge got her to look down at the words concealed by his cupped hand.

Do not criticize Kevin Talley. Are you crazy? Tell him his idea is great. I want to live.

The phone in the conference room rang. Alonzo picked it up and listened for a moment. "Mr. Talley, it seems that Mrs. Talley is on line five. Do you want to take the call in here or in your office?"

Apparently Mr. Talley couldn't just ignore his wife. When he left the conference room, low-voiced remarks about Mrs. Talley ran around the table. But no one talked to them.

Nicole poked Finn, who reached for his notebook.

FYI: Bree Talley is mega-rich. She's the money behind the business—and the real boss of ENJ. I have to get rid of this note before he comes back. I still want to live.

When she'd read it, he tore off the page and folded it several times, sticking it down inside his boot.

Kevin Talley was coming back. He pushed open the door and headed for his seat, looking at Nicole again but not with quite as much enthusiasm.

"So. Turns out the wife changed her mind. She doesn't like Denim and Then Some anymore. Nicole, got any ideas? Besides the magic, I mean."

Nicole swallowed hard. He was the one who'd put her on the spot. He had asked her to be absolutely honest. Well, she would be.

"There needs to be romance too," she said. "It's the best magic, if that doesn't sound too corny. But it has to be shown in a way that makes people believe it."

"Could you be a little more specific?" Kevin Talley fiddled with a pencil.

Nicole looked out the vast window, as if inspiration was going to fly right through it and save her. The afternoon clouds had moved on and twilight had fallen. In the deepening sky the moon appeared. The clear winter air made it sparkle.

"Diamond moon," she said suddenly. "You could have a fantasy setting, very simple, with a woman wearing jeans but not ordinary jeans. She's lit in blue, not so detailed that she seems too real. The jeans seams are outlined with tiny diamonds sparkling faintly. There's a moon above her—a huge moon, covered with tiny diamonds too. The sky is dark indigo blue."

Talley was actually listening. Nicole stopped. Finn kicked her under the table.

"I'm thinking," she told him under her breath. She sat up straight. "A crescent moon would be even better, one that the woman can swing on," she continued. "But all the other elements stay the same. The scene is mysterious and beautiful—it draws the viewer in like a dream. And in the shadows beyond the moon there's a man. We know he's her lover and the moment they see each other is just about to happen. She dreams of him, and we see him about to step forward and take her in his arms and—"

Kevin Talley slapped the table button and his slogan disappeared. The screen behind him went blank.

Nicole snapped back to reality.

"Romance. Magic. Diamonds. Denim. I love it!" he said. "How much will it cost? Can you give me a breakdown by tomorrow?"

Sam saw Nicole's number come up on his cell phone and picked up. "Hey. Haven't heard from you in a while. What's going on?" He tried to sound casual.

"I just got out of a meeting with Kevin Talley. He wants me to do the windows at the flagship store. He intends to pay me a lot of money and give me whatever I need to do it right."

"That's great! What happens next?"

She paused for a moment. "I'm going to need some help, Sam. Your help. Finn's signed on already. But I don't want to work with the ENJ visual team. They are scary, scary people. And they don't like me."

"I can help, sure." He thought for a few seconds. "There's nothing coming up that Greg needs me for. I just talked to him. He said that from here on in it's mostly maintenance of the installations, you know, in case of a storm or something. So I'm free."

"Where are you now?" Nicole asked.

"Down at the lot. Not doing anything important."

"Good. Can you help me right now?"

Sam couldn't help smiling. There was no one to see. He was in the corner with the tall trees. "You bet. With what?"

"I need a moon. A great, big, luminous moon."

There was something dreamy in her voice. He liked the sound of it. A lot.

"Then let's go find one," he said.

Chapter 10

Sam had to hang up when a customer appeared. Nicole called him back ten minutes later. "We have to do this tomorrow. The place is closed."

"Okay. Not a problem. Where is it? And what is it?"

Nicole didn't answer right away. She sounded a bit distracted. "It's a prop warehouse out in Queens. Actually, several of them."

Sam had never heard of such a thing. "Tell me the odds of finding a moon in a warehouse."

"Not too bad, actually. I once found a sphinx and a seven-foot banana on the same day."

"I can't even begin to imagine what you used them for."

"Different projects. I had to keep them in my apartment for a while."

Sam grinned. He had the oddest conversations with Nicole sometimes, but he always enjoyed them. And the lot seemed to be in an afternoon lull, after he'd sold that tree.

"So where are they now?"

"Back in the warehouse," she said, as if anyone would know that. "You don't have to buy. They rent stuff out. Set designers, ad agencies, photographers, TV and movie people—we all go to prop warehouses. Not just window dressers."

"New to me. I'm really looking forward to it." Sam laughed.

"We have to rent a car," Nicole said. "I'll take care of that."

"But you need a big moon. Is that going to fit in the trunk?"

"Hmm. We have to find the right moon first. They might even have a folding one, or one that comes apart somehow. If we need to, we can go back with a van or a pickup."

"What if they don't have a moon at all?" Sam covered the phone when he saw a man stop at the lot and look idly at the trees against the frame. "Be right with you," he said to the customer. "Nicole, I gotta go."

"Okay. Meet me in the morning. I'll text you the time and I'll pick you up in front of your building."

They exchanged good-byes and Sam walked over to the man. "Is there a particular size you're looking for?"

"Nah. I just want a really nice tree."

Sam sized him up. Whoever manned the lot had some leeway on prices. The man probably wouldn't pay top dollar. He needed a haircut and he looked a little scruffy otherwise. The cuffs and collar of his jacket showed wear, and his sneakers were almost worn out.

"How much for this one?" the man asked. He moved to the fir tree in the bucket filled with peat moss.

"That one is set aside," Sam said politely. He pointed to the *SOLD* tag.

"Yeah? But I like it. What if I match the price and go up by five bucks?"

"Sorry. I can't do that." Sam didn't know who had asked Theo to set aside the fir, but he did remember the old man saying it was for a special customer.

"They all look alike. You could switch it for the same kind. Who's to know?"

Sam had the feeling the customer had fixated on the tree for some unknown reason. Or on him. Maybe because of the Stetson. If this oddball took him for a country boy, so what. It took all kinds, especially in a big city, but that didn't mean Sam had to give in. His answer was firm.

"No. It's one of a kind. See the crooked branch on top?"

The man in the shabby jacket grinned unpleasantly. "That's why I like it. I'm crooked too."

Sam's patience snapped. "Move on. I mean it." He took a step toward the man, looming over him. The baseball bat that Theo kept handy just in case was within easy reach. He'd use it if he had to.

The man held up his hands, encased in grimy gloves. "Don't get excited. I was just making a joke. Is that any way to treat a customer?"

"Get out of here. Now."

With a disagreeable sigh, the man turned and sidled away down the street. He threw a last look over his shoulder at Sam, who was moving the tree with the *SOLD* tag away from the curb to a spot where it was less visible.

When Sam looked up again, brushing peat moss off his hands, the man was gone.

Nicole's next call was to Sharon. They got through the hellos and how-are-yous fast. Sharon knew something was up.

"And how's Sam?" Her friend's tone was nonchalant. "You didn't call just to chat."

"Ah—I'm working with him again. Not for pay. We're going to the prop warehouses tomorrow."

"Strong arms. Heavy lifting. Yes, I see."

"Don't tease me," Nicole begged. "It really is going to be work. I need stuff for the big ENJ job I just got. I'm doing new windows for their flagship store. Super rush."

"Now that is news. Good for you, Nicole. That's amazing. Who's in charge of the freelancers? Yes, I am angling for a job. Any job."

"Finn Leary. I'll give you his number."

"I have it. I know Finn," Sharon said joyfully. "I'm going to bug him the second you hang up."

"That would be so cool. We haven't worked together for ages."

"True. So. I've been thinking about Sam—"

"I don't need any more advice on my love life."

"You sure?"

Nicole was beginning to realize that sometimes you just *knew*. A budding romance wasn't going to turn into true love if it was picked apart and analyzed to shreds.

"We decided to be friends." That wasn't a lie.

Sharon took a breath. "Then I won't tell you that there's no future with a guy who lives in Colorado. Sam is here for seasonal work, no matter how tall and brawny and polite and sexy he is."

"How did you know he was polite?"

Her friend hooted. "He hasn't jumped you yet. Dead giveaway."

"Sharon!"

"Bye. I gotta call Finn."

But Nicole didn't, not right away. She spent an hour or more online, looking up Colorado on the Internet. Just about every photo was breathtakingly beautiful. And it seemed like everyone had only good things to say about the whole damn state, whether they were from there or not. She looked up Velde again. Pretty town. His ranch, well, who knew. But she was sure that was beautiful too.

Next morning, he was waiting for Nicole on the stoop, per her text. She drove up in a red rental car, bright and shiny, and rolled down the window.

"How do you like my wheels?" she called.

"Nice. Where'd you get it? Is there a rental place right around here?" That seemed unlikely.

"It's from CarGo. You rent by the hour and pick out the car online. Ready and waiting at a garage near you. They have vans and trucks too. You don't have to pay for gas or insurance. It's all included in the membership."

"Good deal." He walked around the car. It was practically new, from what he could tell.

"It's a great deal. I think it's the future of city living," she said happily.

Sam got in and slid the seat all the way back to make room for his long legs. It was nice to be in a car again. Then he remembered what Manhattan traffic was like. And that a lot of New Yorkers didn't drive at all.

"So," he said conversationally, "how long have you had a driver's license?"

Nicole pulled out into the street, going around a double-parked car. "Since I was twenty-one. But I bet you've been driving since you were old enough to reach the pedals."

"Yeah. Kids do in the country. I guess I was about twelve when my dad let me drive on the ranch roads, but I'd been driving before that. Stick shift, too."

"I can't drive a stick. Never even tried."

"Come out to Colorado. I'll show you how. Bet you could learn to drive my old truck in no time."

Nicole glanced his way, then back at the street again. "Are you serious?"

"Believe me, you couldn't do any damage to that truck that would show. And Colorado's a beautiful place. You should see it."

They came to a red light and she stopped. "I may take you up on that someday."

Sam smiled. "Just say when."

Nicole pushed a few buttons at random until a small

screen in the dashboard lit up. "Pick a station," she said. "Whatever you like. These cars have satellite radio."

"Way to go."

The light changed, and they went across the intersection. Nicole drove smoothly, considering she was negotiating an ever-changing obstacle course of taxis and jaywalkers. Sam mentally timed it: New York drivers gave each other three seconds to make a move. If you hesitated, you risked getting into a fender bender.

They got across town without incident and reached the turnoff to the Queensboro Bridge. Nicole stopped, watching a brawny traffic cop in a safety vest for the signal to go. His white-gloved hands were constantly moving, and he meant business, dropping the ear-piercing whistle on a lanyard around his neck and bellowing out orders when he had to.

"Dude is fearless," Sam said with admiration.

The cop diverted two large trucks and a fur-coated individual in a luxury car to the side, where a flasher-top cruiser was parked. The officer inside got out and approached Mrs. Furry, who was screaming something out the window about a lawyer.

Sam and Nicole looked ahead as they made the turn. In another few seconds they had gone through a death-defying intersection and were heading over the bridge. He looked up and around and out, taking in the view of the East River and catching a glimpse of the aerial tram that ferried passengers across it.

"Is that the tram that was in the movie a while back?"

"Actually, that's a new one. It looks a little different. It's fun to ride—the view is even better than this. Add it to your list."

"I sure will."

They were pulling off into a vast stretch of buildings

that looked something like Manhattan, only not as densely packed together.

"Welcome to Queens," she said. "Astoria is that way. We're not going there."

Sam looked. Maybe he'd make his own way out here one of these days, see where Greg came from.

"Just so you know, Queens is not exactly royal, but it's interesting. More great ethnic neighborhoods than any other borough in New York. And it's a lot bigger than Manhattan."

"Do the subways go out here?"

Nicole nodded. "They do, but nowhere near where we're headed. Besides, it's fun to rent a car sometimes. I like to drive in New York."

"You have nerves of steel," he told her.

Sam looked out the window while she concentrated on the driving. There was almost too much to see, and it was going to be impossible to describe to his folks. So he just enjoyed it for himself.

After a while they were going down a main street that could have been anywhere in the U.S. There were family restaurants, hardware stores, gardening emporiums, and clothing stores. Nothing fancy. But doing well.

Nicole slowed down to check the street signs, making a left turn into a neighborhood of one- and two-story houses on wide lawns, set back from the curb. There were kids riding bikes on the uncrowded sidewalks and some adults out walking dogs.

"Are we still in New York City?" Sam asked in disbelief.

"Yes, we are. Queens isn't much like Manhattan, though. This part of it is really suburban."

She looked ahead to the far end of the street. "We're almost there."

Sam had almost forgotten about the warehouses. "You're kidding me." He didn't see anything but one nice house after another.

"Nope." She turned right at the corner and then sharply left. A low warehouse ran for what seemed to be blocks. Nicole turned into a loading bay and pulled into the parking spaces to the side. Several large trucks were backed into the bay, dropping off items or picking them up, Sam couldn't quite tell.

She switched off the ignition and got out, waving to the men working on the bay.

"Okay if we go in this way and skip the showroom?" she asked.

"Sure, Nicole." The men looked curiously at Sam, who tipped his Stetson to them.

"They probably think you're an actor," she said out of the side of her mouth. "You may get asked for an autograph."

"Yeah, right."

She clomped up an open metal staircase, followed by Sam.

The interior of the warehouse was drafty and dim, crammed with all kinds of stuff. There were rows of chairs, some in sets, some different, as well as every other kind of furniture. On top of the bigger pieces were one-of-a-kind items.

Sam didn't see a sphinx or a seven-foot banana, but they had to be around here someplace. He passed under a white metal palm tree hung with metal coconuts.

"Check out the moose head to your right," Nicole said. "I rented that once. The eyes move and so do the antlers. There's a battery-powered motor inside."

Sam found himself face-to-face with it. He hadn't expected the huge head to be hung so low. The glass eyes glittered, but he guessed the battery had died. He was thankful for that. "Does it talk?" he asked.

"You could probably rig something," she laughed.

They kept walking through more furniture.

"A lot of this is just boring stuff from TV show sets. When it gets too shabby looking, the prop director gets rid of it. But don't worry. We're on our way to the crazy stuff."

"Don't see any moons yet."

Nicole looked around. "I have scrounger's luck. Let's see what they have. There's more than one warehouse out here."

Sam had stopped at an armchair.

"You can't fit anything into that sublet."

"I don't intend to." He looked more closely at the chair. "This looks familiar for some reason."

"Check the tag. You can find out what show it comes from. Prop people don't like to use things that have been featured on other shows."

Sam found the tag and read it aloud. "*They Live to Love*. I don't believe it. My mother used to watch that soap. This chair is part of TV history."

"I can't imagine anyone on a ranch watching soaps." Nicole came over to look at the chair, curious herself.

"Hey, my mom got up at five and worked most of the day for as long as I can remember. When she sat down to watch *They Live to Love*, we knew it was quittin' time for her. We weren't allowed to bother her—she loved that show. I swear she knew the characters better than the writers did."

"Really? That's funny."

Sam walked slowly around the chair. "And I even remember which one used this chair. The kindly doctor."

He brushed off some of the dust and sat down. "You have to take my picture. Mom won't believe it."

Nicole took out her phone. "Smile."

"It's all coming back to me." His voice became almost reverent as he rested his hands on the arms. "Dr. Glick sat right here when he told Lucy Kay she had an incurable disease that would cause her to morph into the body of her long-lost evil twin."

"You have to be kidding. Smile again."

The phone camera clicked several times as he talked.

"I actually watched that episode. Fell off the couch laughing, too, until my mother whacked me with a pillow. I still have the scar."

"Sure." Nicole came over.

"Let's take one of you and me," he said. "Right here in the chair. I'll hold the phone. I have longer arms than you do."

She held back after she handed him the phone.

Sam could read her mind. "Granted, there isn't much room. But are we still just friends?"

"Are you still sorry you kissed me?"

He sighed. "Is that why you've been so skittish? Girl, come over here."

Nicole didn't fight him as he pulled her onto his lap. But she did wiggle off until she was safely squeezed into the side of the chair cushion. Her hand curled around her phone and took it from him.

"I'm not taking a picture of us until you answer my question. Are you still sorry you kissed me?"

"No. And I never was sorry. As I remember, I was just saying that to make you mad." His gaze was steady. There was no escaping it. Their noses were only inches apart.

Nicole looked at him warily.

"Comfortable?" he asked her.

"Squeezed like this? No."

"How about if I turn this way?" He adjusted his body so that he was somewhat on his side, his long legs stretched out. The change in position knocked the Stetson off his head. Without looking, Sam made an overhand pass and set it on top of the armchair.

Nicole had room to move. But instead of getting up, she turned on her side too. She reached out, but not to push him away. Her hand gripped his muscular upper arm and drew him fractionally closer.

Sam took advantage of her unspoken invitation. His lips touched her mouth, gently at first. She opened her lips to his exploring tongue, and the kiss was on.

The armchair rocked a bit when he moved his free arm around her waist just above her hips and lifted her up onto him. Nicole arched, shamelessly enjoying the stolen moment of pure pleasure. No one was looking. They were all alone in the vast, dim warehouse.

His hands began to move over her, bold caresses that heated her skin without him getting under her clothes. She cupped his face, kissing him harder.

Sam let her do whatever she wanted, holding her just right, responsive and tender . . . and strong. It was almost too much for her.

Nicole sat up on his lap and put her hands on his chest, just looking at him. His smoky blue eyes were half closed but very, very focused on her. She touched a fingertip to his mouth, following its hard curve.

Then she rolled off, sitting primly beside him and looking straight ahead. Sam straightened in the chair and put his arm around her shoulders.

Nicole was a little out of breath. "Well, that was nice. Very nice."

Sam stroked her hair and smiled down at her, cradling her in the crook of his arm. "More than nice and you know it. There must be something else on your mind."

She looked at him dreamily. "We were looking for a moon."

"Yeah."

"Oh, no. I totally forgot." She sat up. "We have to go moon-hunting some other time, Sam. One job is all I can handle or I'll lose my mind."

Of course, Sam might not be helping with that. He looked like he was waiting for her to explain.

"The second window at Now—I have to do it before Darci comes back from Aspen."

"As in right now?"

Sam helped her stand. She brushed at her clothes and pulled down her sweater. "I want to get it out of the way. This was a wasted trip," she fretted.

Not to Sam.

"Maybe I can find a few things for Now." She looked around at the stored furniture. "Not here, though. You up for a fast scavenger hunt?"

He had the feeling she needed to be busy.

"Why not? And don't worry about the second window. You have the measurements in your notebook? I saw you keeping a running log of everything."

"Yes but—"

"Call Bob. Or I'll call him on the way back and give him a heads-up. First things first. He can build the framework from your notes."

"If he has time."

"I'll build it if he can't."

Nicole sat down in another chair with no arms and crossed her legs, yoga style. She closed her eyes and let her hands rest on her knees.

"Breathe," she said softly. "Delegate. Breathe. Delegate."

Sam laughed out loud. Her eyes opened, flashing with indignation. "Shut up!"

Someone had left several mannequins resting against the back of the window bay at Now. The last assistant to leave had let them in, then handed the keys to Nicole with instructions to drop them off at her apartment in the morning.

Sam went to move them. "You're not going to use these, right?"

"No."

Sam went to move them. He put his hands around the waist of one, feeling a little foolish, but there was no one to look. He lifted it easily. "These are light. I thought mannequins were made of plaster."

She shook her head. "They haven't been made of plaster since forever. That stuff shatters, and mannequins get dropped a lot."

He looked into the haughty face of the mannequin, holding the torso away from him. "So how much do you weigh, honey?"

"About forty or fifty pounds. It's made of plastic composite resin. But don't hold it that way."

Sam brought the mannequin close to him as if he was giving it a hug. Its arms rotated somewhat and stuck out over his shoulders. "Like this?" He turned around a little too quickly.

The left arm came off and fell to the floor.

"Oops. Sorry."

"Every newbie holds a mannequin wrong. There's only one way to get a good grip on those things."

Sam was afraid to let go. The right arm had snagged on a clothing rack. He looked at the metal plate in the torso where the left arm had come off. "I don't think I broke anything. Yet." He looked down at the arm on the floor. "Still has all the fingers. That post in the arm locks into this plate, right?"

"Hang on a sec. I'll help you. I just can't let go of the framework right now."

"Take your time. Me and the one-armed lady here are just getting to know each other." He eased the awkward object a little away from himself and a leg came off. It hit the floor and rolled around, also undamaged.

"Damn!"

Nicole laughed heartlessly.

"What the hell do you want me to do with this?" He couldn't move without stepping on a detached limb, so he just stood there.

She put down her hammer and found a two-by-four to support the framework. "Here I come." She made her way to him, picking up the leg and the arm and setting them aside.

Sam turned his head to look when she carefully eased the clothes rack away from the mannequin's arm. To his relief, it stayed on. But his slight motion to observe Nicole had caused the mannequin's wig to slip down over its painted eyes.

It didn't seem right. He held the mannequin tightly around the waist and gently adjusted the wig. The head fell off, landing in a pile of neatly folded sweaters.

Nicole burst out laughing again. By now he was too.

"Sorry, honey," he said to the head on the sweaters when he could talk again. "Didn't mean to be so rough with you."

Nicole took a deep breath. "Okay. I'm going to show you how to pick up a mannequin like a professional."

Sam rolled his eyes. "I'm happy to learn, but just so you know, I have no intention of starting a career as a window dresser." He shifted a hand. What was left of the mannequin teetered on the remaining leg. "I can't let go!"

Nicole put her arms around the torso's waist and lifted the whole thing off him, stepping to one side.

"First of all, you carry it with the back to your front."

Sam was happy to be relieved of his burden. He pretended to kiss the mannequin's gracefully outstretched hand—without actually touching it.

"Because you're holding it from behind, you can see where you're going and keep the arms from catching on things," Nicole said. "Now here's how to do the actual grab."

Her hand slid down over the smooth front to where the fake legs joined the plastic torso. "Right here. In between."

Sam guffawed. "I shouldn't watch. This is not PG-13."

"That's how you have to do it," she insisted.

"I can't. My momma would slap me into the middle of next week if she ever knew." He had to lean against the wall, he was laughing so hard.

Nicole was laughing too, but she was determined to teach him. "Don't say that. You may have to help me move the ENJ mannequins."

Sam composed himself and listened up.

Nicole hoisted the mannequin. "Got the idea? This way it leans against you close to your own center of gravity but it's high enough so you aren't dragging it. It doesn't seem as heavy and it won't separate."

She carried the mannequin to a heavy base and attached the remaining foot and leg to it in one swift motion.

"Live and learn," he said, wiping his eyes. He picked up the fallen arm and leg and brought them over. She fastened them to the torso and adjusted the position.

Sam went back for the head, handing it to Nicole. She positioned it on the neck but stopped a half turn short of screwing it on completely.

"There," she said mischievously. "It looks better with the head on backward, don't you think?"

"Stop," he gasped. "Just stop. I hurt from laughing."

There was a knock on the door. Nicole looked through the glass to see Bob, with the framework over his shoulder.

She let him in.

"Thanks so much," Nicole said to Bob. "You're a life-saver."

"Happy to help. Hi, Sam." He walked over to the second window bay and set down the framework. "Did you cut the vinyl for this yet, Nicole?"

"No," she answered. "I'm going to run outside and take photos of the storefront. Then I'll e-mail it to my sign guy, and he'll have it printed out super big for me tomorrow. Won't take long to install." She turned to Sam.

"Fill me in," he said.

Nicole found her notebook. "It's fundamentally the same idea as the first window, but I'm changing the time and mood to the present. So the windows by each side of the door really will be Now and Then. And the now side will include an image of the then side. Best I could do, considering the time crunch."

The two men looked at each other. Sam spoke for both of them when he said, "That's a great idea. And easy."

"Glad you think so. This could be my last boutique job," Nicole said with a smile. "I'm meeting Finn in the morning. He's going to get me up to speed on corporate retailing."

Chapter 11

Finn was standing outside the ENJ flagship store, his neck wrapped in a thick muffler and his red hair concealed under a hat that more or less matched it. Nicole guessed from half a block away that his girlfriend, Janey, had knitted both for him and run out of yarn at some point. One end of the muffler was a different color and it didn't match. She hurried to his side, keeping her thin pashmina scarf wrapped around her head and pressed to her mouth. The wind off the East River was bitingly cold.

She pulled the folds of the scarf down to say hello to him. "How come you're not inside?"

"I was waiting for you," he replied through his muffler. "I thought maybe you would have a few questions before we go in."

Nicole nodded, feeling guilty. Finn's feet had to be freezing, even in the heavy boots he wore. There was no friend like an old friend.

"Just a few. Real quick. Is anyone from the visual team at headquarters going to be here?"

"No. But I did hire your friend Sharon Levitt."

"Thanks!"

"She does good work. Even if she talks too much."

"Is Kevin Talley coming in?"

"Not right away."

She smiled and grasped the handle of the door, pulling it open. "How'd I get so lucky?"

"You're not the only one. Talley's assistant said I could choose your support team. Besides Sharon, I hired everyone who was there the other night. Good group. But they won't be showing up until later tonight."

Finn reached over her head to hold the door. She ducked under his arm and entered.

The store wasn't open for business. Staff members and sales associates were milling around the coffeemaker, drinking from paper cups, then discarding them quickly.

"You've never done a morning meeting, right?"

"Nope."

He pulled off his hat and his red hair stood on end with static electricity. Then he unwound the seemingly endless muffler. Nicole could see why Janey had run out of yarn.

She followed him to a room where everyone had already dumped their outerwear and backpacks or purses, and took off her own warm things, helping herself to the last remaining hook.

"Okay. This is what happens. Morning meetings don't last long but they are a big deal. Attendance is mandatory. Everyone has to show up—visual team associates, sales staff, business operations people, you name it. Even the cleaning personnel."

She looked out the door of the coatroom. A uniformed woman was walking by, dragging a vacuum that hadn't been switched on.

"So I see."

"There's a hierarchy. You're near the top, thanks to Talley. You outrank me, actually."

"I do?"

He winked at her. "Yeah. You can boss me around all you like."

"Good."

"Okay, the pecking order. The store manager is in charge of practically everything, but the visual team—that's us and all the scroungy people we knew in college—"

"Thanks a lot."

"Am I wrong?"

"No," she laughed, looking out the door again.

"The visual team is usually assigned by the home office and doesn't answer directly to the store manager. Managers work on a rotating schedule. The most in-charge person who happens to be there first can start the meeting, and managers rotate responsibility for these meetings."

Nicole was following him, but not with much interest. Putting up with Darci's occasional tantrums suddenly seemed like a piece of cake.

"As far as the money flow, operations controls the financial part of the business."

"Seems reasonable." Maybe there was a reason she'd been a freelancer for so long.

"Moving right along, there are department managers, and a little lower down the totem pole, sales associates. But it's all for one and one for all. Your windows are bait to bring in customers and boost sales. Everyone works together to make that happen. Everything gets tracked. Everyone has to be on their game."

Nicole felt a flash of nervousness, even though she knew they would only start work on the windows after the store closed.

"I still haven't found my moon, Finn. How long do I have to be here after the meeting? Am I supposed to help anyone else?"

"Not long. I'll walk you around, explain stuff. And no to your second question. Visual employees do not work register or dressing rooms unless we're supercrunched. And with nothing in the windows, we're not exactly attracting hordes of customers. Like Talley said, the week-to-date sales numbers are falling."

Nicole nodded. "No pressure or anything."

"Of course not." He patted her shoulder. "December is only the most important selling month of the year. Repeat after me: I will survive."

"I will survive," Nicole said.

A high-pitched, somewhat artificial female voice wafted their way.

"That's Babs Chroma." Finn looked at the chunky watch on his wrist. "Right on time."

The store manager was tall and slender, clad in a skintight, charcoal-wool suit that didn't leave much to the imagination. The tiny jacket plunged to a deep vee in front, and the skirt was breathtakingly short. Her long legs were sheathed in black tights, and she sported platform stilettos—black patent leather, no less—that added a good five inches to her height.

Babs Chroma knew how to stand out.

Nicole caught a glimpse of herself in a mirror placed at the end of a rack for customers who didn't have the time to wait for dressing rooms.

By comparison, she resembled a fire hydrant. Not red, just short and thick. Which she wasn't.

She shouldn't have looked. Nicole knew that store mirrors had the magic power to make unsuspecting shoppers cringe, probably so they would buy something, anything, that was different and new.

In her own mirror, Nicole had rated herself as an 8 on a Registered Cuteness Scale of 1 to 10. Her best jeans and shrug sweater over a rock-band T-shirt didn't look the same here.

Nicole told herself she was here to work. And to learn. She stood in the back just in case, half concealed by an

open shelf stacked with folded jeans. She didn't want Babs
to point a manicured fingernail at her and ask her to introduce herself.

Other people, mostly young, male and female, quickly
joined the gathering.

A few sat down. Babs looked like she never did. With a
glance at her watch she began the meeting, pacing back
and forth on those killer heels. Nicole wondered what Sam
would make of her. Babs reminded her of a tall, long-
legged bird. The kind that speared frogs.

But her tone was friendly enough.

"Hey, guys. Welcome. So nice to see you all—I'm sorry,
I'm not too good with names, but when I say you, I mean
you and you and you!"

She pointed to people at random. No one smiled.

"Okay. Let's get started. We had a great day yesterday.
We finished up five percent to our goal, which means we're
up seven percent from last year. In order to make our
week, here's what we need to do today."

Babs had it all memorized, Nicole figured.

"We have to do at least twenty-five thousand dollars to
meet last year," Babs said. "We have to do thirty-five thousand dollars to make goal—and that is a projected but re-
alistic goal. Everyone with me so far?"

Affirmative mumbles. No one wanted to seem clueless.
This was not a question-and-answer session.

"That's great. Now, Christmas is just around the corner,
and a lot of customers are thinking about how to spend
their upcoming bonuses. Plus there's a payday at the end
of the week. And the forecast is for clear, cold days."

Nicole raised a questioning eyebrow.

"She has to factor in everything that affects sales," Finn
whispered.

"That's great shopping weather! No slipping on ice. No

rain or snow to slog through to get to ENJ. I think we could make a stretch goal of forty thousand dollars!"

No one cheered.

"But let's think big. As in superstretch goal! No, better than that! Super-duper stretch!"

Nicole looked around at the mostly glum faces. Sharon had worked as a sales associate until she'd burned out on the low wages and punishingly long hours.

"I do have some fabulous incentives that the home office has authorized me to offer," Babs cooed. "If you can reach your individual sales goals"—she paused meaningfully—"each and every one of you could be eligible for a day off. Or a comp day added to your sick leave. Or even dinner at a fancy restaurant on me!"

Finn cleared his throat. Nicole hadn't realized he was standing that near to her.

A junior manager in preppy casual attire stepped forward.

"Doesn't that sounds good?" he said encouragingly. "Remember, the higher your numbers are, the higher the manager's bonus will be for Babs. What she's talking about is paying it forward to all of you."

There was a barely discernible ripple of enthusiasm. Most of the sales associates seem to understand that the main beneficiary of their extra effort would be (a) the company and (b) Babs Chroma.

The junior manager went on with the same breathless enthusiasm.

"ENJ really wants to motivate everyone to work together for our holiday bonus package. And don't forget that Babs also gets a year-end, quarterly bonus to share. She's counting on you!"

Finn scowled. "I hear that Babs doesn't like to share all

that much," he whispered to Nicole. "Walk backwards. Slowly. We don't have to listen to this. If we even get a bonus, it has nothing to do with hers."

The junior manager was clapping for attention. "New product time! Let's listen up!"

Nicole took a step backward but continued to look forward.

"Should we stay?" she murmured to Finn.

"Guess we have to. Babs is looking at us."

Jeans and jackets were brought out and presented to the assembled group, along with instructions for positioning them on the selling floor. Babs Chroma and a couple of the department managers offered suggestions on how to wear things. A couple of sales associates served as models.

Nicole raised her head and looked around. Music played faintly through hidden speakers, getting louder.

"Do you hear what I hear?" Babs exclaimed. She answered her own question. "Yes! Christmas carols for our demographic!"

The volume swelled, pumping to a rock beat. Finn talked directly to Nicole, safe from being overheard. "The soundtrack does change. Just get used to it. You'll hear something different when the shopping slows down."

Nicole shook her head. "So much for tradition."

Finn gave her a what-can-you-do look. "Home office does a lot of research on things like in-store music. ENJ wants their customer to feel right at home."

The meeting seemed to be almost over. The few people who'd sat down were getting up.

But Babs Chroma had to have the last word. "All right! We can do this! Turn up the music! Open the doors!"

Sam and Nicole edged away as the sales associates moved to their stations.

Nicole looked back at Babs, who was talking to the junior manager. "She has pep to spare. I don't use that many exclamation points in a year."

Finn shrugged. "Managers have to motivate."

Nicole hung around the flagship store for the rest of the morning, observing how shoppers interacted with the merchandise displays in place—or ignored them. Finn and his team would be picking up the theme of her windows and repeating some elements on the selling floor.

ENJ wanted to help customers connect with the brand in a new way, and Talley was prepared to pay for whatever Nicole wanted for the window displays. The first item on the list was the moon.

Finn was going to get the custom ENJ mannequins from wherever those were stored, and the paint, and whatever props he thought might work. Other members of the team were putting together an assortment of clothing for the window, all new designs. The person who was doing the studding had gone out to buy two huge boxes of tiny fake diamonds—the moon would be studded too.

She moved over to one of the papered-over windows and called Sam.

"Ready to go hunting again?" she asked.

"Yeah. I'm at the deli, picking up sandwiches for the guys at the lot right now—you want anything?"

"No. Thanks, though."

"After I drop them off, I'm a free man. Did you rent a car?"

"CarGo had a truck available," she said happily. "It's at the garage around the corner. You'll probably get there before me."

He spoke to someone at his end, then came back on. "What did you say?"

"I rented a pickup truck."

There was a pause. "What if we don't find a moon?"

"I did already," she said. "But I haven't seen it yet. I asked around and someone I know at a different warehouse e-mailed me last night. Getting back to the truck, I can put you on the insurance for a day with one phone call. Want to do the driving?"

"Sure."

"What's your driver's license number so they can verify you?"

"Hang on." She heard the sounds of a paper bag being set down. "I don't have it memorized. I'll text it to you, okay?"

"Okay. Meet me at the garage."

She hung up and called CarGo and took care of business, then checked in with an old pal at the warehouse.

"Hi, Joey. It's Nicole. I'll be there in about an hour. Is anyone else interested in that moon?"

The answer was a growling laugh. "Nah. Ya kidding me? Come get it."

"It's big, right?"

"Hell, yeah. As in way too big. I wanna get rid of it. Ya got someone ta help ya move it? I'm shorthanded today."

"Yes, I do."

"Just go round to da back part of the warehouse. Where I stick the stuff I can't sell."

"Thanks, Joey. See you soon."

Sam was waiting at the garage, finishing his sandwich as she approached the open entrance. He tossed the foil wrapping into a can and waved to her. "I'm here. I don't see a pickup, though."

Nicole held up a plastic card with the CarGo logo. "It's here. The attendant will bring it. This unlocks it and charges the rental to me automatically."

"How about that."

An attendant in black pants and white shirt with a bowtie

came running. "Hello, miss." He took the card from Nicole. "Which one?"

"The blue pickup truck, please," she told him.

Sam stood with her, listening to the sound of the giant elevator that brought vehicles up and down inside the garage building. "How did the morning meeting go?"

"I learned a fair amount about how the store operates. The finished windows will tie into smaller in-store displays, but we aren't creating those. Just the big picture, so to speak."

"Nervous?"

Nicole managed a very small smile. "A little. But once I start working, I pretty much forget about everything besides getting it done." She looked up at him and her smile got wider and warmer. "I'm glad you're going to be there."

Sam didn't get a chance to reply. The elevator door rolled up and a shiny blue pickup rolled out. The attendant drove toward them, threw it into park, and jumped out, leaving the engine running. He handed the plastic card back to Nicole and she tipped him a dollar, then walked around to the passenger side.

"Key's in it," she told Sam.

"Ready to roll?"

She took a length of coiled rope out of her purse and slipped it over her wrist. "Yes. We'll need this when we get there."

"Is it long enough? I never tied down a moon before."

"It's thirty feet. The moon's only five feet high."

"That oughta do it." Sam pulled the driver's side door open all the way and swung himself up into the seat.

He looked at the odometer. "Under a thousand miles— this is new. Great." He looked down at the gearshift. "Automatic. Okay."

They drove off. Sam had liked being in a car again, but he felt right at home in the truck. The narrow streets weren't that bad—you just had to go slow a lot of the time, that was all. Nicole gave him directions, and it wasn't long before they were going over the Queensboro Bridge. The pickup's high cab gave him an even better view this time.

"Lots of bridges," he commented, noticing the spans over the East River.

"The Brooklyn Bridge is my fave. Look way down."

He barely caught a glimpse of the famous structure as she told him to change lanes.

"I'll get you out to Brooklyn," she assured him. "Whole different world, not like Manhattan. You'd like it."

"You're on. What's that tall building back there?" he asked, looking in the rearview mirror. "On your right, by the river. Actually, it's a tall one and a short one together. I know I've seen both."

She rolled down her window and glanced back.

"That's the United Nations," she said. "The park around it is really nice, and there's a huge rose garden. No roses now, though."

He looked over at her. "The wind just put them in your cheeks, that's why. Did I tell you today how beautiful you are?"

Nicole rolled up her window. Her cheeks glowed even brighter as she shook her head. "No. And thank you. I won't be when I'm covered with blue paint and glue."

"That oughta be interesting." He laughed.

"Wait until you see me." She changed the subject. "Are you ready for Joey Traverso? He's as New York as it gets."

"You bet."

Joey Traverso turned out to be a thickset guy in his late fifties with a Mets ball cap and a laugh like a bear, if bears laughed. His dark eyes were set in friendly wrinkles, and his gap-toothed grin when he saw Nicole made it clear he'd known her for a while.

"Nicky! How are ya?" Joey gave her a hug.

"I'm fine. Working hard."

"Good, good. That's good." Joey turned to look at Sam. "Who's this guy?"

"Sam Bennett. He's a friend of mine," she answered quickly.

"That's nice. From around here?"

By now, Sam knew that the other man meant the five boroughs of the city. There was no "here" beyond the Hudson River to real New Yorkers.

"No. Sam's from Colorado."

"Oh. I get it. Da West," Traverso said.

"That's right," Sam said. "Last time I looked at a map, Colorado was definitely to the west."

Joey hooted with laughter. "Funny. Ya like a cowboy or what? I like da hat."

Sam tipped his Stetson to him. "Howdy. Did I say that right?"

"Ya did," Joey replied solemnly. "Ya know, I used to watch shoot-'em-ups when I was a kid. *Gunsmoke* and *Bonanza* were my favorites. The Cartwrights coulda been from Brooklyn. They hung tough."

"Great shows," Sam agreed.

Nicole was looking at both of them as if she had no idea what they were talking about.

"Before your time," Sam said to her. "But you can watch both on Colorado cable."

"Oh."

A cell phone in Joey's pocket began to buzz. He took it out and peered at the screen. "Eh. That's Ed Fox. Big movie man. He drives me crazy, but—aha. The shooting permit musta come through. Gotta stay on this one."

He read the text and then called Fox back, while Nicole and Sam looked into the dark, cavernous warehouse.

"Yo, Ed," the thickset man said. "Yeah, this is Joey. Who else, your mother?"

A rapid-fire response from Ed followed.

Covering the phone with his palm, Joey spoke to Nicole.

"Ed never shuts up," he said to her. "I gotta pay attention. But ya know where the moon is. If ya wannit, take it. Don't thank me. G'wan, get outta here. I'll send ya a bill. But don't be a stranger. Nice to meetcha, Sam."

He extended a meaty hand.

"Same here." Sam shook. "Thanks for your help, Mr. Traverso."

Joey put the phone to his ear but spoke to Sam. "For Nicole, anything. She says jump, you ask how high. Ya unnerstand?"

"Yes, I do."

Nicole led Sam away, hiding a smile. "I didn't know Joey thought that highly of me," she said.

Sam chuckled. "I consider myself warned. So where's the moon?"

It was late enough in the day that he wouldn't have been surprised to see one rising over the distant skyline of Manhattan.

Nicole took him by the hand and led him into the depths of the Traverso Bros. Warehouse.

They found the moon behind a vintage Texaco star.

Nicole looked at it with shining eyes. "Unreal. That's exactly what I wanted. It's part of an old sign."

Sam pushed the old gas station star a few feet away from the moon. It was nothing more than a flat, round sheet of unpainted metal with a four-inch rim, about five feet high. It looked like junk to him. The surface was dinged, as if someone had thrown a baseball against it for about twenty years. There was a noticeable amount of surface corrosion, what with the pits and streaks and whitish discoloration.

"Don't you think it's beautiful?"

"You want my honest opinion? No," Sam replied.

"Wait until I paint it silver," she argued. "It'll look just like the real moon."

Nicole did have a point. The last full moon Sam had seen—in Colorado—had a few imperfections. But its pure white light had filled the night sky and shone brightly over the snow. If she could get a banged-up old metal disc to do that, she was a miracle worker.

"Maybe so," he said. "Want me to move it? It oughta roll."

"Gee, I hope so," she said wryly.

He dragged the Texaco sign to one side and brought the moon forward, holding each side with a hand. "Hey, look at me. I'm waltzing with the moon."

Nicole giggled. "Teach it to two-step."

"Do you know how?" He kept on with what he was doing.

"Nope."

"Then add it to your list of things I'm going to teach you to do," Sam said.

"Driving a stick shift and learning to two-step—it's a pretty short list."

"You're a pretty busy lady."

Once he was clear of the big things that might catch it, they maneuvered the moon between the two of them, rolling it down crowded aisles of dusty furniture and odd items.

"I think this is how cavemen invented the first wheel," he joked.

"Don't forget the cavewomen. They invented the first stroller and the first rolling suitcase."

Light brightened the gloomy interior of the warehouse. "We're coming to the loading bay," Sam said, looking over his shoulder.

A large truck was pulled up to the bay, and several guys were loading it.

"Okay." She stopped, holding onto the metal rim. "You can bring the truck over."

"Hope it fits." Sam went down the stairs at the side.

The loading process went smoothly, and the rope proved to be more than long enough.

Testing the final knot, Sam turned to her. "What now?"

"Let's go to a diner out here so I can get a late lunch. We'll be able to keep an eye on the truck without having to pay for parking in Manhattan."

"Fine. Tell me how to get there."

She looked up *Diners, Queens* on her phone and directed him to the nearest one as he drove. Sam backed into a parking space in front of the uncurtained windows. The moon gleamed dully under the bright lights of the parking lot.

Nicole checked it when she got out of the truck.

"I didn't hear any clanking around back here." He tested the rope. "We should be able to get it back to Manhattan with no problem."

She nodded. "I guess it won't break. It'd better not."

"Don't worry."

"It's going to look amazing when I get done. Traverso Brothers is where I always find the best stuff."

With a happy sigh, she wiped away dust from the moon's surface as Sam went up the stairs and held the door open for her.

Nicole went in, looking at her hand. "Brilliant. Now I need to wash up."

Overhearing, the hostess came toward them. "Right

that way, miss." She nodded toward the door as she reached for menus. "Two?" she asked Sam.

"Yes. Thanks."

The diner was an old-fashioned place, with chrome-trimmed tables and banquettes done up in harlequin-pattern vinyl. He slid into the booth the hostess indicated and looked out. They would be able to keep an eye on the moon. But nobody seemed to notice Nicole's treasure.

Nicole came back, peering out the window before she slid into the opposite side.

"Stop hovering. Nobody's going to steal your moon," he laughed.

"Hey, it's one of a kind," she protested. "And it's the right one. Don't you know how it feels when you find something that good?"

Sam only nodded. There were a lot of answers to that question.

Nicole read the menu. "It's going to be a long night. I need fuel." A waitress appeared. "I'll have a cherry Coke and the fried chicken basket with a side of mac and cheese, please."

The waitress jotted it down and looked expectantly at Sam. "Ah—same thing for me." He was feeling hungry again. Hauling that moon had given him an appetite.

Nicole handed back both menus and the waitress walked away.

"Are you really going to eat all that?" he asked.

"Watch me."

Finn's team was good. The ENJ flagship store closed at nine and they had the mannequins painted blue by ten. Several were positioned in front of a space heater to dry. They needed only two for each window, but Nicole wasn't taking any chances on body parts falling off.

The mannequins were different from the ones at Now.

The facial features were not painted but only suggested with abstract curves, and the bodies were flexible.

Sharon was in charge of the dressers, handing each a rhinestone setter to affix tiny fake diamonds to the jeans. She sat down with the box full of them and ran her fingers through the glittering pile.

"Just what I always wanted to do," she said to Nicole, who barely paused to listen. "Play with diamonds. So where is Sam? Didn't you say he was going to be here?"

"He's working in back."

One pair was completed and hanging alone on a rack. The effect was subtle, not gaudy. Other ENJ denim items were crowded together on a different rack, awaiting their turn. Nicole had some leeway as to which ones she would ultimately use in the windows. She was as nervous as a cat, running everywhere, seeing to every detail.

A couple of guys were up on ladders rigging lights high up in the ceiling of the window bay. She called out yes or no as the riggers moved spots of white around, not satisfied with any until square sheets of gel went over the brilliant lights and turned the scene into shades of indigo.

Sam was drilling through the rim of the moon so it could be securely hung. Once that was done, it would be taken down and covered in tiny fake diamonds, then re-hung from the steel beams above. The ENJ window setup was professional, and there was a lot less improvising to do than at Now.

But the work seemed endless. Some members of the team were stretching canvas over high wooden frames to create panels that would be painted in darkening shades of a different blue to create a receding effect when the panels were set up inside the window.

They were building everything onto two platforms that would slide into the bottom of the window when all parts of the design were completed. Finn moved among the chaos in an unhurried way, his red hair like a torch against the cool jewel blues. He directed the construction and the painting, checking with Nicole on every detail, occasionally talking to someone else when the wireless receiver he wore in one ear flashed. They both took innumerable photos and compared notes.

Nicole was down to tank top and jeans and some accidental splotches of blue paint on her face. Sam tried not to look at her too much. She was too busy to talk.

Finn stopped to take a few photos of Sam as he adjusted the position of the hanging moon. "That's going to look great when it's finished."

"I'm willing to believe it," Sam said.

Finn smiled. "Thanks for helping out, man. The simplest windows are the hardest. And Nicole is a perfectionist."

It was hours before the first tableau was set up. By then Sam was able to take a break and observe.

He didn't notice Sharon observing him, standing with Nicole too far away to be heard.

Sharon whispered anyway. "So that's your cowboy. My, oh my. Sam Bennett really is something. Now I understand why you were so confused."

"I'm not confused. I mean, we do hang out and all that." In armchairs. Kissing their way into heaven for two.

"Uh-huh."

"It's just for fun, not the future," Nicole went on. "I'm not going to marry him or anything."

Sharon turned to her. "Marry? I don't think I ever heard you use that word."

"Don't read anything into it, okay?"

Sharon seemed doubtful. "Too bad he's not staying."

"I guess we can agree on that," Nicole said with a sigh. "All right." She looked over at the freelancers working on the moon. "Back to work."

They went their separate ways.

The shining moon, transformed from its battered state by the painstaking efforts of the team, leaned against a heavy ladder. When the platform was moved, it would hang low in a deep blue sky over the graceful figure of a young woman, her face in half profile as she turned to glimpse the man behind her. Tiny diamonds traced the outlines of what she wore.

The mood was intensely romantic and also sensual.

Several of the women on the team sighed with appreciation when they saw the final setup.

"It's like a dream of love," one murmured. "You know in another second that he's going to sweep her up in his arms or something."

Nicole looked over their heads and winked at Sam.

"You did good," he said.

"We all did."

She moved to the platform containing the second window scene to check it against the drawing in her sketchbook, making more notes around it.

It would be a continuation of the first window, its lights set up so that the stylized moon would seem to illuminate both scenes, creating a convincing illusion.

Nicole stepped up into it, adjusting the position of the female mannequin. "She needs to really look at him," she said to the guy who had just moved the male figure into the background. Nicole got the positioning the way she wanted it and jumped down, studying the scene carefully.

Sam felt the cell phone in his shirt pocket ringing. Who the hell was calling at one in the morning? He took it out and looked at the screen. His mother. It was only eleven o'clock in Colorado.

She did sometimes check in with him around then, when the evening chores were long since done and she had a quiet moment to herself in the ranch kitchen. He answered, moving away quickly to the other side of the store.

"Kevin Talley wants the new dark-wash jeans on the blue guys," Finn called out.

"No one can tell. You can barely see what they have on in the background," a dresser said. She wasn't arguing, just pointing that out.

"True. But Talley has to get his two cents in." He signaled one of the men on the team. "Help her lift that down."

Nicole had heard the conversation. The change wouldn't affect the look of the window at all. But it did feel strange to see the blue girl looking at nothing.

Sam came back to where she was standing. "Can I talk to you alone for a sec?"

"Sure." She picked up on the somber tone of his voice. "What's the matter?"

They walked away from the others. "My mother just called. My dad's broken his leg. He slipped on a patch of ice out by the barn."

"Oh no!" Nicole looked up at him with heartfelt concern.

"I'm guessing there were some complications—he is almost sixty-seven. Anyway, he's home. Apparently he's going to be laid up for a while. My sister, Annie, drove down from Vail while my folks were at the hospital for the X-ray and cast."

Nicole absorbed all that in stunned silence.

"That's good that your sister is there."

No matter what had happened between them, she'd always known that Sam was going back to Colorado right after New Year's.

"Yeah. But Annie can only take one day off from the ski lodge, and my brother, Zach, can't get there until the weekend. So I'm flying home."

Nicole hoped her voice didn't sound as numb as she felt. "Of course."

"My mom's online right now, looking for morning flights. She's going to get back to me."

Family trumped fun. She would do the same for hers if something like this happened.

Nicole composed herself somehow. "Are you leaving right now?" He wasn't being paid for his work tonight. He could go whenever he wanted to.

"I think I should. Who knows what the next call will be about?"

She looked around for Finn, not seeing him. "I'll explain to Finn. Let me walk you out."

"You don't have to."

She gave him a wistful smile. "Don't you always walk me home? I'm just doing the same for you. To the curb, I mean. For a taxi."

"Fastest from here, right? And it's the first part of the trip back," Sam said. "So I guess that does count as walking me home."

It occurred to Nicole that they were both putting a brave face on their unexpected parting. She told herself silently what she'd just told Sharon. *Don't read anything into it.*

"Your folks will be glad to see you. I really hope your dad's going to be all right."

Sam gave her a rueful look. "They don't come tougher than Tyrell Bennett. The hard part is getting him to slow down."

"Make him," she advised.

"My mom is a lot better at that than I am." Sam murmured.

She walked with him over to where everyone had slung their coats and bags. Best to stick to routine remarks, she thought. She didn't want to bawl. Nicole was so wound up she just might. "How long is the flight?"

Sam started looking for his jacket and found it under a parka. He'd put his Stetson safely above it all on a high shelf.

"About five hours nonstop," he said as he reached for the hat. "But more like seven or eight if I have to connect. Last minute, I probably will. I told my mom to book the cheapest ticket that would get me there by tomorrow."

Nicole looked up at him. He caressed her cheek, rubbing his thumb over a streak of blue paint. "Don't forget to wash your face."

"I'll add that to my to-do list."

Sam smiled faintly.

"Try and get some sleep before you leave, if you can," she added.

"Not a high priority."

He shook out his jacket and put it over her shoulders.

"What are you doing?"

"You're only wearing a tank top. I have a shirt on. And I'm going to wear my down jacket back to Colorado. It's way below zero there."

"But—" Nicole made a move to shrug it off.

Sam stopped her with a hand on her shoulder. He buttoned up the metal buttons and chucked her under the chin. "Don't argue. Let's go."

They kept a little distance between them as they walked out together, in unspoken agreement to not become the subject of gossip. Outside of Finn, who didn't say anything, no one noticed them exiting the store as the security guard turned the key in the lock to let them out.

Nicole shivered despite the jacket. Sam didn't. He looked down the empty avenue for a taxi, seeing one only two blocks away.

"I don't know what to say. Happy trails? I'm so sorry

this happened," she began. Then she stopped, fighting a catch in her throat.

"My dad will be fine. And I'm coming right back. Don't know exactly when, though."

"Stay in touch," Nicole said. The world wasn't coming to an end, she reminded herself.

"I will." The taxi went through the intersection and flashed its lights at them.

"Call me when you land. Or text. I might still be here." She gestured toward the store.

"Send me a photo of the windows when they're done."

"I will."

"On second thought, don't. I'd rather see them for myself, standing right where we are now. Then we can go out to dinner and celebrate your first big job."

The taxi pulled up.

"It's a date, I guess." Her intuition told her that he wasn't all that sure he would be back to make good on the invitation.

Sam looked down into Nicole's eyes, sweet and soft, the color of dark honey under the streetlight. His ungloved hand cupped her warm cheek and he tilted her face to his, kissing her long and lovingly.

Nicole was breathless when he finished. Sam meant her to be.

"Good-bye," she whispered as the taxi driver unlocked the door for him. He got into the back of the taxi.

That wasn't a word Sam was going to say to her. He looked through the window as she pushed the door shut and put her palm against the glass for a second. He did the same on the other side.

Nicole stepped back. She let him go.

Chapter 12

Sam dozed through nearly all of the nonstop flight, not drinking or eating. He was grateful when he awoke for having had the chance to catch up some on sleep. The last-minute ticket and the empty seat next to him had been pure luck.

A flight attendant was delivering the usual information over a microphone, which turned her soft words into a warning squawk.

"Passengers, please return seats and tables to the upright position and prepare for landing. Welcome to Denver. The time is . . . and the outside temperature is . . ."

Sam wasn't listening. He reached for his seat belt and realized he had never unbuckled it.

The plane landed and taxied to the gate, and they deplaned quickly enough. The Denver airport was relatively empty. It felt a little strange not to be shoulder to shoulder with everyone. He'd gotten used to crowds in New York.

Sam ducked into a restroom, then washed up. He scrubbed the sleep out of his eyes, then combed his hair. His mother would fret if he showed up looking scruffy.

Back in the long, high-ceiling corridor that led to the baggage claim where she was meeting him, he walked faster.

Sam adjusted the gym bag over his shoulder, which was

relatively heavy for its size. He had to slow down. The difference in altitude between Denver and New York was noticeable.

Louisa Bennett, Lou to her family and friends, was just entering the door in back of the gates around the baggage claim area. He saw passengers from his flight waiting by a carousel that shuddered to life. The tilted ramp in its center started sending suitcases out and down.

She spotted him and threw open her arms. "Sam! Welcome home!"

Sam exited and wrapped his mother up in a great big hug.

Petite as she was, his mother tended to disappear inside most hugs. He looked down at her. The same bright blue eyes looked back, sparkling with happiness. Her pixie haircut, white mixed with gray, didn't seem ruffled at all by the embrace.

"It's so good to see you, son. No luggage?"

"Nope. Just this." He hoisted the gym bag. "I didn't need to pack. I have plenty of clothes at the bunkhouse."

Which was true. Sam didn't want his mother to think that he wouldn't stay on if they needed him. That was a given.

"Do you? I never go in the bunkhouse. You boys are grown and taking care of yourselves, and I'm thankful for it. That was a happy day when we bought a washer and dryer for out there."

Sam followed her out the electronic door, inhaling the frigid mountain air. Its dry, bracing coldness was a tonic.

"Now, I hope you're not too worried about your dad," she said as she walked. "It looks like he's going to be all right. But I wanted to talk to you before you walked in the door. That's why Annie didn't come."

"Aha. I wondered about that for a second."

"The long and the short of it is that your dad isn't going to heal up quick the way he used to."

"I had a feeling I didn't get the whole story over the phone from you," Sam said.

"I didn't want him to hear me, and I didn't know if I'd have a chance to call you back when you were still awake out there."

"Just tell me, Mom."

Lou's reply was brisk, a sure sign of strong emotions right under the surface.

"Your father went to the barn sometime in the afternoon that day, to check on a sick calf. The temp was down in the teens. I didn't know he was going—he didn't bother to tell me."

"When does he ever?" Sam wanted to know.

"Anyway, he slipped on ice and broke his leg. But he was there for a while before I happened to look out the bedroom window."

"How long?"

"I don't know exactly. It was still light out. He was conscious, just kind of confused. The doctor said it was probably mild hypothermia. Thank heaven he had his long johns on and insulated overalls."

Sam shook his head. "That's not good."

"We didn't know the prognosis for the break when I called you. The orthopedist said your dad might or might not need a pin put into the bone, depending. So it's wait and see."

"Got it." Sam's tone was serious.

Lou Bennett's voice was light as she changed the subject.

"I just need you to sit on him," she laughed. "He keeps wanting to get up and do. Every time I say don't, he huffs at me."

"That's to be expected."

He shortened his strides to match hers as they went up the parking lot ramp.

"He's looking forward so much to seeing you, Sam. It's going to be wonderful to have all our children under one roof again. I know, I know—" She held up a hand before he could say anything. "You and Zach haven't been gone that long, and Annie wasn't far away in Vail. But it still feels strange when none of you are actually on the ranch."

"I can understand that."

They had arrived at a battered vehicle that looked like a cross between an SUV and a station wagon and a truck, all from the same manufacturer. Sam's dad loved to tinker and knew how to weld. He never threw away a fender or an auto part if it wasn't rusted. The result had been named The Banger.

"This thing running okay in the cold?" Sam asked. "I heard it got down to twenty below in Velde."

"It runs fine," was Lou's indignant answer. "Always has."

"One of these years I'm going to buy you something brand-new and all your own."

"I like The Banger," she said loyally. "And it is mine. Your father has his truck. Want to drive?"

"All right." Sam tossed his gym bag in the back.

It was hard to believe that he hadn't been gone that long. The drive to the ranch made him feel like he'd been away for months. He knew every curve, and yet the landscape seemed different.

The snowfall since his departure had covered more of it, that was for sure. It lay in soft, sculpted drifts of the purest white everywhere he looked.

He responded now and then to his mother's affectionate chatter, preoccupied by the information concerning his dad's fall. He and Zach were going to have to get around to repairs to the ranch house and the outbuildings.

Sam had noticed excessive thawing over that corner of the barn roof last spring. There might be cracked shingles trapping snow that melted and formed ice on the ground. The afternoon sun lingered on some parts of the barn for hours, even in December.

"We didn't expect to hear from you every day, but you almost never called. We figured you were working hard."

"Like a dog. A happy dog," he amended. "But sometimes we didn't quit until close to midnight."

"You're young enough to do that. Not your old man, not anymore. He's going to be sixty-seven in January, you know."

Lou Bennett was six years younger. Sam glanced her way. She might not take it kindly if he told her that she and his dad needed to start being more careful. Anyone could slip on ice.

"So what's New York like?" she asked.

"Quite a city. I don't think I'd ever want to live there, though."

Lou didn't respond to that right away. "Your dad and I figured you were busy, but we were also wondering if you met someone."

"Mom—"

"I knew it," she said triumphantly. "I told Tyrell so. So who is she?

Sam sighed. There was no escaping feminine intuition. It was better than radar and more precise than a GPS system.

"Her name is Nicole Young."

"Oh. And what does she do?"

He slowed down to drive The Banger into a switchback brimming with drifted snow and back around onto a straight stretch of road. "Nicole creates window displays. She just got a big job for a national jeans maker. I was helping out with her team when you called."

"You didn't mention that."

"I would say that dad's broken leg is a little more important than decorating store windows."

He could sense his mother smile in the darkness. "Well, yes. I'm glad you came back, Sam. So . . . Nicole, is it?"

Sam knew his mother would remember the name. "I just met her. It's nothing serious."

"Of course not. But what she does sounds so interesting. I hope you have pictures on that phone of yours."

"Yup. On it and online. I'll download them later so you can really see them."

"Thanks, honey." Round eyes reflecting their headlights seemed to be caught in a thicket at the side of the road. "Watch out for deer. I almost hit a doe the other day. She cleared the front in one jump, but just barely."

Sam drove past the thicket, slowing down.

He entered the house after his mother, who called softly to her daughter. "Annie? Where are you?"

"In here with Dad."

A mellow glow came through the entrance to the large living room. Sam knew their Christmas tree was up and decorated, strung with big colored lights.

Sam went in. The sight of that big, gorgeous tree with all the ornaments they'd had for years was worth the long, tiring flight. He was home.

Sam turned to see his dad, asleep in his favorite armchair with a book on his lap. His casted leg was propped on a footstool.

Annie got up the second she saw Sam, throwing her arms around him just like her mother had. She kept her voice low when she said hi, but that didn't stop her from trying to beat him up.

Sam laughed under his breath. He barely noticed the ineffectual blows to his midsection. That was just Annie's way of greeting him and Zach. But she seemed stronger.

"Quit it," he murmured, ruffling her long hair to make her mad. "You'll wake up Dad. How is he doing?"

"Better today. More tired than he wants to admit. Thanks for getting here so soon."

He nodded toward Lou.

"Mom saw to that," he said. "It's good to be home."

Annie took his arm and walked him out of the living room. "I don't want to wake Dad up. Let's talk in the kitchen."

His favorite place on the ranch and barely changed since it had been built. Several generations of Bennett wives and daughters had kept it close to spotless, though his grandmother had been the last one to cook in the woodstove in the huge fireplace. Before that, the women on the ranch had used a spit, a grill, and a hinged iron pot hung over the fire to prepare meals.

Cooking had been an arduous process for them, remembered with respect but not missed by those who came after. Stoked, the old woodstove still provided heat, and his mother occasionally raised bread dough on the high shelf above the lids that tamed the heat of the fire within, but that was about it.

His mother was putting the kettle on for hot drinks. He and Annie and Lou Bennett stayed up talking until well after midnight.

The conversation shifted to the female side and Sam listened, thinking about where he would sleep. The main house seemed like the best bet for his first night back. Without Zach in residence, giving him the usual aggravation he didn't need, the bunkhouse would seem lonely. He would pay it a visit tomorrow and make sure there was firewood by the pot-bellied stove for when Zach returned.

His younger brother would howl if all he found was two split logs and a handful of kindling, even if that was how he'd left it.

Sam knew he wasn't going to miss the elf-size foldout bed in his New York sublet. Staying in the same house with his folks and Annie just seemed like the right thing to do. Though he had to admit he'd gotten used to the faint noise of people in the apartment above and on the street. The new moon he'd seen on the drive home would have to sub for the light from the street lamp that streamed into the sublet's one room.

"Turning in?" his mom asked when he rose from the old deal table.

"I should. I might wake up in the middle of the night, though."

"Then go into the kitchen and make yourself a snack," she said. "Everything's in the same place," she teased him.

"Good to know. G'night, Annie." Then Sam remembered. "Shoot. I bought you a present in New York but I left it in my apartment."

"Then you have to go back," Annie said firmly.

"Let's see how Dad does," Sam replied.

He took his dad out for a ride in the truck the next day. Tyrell Bennett could get around outside with a cane and waterproof wrapping over his cast, but Sam didn't want him risking another fall.

"Head for the back road," his father said. "That got plowed out the day before I fell. The snow after that filled in the ruts some."

The truck's heavy tires gripped the slick patches, and Sam went slowly to avoid jolts. Bits of hard-frozen snow and hoarfrost stuck to the windshield that the wipers couldn't budge.

His father surveyed his domain through the white-speckled glass.

"We got more'n two feet after you left. Drifted higher out here, like always."

"I can see that. The land's disappeared. Sure you didn't sell off some in your sleep?" Sam joked.

"Son, you know me better than that. This ranch stays in the family. You and Annie and Zach are going to inherit it just as it is."

"May that day be a long way off," Sam said.

His father sighed. "What us Bennetts do is one thing. But I heard just the other day that the folks down the hill are talking to developers."

"That's a shame."

"Can't stop people from doing what they want with their own land. But you're right, it is a damn shame. Don't you worry, we're not selling up. I'm healthy as ever and so's your mother."

Tyrell winced when the truck went over an invisible bump. "Ouch. Didn't think this leg would hurt so much once the happy pills wore off. I'm as brittle as an old fence post."

Sam was reluctant to bring up what his mother had told him about his father's injury. He searched for the right words.

"Mom said you lay there for a while. She thought you were in the house."

"That's right. I didn't tell her I was going out. No need. I just wanted to get some medicine into that sick calf before he started bellerin' again. Then I slipped. Accidents happen."

Sam stopped the truck and let the engine idle.

"You got lucky. What if Mom hadn't looked out that window before nightfall?"

"She did, though," his father said stubbornly. "I remember her coming out to me. You know, I felt warm by then. But I couldn't think right. Or move."

Definitely hypothermia. Sam had checked the symptoms online last night. Before you lost consciousness, you didn't feel the cold sometimes.

"Dad, do you even know how long you were there, hurt?"

Tyrell answered with dignity and no contrariness. Unusual for him.

"I do not. And I understand what you're gettin' at. I'm old, that's all. Not a damn thing me or the doc or your mother can do about it." He looked out over his snow-drifted fields. "Don't know what I'd do without Lou. She's my rock."

Sam didn't want to think about the possibility that either of his parents might ever be alone. "She loves you."

"Sometimes I wonder why." Tyrell gingerly stretched out the casted leg into the footwell of the old truck.

"Take it easy."

"That's what I'm doin'. This damn thing slows me down, but it can't stop me. Do you know how many bones I broke in my life?"

"No."

"I counted once. Seven, and that includes a coupla ribs and a collarbone from my rodeo days."

Being indestructible was a badge of pride for his old man.

"Annie isn't even close," Sam said. "Only one broken leg so far and a chipped elbow when she wiped out on the black diamond run."

"Skiin' is a little safer than rodeoin'. Annie's a hellcat on the slopes," Tyrell Bennett said with obvious pride. "You goin' to ski while you're here?"

"Maybe. If I have time." Sam didn't feel like discussing repairs with his father, who liked to do everything himself.

"Well, we could all just chill out and do nothing," Tyrell said. "Might be a nice change."

"Chill out?" Sam chuckled. "Where did you pick up that expression?"

"Annie. That's what she keeps telling me to do."

Sam started driving again.

"I haven't been out this way for a while." The older man looked out the window. "The snow covered the stump, but that's where we cut the blue spruce." His voice was cheerful. "The money from that already paid for feedcake and extra hay. Now drive on a little more."

Sam grinned. He knew what his father wanted to see.

"Stop here. There's the tree we didn't cut," Tyrell Bennett said with satisfaction. "Hey, I said stop. I'm getting out."

Sam braked. "You shouldn't."

"Don't tell me what to do," his father said irritably. He swung open the heavy door of the pickup and eased down, very carefully. Then he thought better of it and stayed where he was, using the door for support.

Sam set the parking brake.

"I guess I can see okay from here," Tyrell said resignedly. "Bet that tree's a foot taller than the one you took to New York, Sam."

"Looks like."

His father studied the spruces a little while longer. "You gotta hang on to the best. That's the future."

"You're probably right about that."

"I'm just plain right," his father said with conviction. "You see the saplings around the big'un? Spiky little bastards. Tough as they come. They'll be taller still." He chuckled.

"I expect so."

His father fell silent. A few years ago Tyrell Bennett would have pulled out his favorite smokes and lit one, but he'd given up that bad habit. In another minute he used his arms to pull himself up into the truck, staying off the casted leg entirely.

He eased down onto the bench seat beside his oldest son. "I may not be around when they get tall, Sam. But you will be."

"Count on it." Sam wasn't saying so to make his old man happy. The Bennett ranch was truly home. He had missed it.

His mother and Annie were sitting on kitchen chairs, watching Sam download photos from his phone onto Lou's laptop. He added more from friends who'd posted theirs online and set it all up as a slideshow.

"There you go. Click to continue or pause it whenever you like," he said.

"Oh, I love this," his mother said. "Annie, scoot over so you can see."

Sam stood up, looking over their heads.

"That's the window I worked on. Just for one day. The shop's right up the street from the installation I was doing with Greg."

"I hope you got a picture of our tree."

"Greg did. You're starting in the middle. That blue spruce is a standout."

His mother stayed where she was in the slideshow. "My word, look at the city scene. And that little rink—isn't that clever. What's the name of the boutique again?"

"Now."

"You mean just that one word? Now?"

"That's right."

"Oh, I see it. There, in the corner of the window." Lou used the zoom function under the online photo to take in every detail. "This is so much fun."

The laptop she was looking into had been her Christmas present from her three grown kids last year. She'd taken to it instantly.

"Is that where you got my present?" Annie wanted to know.

"How did you know?" Sam was startled by the question.

"It looks like the kind of place I'd go into. You're smarter than you look, Sam."

"Thanks a lot, princess."

Lou paid no attention to their verbal sparring. She'd been listening to it for years.

Annie grinned. "Seriously, there are boutiques just like that in Vail and Aspen. Denver too. Colorado is getting to be full of rich people who love to shop."

Sam thought of Nicole. She might be interested to know that.

"Speaking of presents," he said to his mother, "I was thinking of getting you a digital camera."

"Not a surprise, then, is it? But I don't care," Lou said happily.

"This is going to be an electronic Christmas," Annie informed her older brother.

"Huh?"

His mother interrupted. "Sam, do you have a digital camera or did you just use your phone?"

"I used the phone. I don't have a digital camera. A lot of these are from friends." He'd had fun last night looking at them all before he'd chosen the ones for the slideshow just now. "Greg took those."

She'd gone back and was starting again in the correct

order. "The blue spruce looks great with all the lights and the big star on top. I wonder how it likes being in New York," she said playfully.

"The kids love it. I was the one who flipped the switch and lit it up when we were finished with the installation. You should have seen their faces."

"I wish I had been there," his mother said with a sigh. "Tyrell too. Maybe next year."

Sam looked over her shoulder. "Keep going. See those blue scenes? That's what I was working on when you called."

"Will you look at that color," his mother murmured. "That's a real fairy-tale blue. Just beautiful. Now, that young lady is a mannequin, but I know the other is real—"

"That's Nicole."

"She's lovely. Even with those streaks of blue paint on her face. Annie, look. That's who Sam was working with at Now and this ENJ place. Nicole is a window designer."

Lou gazed into the laptop screen, but Annie turned around, ready to start a little trouble with her big brother. She mouthed the words *she's lovely* and fluttered her eyelashes at him. Sam scowled.

"I didn't know you liked city girls," Annie said innocently. "Are you dating her?"

"That's none of your business."

"I have my ways. I will find out." His sister grinned at him over their mother's shoulder.

"Is Nicole from New York?" Lou asked.

"Born there."

Lou seemed thoughtful. "I heard that a lot of people who live in New York are from somewhere else. That's true of Colorado these days, though."

"I suppose so."

Lou kept clicking. "And there's that gigantic thing you

two found. Look at that before and after. What a difference."

"It came out really well. Finn—he's a friend of Nicole—posted those. Hang on. Can I look at that one? I don't remember him taking it."

Sam was on a ladder behind the decorated metal disk, which glittered so brightly that his face was partly obscured.

Nicole was standing in front of him, smiling.

"What a beautiful smile. She's looking at you like you hung the moon." Lou turned to her son. "Which is exactly what you did."

Nicole felt something in the pocket of Sam's jacket prickle her fingers. She closed them around a twig and removed it. It was from some kind of evergreen tree. The needles were pale under the streetlight, still thickly clustered and fresh.

It must have come from the blue spruce. She'd seen it on his phone once, but she had never gone to see Sam's tree in person.

Nicole rubbed the needles between her fingertips, putting the twig under her nose to enjoy the piney fragrance before tucking it back in the pocket. She turned up the collar and caught a faint whiff of Sam's scent. Not aftershave, just clean. With a note of man. Maybe it wasn't a good idea to wear his jacket. Sam was enough of a distraction when he was actually around.

She continued walking past several cross streets south of Now to where she thought the tree might be.

The small park divided a busy street. There were other trees behind his, but not the same color. They were dark, and Sam's tree was an unusual light blue. The spruce stood tall and strong amidst the high buildings surrounding it and the constant racket of traffic that flowed by.

The star atop the spruce glowed a steady gold. It was the only one of the group with a star, though all the trees twinkled with color. She half wished she could climb up into its branches and see if she felt as safe as she did in his arms.

Nicole settled for the bench underneath it. It was freezingly cold. She wouldn't be able to stay there very long.

She had been stunned to find out that Sam had to fly back to Colorado, although of course he'd had no choice. Nicole had kept her promise to call him, but when he'd answered the Bennetts had been just sitting down to dinner. She'd forgotten about the time difference.

Sam had called her back later that night, not saying much. His father's injury had been worse than he'd been told. There might be complications. He wanted to get to repairs that had been put off, make sure that his parents were safely set up before he could think about coming back.

One thing for sure, he wasn't making any promises to her.

She understood why. She respected him for putting his parents first. But a question that made her sick at heart assailed her. What if he never came back?

He'd planned to stay in New York until New Year's Eve, but a family emergency was likely to keep him in Colorado indefinitely.

Miserable, she huddled into his jacket. Might as well get used to missing him, she told herself. But Nicole knew that might be impossible.

Her cell phone rang, and she scrabbled frantically through her purse to find it. Not Sam.

"Hi, Sharon."

"Just thought I'd call."

Nicole suppressed a sigh. It was good to hear a friend's voice, and it was nice of Sharon to check in with her.

"What are you doing?" she asked when Nicole didn't say anything.

"Sitting in the middle of the street feeling sorry for myself."

A taxi blared its horn and swerved around a car that had stopped short. Startled, Nicole dropped the phone.

"Nicole?" Sharon's voice was high and anxious. "What the hell is going on? Nicole?"

She picked up the phone and dusted it off. "I'm fine. Sorry. I am in the middle of the street, but I'm in a pocket park. I'm sitting on a bench with Sam—I mean with the tree that Sam—I don't want to talk about it."

"Tell me exactly where you are," Sharon said firmly. "I'll be there as soon as I can. Just gotta get my boots and find a twenty for a cab."

Nicole did. Then she swallowed the lump in her throat and waited.

Chapter 13

Zach flew into Denver the next day. Annie picked him up, and not long after he and Sam were finishing a huge lunch prepared by their mother.

"You two look more alike every year," she sighed.

Annie assessed her older brothers. "Zach's hair is lighter. And he's a little taller," she pointed out. "Other than that, you're right, Mom." She got up to clear the table.

"Pie, boys?" Lou asked. "How about coffee?"

"Later for the pie. But we'll take a thermos of coffee out with us," Sam said. "Thanks for lunch."

"The casserole was really good," Zach echoed.

They got to work directly, going out to the barn in companionable silence. The first task was to smash the ice below the dripping corner of the barn.

Zach and Sam found sledgehammers in the barn's tool cabinet and went to it with a vengeance. Then they sprinkled rock salt to break up the ice some more and threw down a thick layer of dry hay for traction.

"Oughta do for now," Sam said. "If it ices over, we can do this again."

"I hope the ladder doesn't slip." Zach put a tall sectional ladder into position.

"That's why you're going to hold it for me."

Zach gestured toward it with a thick-gloved hand. "After you."

Sam went up, not listening to the rattling of the ladder. At the top, he leaned forward to inspect the shingles, digging a chisel under the loose ones and chopping at the hidden ice.

The repair took a while. By the time Sam climbed down, the winter sun was slanting across the drifts, not touching the blue hollows.

"You all right?" Zach asked when he was on the ground.

"Sure. That was fun," Sam said sarcastically.

"We don't have to finish it today. Let's go back to the house and warm up."

"Good idea."

They trudged over the cleared road, kicking lumps of frozen snow to the side when they encountered one.

"So how have you been?" Zach wanted to know. "Did you have a good time in New York?"

"Yeah, it's a great city. I met some really nice people."

Zach grinned. "So I heard. Mom thinks you're sweet on someone."

"That would be Nicole Young. Nothing serious. We hung out, ran around the city, saw the sights. I came back soon as I could when I heard." He sighed. "I barely got a chance to say good-bye to her."

Zach shot him a look. "Annie showed me the photos. Bet you didn't want to."

Sam didn't reply right away. "I'm not moving to New York, Zach."

"Oh. Well, you were always the responsible one. But I am here. You could go back. Wasn't that the plan?"

Sam looked out over the frozen fields, his smoky blue gaze distant and serious. "Plans change. I don't know if you noticed, but Mom and Dad are getting older. This place needs work if they're going to stay on."

"Can't do it all in winter," Zach said peaceably. "I don't have to go back to Oregon. How about you? Does Greg need you on his crew?"

"We wrapped up all the jobs under contract. He has plenty of guys to do pickup work and maintenance."

Zach flipped up his hood. "Whatever you say."

They continued down the road. The ranch house was in sight.

"I wouldn't mind seeing Nicole again, though," Sam said. "I can call. We could get together on Skype."

"Not the same but better than nothing." His brother shot him a sidelong glance around the hood. "Go for it."

Sam felt the phone in his pocket vibrate. He pulled off one glove to take it out.

"Never fails. That must be Nicole," Zach laughed.

Sam frowned at the screen. "No. It's Annie. I can see her in the window."

Both brothers looked toward the house and waved to their younger sister, who had her cell phone to her ear.

Sam picked up the call. "Hey."

"Mom wanted me to tell you we're having pot roast for dinner. Plus more mashed potatoes than even you two can eat."

"Thanks." Sam hung up, but he held onto the phone.

In another minute, Annie came out, dressed in a close-fitting ski jacket with a trimmed hood that framed her striking high cheekbones and dark hair.

"You two done?" she called to them. "You've been out here forever."

"No, we're not. Anytime you feel the impulse to help us, don't fight it," Zach called back.

Annie walked to them. The wind kicked up. She was slender enough to be blown most of the way there.

Sam searched in his pocket for the glove he'd taken off,

putting it on but jamming both hands into his jacket before he flipped up his hood too.

Annie reached them. She pointed to Sam's feet. "I think you dropped something."

He looked around, saw nothing but packed snow, and took a step back.

There was a crunch.

Annie reached around him and bent down. "Is this your phone, Sam?"

He cursed a blue streak.

"Calm down," Annie said mockingly. "I understand the company manufactured about ten million of these." She handed him the cracked remains.

"Funny. But I'm not due for a trade-in yet."

"You won't have to pay," his sister assured him.

"Yes, I will. Unless you know something I don't know."

Annie turned her back to him and took the lead. Sam exchanged a glance with Zach, who only shrugged.

They went into the house, shedding their jackets and gloves and stamping the snow from their boots.

"You two sound like buffaloes," their mother teased, coming out of the kitchen. "Ready for that pie now?"

"Sure. And some more coffee to go with it, please. That pot roast sure smells good."

Sam bent down to kiss his mother's cheek.

"Goodness, your nose is cold."

His father was in the kitchen when they entered, a half-eaten piece of berry pie on a plate in front of him. He was gazing into the laptop.

"I showed Dad how to start the slideshow," Annie said, coming into the kitchen. "He's been through it three times now."

"Four," Tyrell Bennett corrected her. "Going for five. Lou, you're right. This is a great way to look at pictures."

Sam and Zach pulled chairs away from the table and sat down, leaning back.

"Is that Nicole?" His father turned the laptop around. By coincidence, to Sam's favorite picture of her.

"Yes."

"Good-lookin' gal."

"She is."

"You should give her a call," his mother murmured casually.

Sam caught Annie's eye. She seemed to be thinking of something. "Um, Sam just stepped on his phone."

Lou and Annie exchanged a glance. Then his mother nodded.

Annie got up and went to the sideboard. There was a wrapped present on it. Something small. She handed it to Sam. "A little early, but Merry Christmas."

Sam looked at her and his mother. "What's going on?"

"It's a present," Annie pointed out, a tinge of exasperation in her voice. "You rip open the paper and there it is."

"Go ahead," his mother encouraged.

Sam unwrapped it and saw the phone of his dreams.

"Has everything," Annie pointed out. "Video enabled too. You can Skype on it."

Sam grinned. "It's fantastic." He got up to give her a hug and sat down again. "You must be psychic. How did you know this was compatible with my plan?"

"There was an opened phone bill of yours in one of the side tables, so I called the company and checked. And I didn't look to see who you call either. I'm not that much of a snoop."

"Right now, I don't care. Thanks, Annie. This is great." He turned it on. "Lots of apps. Games too."

"You can add more whenever you want."

His father was looking into the laptop again. "You

know, son, I did some thinking when you and Zach were out at the barn."

Sam looked his way. "The roof can be fixed. We're almost done."

"I appreciate what you're doing. But now that your brother's here, you don't have to stay. Looks to me like you were having a mighty good time in New York."

"You and Mom need help."

"I suppose we do. I was just saying." He turned his gaze to his wife. "Lou, when is that pot roast going to be ready?"

"Not for another hour and a half."

"Guess I'll take a nap then." He rose stiffly and found his cane, then stumped off to the living room.

For the next few days, Sam fixed things. Armed with a bucket of tools, he drove all over the ranch, usually accompanied by his brother.

Annie had gone back to Vail, but before she'd left, she managed to extract his contacts from the memory of his damaged phone before it died forever and get them into the new model. They'd given the old one a decent burial in Tyrell Bennett's box of busted gadgets, down under a tangle of sprouting wires and rusted hardware.

He'd used the new phone only once: to call Annie and make sure it worked. When he was working around the ranch, he kept it in the house.

Today he was alone in the barn. Anything he saw that needed hitting with a hammer had been hit. He turned his attention to an old, disused feed crib. No telling if his father wanted it, but the sagging side and bent legs clinched the decision. Sam took a swing at it. The crib collapsed into a heap of jagged shards and cracked planks.

He looked up to see his father standing in the open doorway of the barn.

"How'd you get here?" Sam asked.

"Zach. You were so busy making noise I guess you didn't notice. The truck's over on the other side with him in it. Just thought I'd walk around. You boys did a good job breaking up the ice." Tyrell peered at the destroyed feed crib. "What did that ever do to you?"

Sam moved a broken plank with his foot. "It was about to fall down."

"We can use it for kindling," his father said. "Anyway, I came here to tell you some good news. Your mother and I just got back from the orthopedist. He did some X-rays and a special kind of bone scan. Cost a mint," he complained.

"What did he say?" That was all Sam cared about. He could help cover co-pays.

"That I'm healing better'n he expected. These days they can snoop on your cells. It looks like the bone won't need no pin."

Sam felt relief wash through him. "Dad, that's great."

Tyrell nodded. "Thought you'd want to know right away. Now—I have something to say to you."

An awkward moment passed.

"Your momma and I have discussed this and we both agree, so you don't get to argue. We want you to go back to New York." He held up a hand to forestall Sam's protest. "You were having a fine time, you got yourself a little place there, and a beautiful lady. We know you planned to spend New Year's Eve in the big city and you're going to."

"Dad—"

"Lou and I don't want you moping around. Truth be told, we don't need you right now. Not with Zach here and Annie not far away. You did your part."

Sam took a deep breath, marshaling a reply.

"Son, I don't happen to be interested in your opinion on the matter." Tyrell's voice was stern, but his eyes twinkled.

"Get yourself on the next plane to New York before I kick you there myself. With this."

He tapped the cast with the tip of his cane.

Sam was at the top of the standby list for a one-stop flight into New York by the end of the day. Zach had dropped him off at the airport.

He still had a couple of hours to wait. He took out the new phone. The icon for video calling caught his eye. He wanted to try it, but he wasn't sure anyone he knew had the same kind of app.

Didn't matter. That could wait. Sam scrolled through his contacts, stopping on Theo's name. The old guy wasn't too good with cell phones, but Greg kept giving him new ones.

He tapped the screen, letting the number ring, idly looking around the airport. He had the flight gate to himself.

He looked down again when the ringing stopped. Everything had changed. He heard voices he knew.

A kindly brown eye with wrinkles around it filled the screen. Sam thought of a walrus and realized it was Theo. The old man's nose appeared next, larger than life, then the brown eye again.

Then he heard Douglas pipe up. "Theo! Don't hold the phone so close to your face."

Sam laughed. "Takes a little practice." He wasn't used to video calling either. "Greg, is that Theo's Christmas present?"

"Yeah," he heard Greg say. "What the hell. I don't care if he loses it."

"Can I have the phone?" Doug's voice. He didn't appear in the screen but Theo did, with Greg next to him. And Nicole.

His heart flip-flopped.

"New phone?" she asked Sam.

"My sister gave it to me. I stepped on mine."

"Oh. I tried to call you a couple of times. So, um, how's your dad?"

"A lot better."

Greg and Theo leaned in. "How's Colorado?"

"Beautiful. Colder than New York." Sam saw Nicole ease to the side and out of the group.

"So come back and warm up," Greg joked. He held up a gloved hand to the sky and showed Sam his empty palm. "Nothing to brag about yet, but when we get a storm, watch out. Our snowflakes are bigger than your snowflakes, man."

"Like hell they are."

Doug moved into the group on the screen.

"Sam, we're making a plywood cutout of a tree with Nicole. Little kids can put their faces in and pretend they're a tree."

A feminine hand—it was Nicole's, he knew the glove—was sliding the thing in front of Douglas, who demonstrated, a big grin on his face.

"That's great," Sam said.

"Good for business too," Theo boomed. "We're selling more."

Sam didn't want to ask about the lowlifes underselling them from trucks. Maybe the cops had run the creeps off.

Nicole stepped back in. He drank in the beautiful sight. Her dark eyes were shining, and her hair streamed out from under a patterned knit cap.

She was wearing his jacket.

"Puff wants to say hi." Douglas moved out from behind the plywood and bent down so low he disappeared. The next thing Sam saw was a blurry tongue licking the screen.

"Douglas, put Puff down."

He didn't recognize the gentle voice at first, then realized it was Maureen Fulton, Doug's mother. "Hello, Sam."

"Hi, Maureen."

She tucked herself into the group, and they all waved at once.

"So . . . where are you?" Nicole asked.

God, how he had missed her. He'd missed them all.

"I'm in the Denver airport," he said. "I'm on the standby list for the next New York flight, but the agent told me she's sure I'll get on. I'll be back late tonight or tomorrow, not sure about that part."

"You're coming back?" Nicole asked.

At that moment, he saw only her. But he could hear the group around her cheering.

"Yeah. Can't wait to see you, city girl."

The agent and another airline employee had returned to the counter in front of the gate, and the large screen above them came to life, showing the standby list.

"Sir?" The agent looked his way.

"Gotta go," Sam whispered. Nicole blew him a kiss.

He got up and went to the counter. "I can confirm you now," the agent said. "But you should know we've been informed of a severe weather system entering the flight path. The plane may have to make more than one stop."

"That's okay." Sam handed over his boarding pass.

Making the connection proved to be no problem. There was some turbulence on the flight, but his soda stayed in the plastic glass. Then the weather got worse from there on out. The pilot announced a second stop in a tone of smooth regret. No one complained. Then the storm roared around them, shaking the plane until even Sam was scared. They had finally made an unscheduled landing at a small regional airport somewhere in Indiana.

And stayed there.

Other passengers from his flight were wandering around the chilly terminal or slumped in bolted-down chairs.

He looked at his phone, checking the time. No telling when they would get out.

Sam walked over to a vending machine, his gym bag over his shoulder. He stood in front of it, contemplating the options. There were neon-orange crackers filled with peanut butter. Had to be a molecule or two of protein in those. He slipped in the required number of quarters and pressed the code buttons. A spiral server moved the cracker packet forward and jerked, dropping it too fast. He looked through the little window in the bottom flap, frowning. Inside the wrapper the crackers were crushed.

He found a buck and fed it to the bill slot, figuring he'd skip the messy crackers and have a snack cake. Both were off-brands with the same label. Eagle Cakes, Cookies, and Crackers.

He pressed the code buttons and waited.

The spiral moved the cake forward and stopped.

Sam thumped lightly on the glass. Nothing happened.

Frustrated, he reached toward the bottom flap, bumping his fingers. It didn't open. He couldn't even get at the crushed crackers.

Sam was tempted to rock the vending machine, but he figured it would fall on him, with his luck. He was going to send a nasty e-mail to Eagle CCC when he got out of here.

There was nothing to do but sit until the storm passed and they got clearance to fly. The colorful glow of the vending machine was about the only cheerful note in the terminal. He took a chair near it, crossing his legs and stuffing his hands into the sleeves of his down jacket.

Sam fell asleep.

A bang awoke him by dawn. Aching all over from sleeping sitting up, he looked groggily at the vending machine. The spiral was moving. It dropped the snack cake.

The Eagle had landed. He got up to try the flap door again. For some reason it opened this time. He took the cake but left the smashed crackers.

An announcement came over the PA system that made him even happier. The storm had passed. The next leg would take him all the way to New York.

Chapter 14

Sam stood outside LaGuardia Airport in the taxi line, which was moving slowly. He got in the back of a real rattletrap when it was his turn.

"Where to, mister?"

He gave the driver the cross street and the avenue, and left it at that. Sam wanted to stop at the Christmas tree lot before he went into his building.

The drive west on the Grand Central Parkway gave him a chance to get reacquainted with the Manhattan skyline before the taxi went into the Midtown Tunnel that ran under the East River. The sky was already dark gray, and millions of windows were lit up, a checkerboard of yellow against the somber colors of the buildings.

He was able to pick out several. There was the Chrysler Building, an Art Deco landmark, its spire decorated with cool white spikes of light. The Citigroup tower had a sliced-off roof. Above them all rose the Empire State Building, a midtown monument. Sam couldn't help mentally adding King Kong to the needle-like thing at the very top.

They went through a tollbooth into the cream-tiled, featureless tunnel, coming up on the east side of Manhattan. Once they were across town, Sam changed his mind.

"Let me out a block away, not on the corner, please."

"Okay."

He almost couldn't believe he was here. Or how familiar it seemed. After a stretch of time in Colorado, the jammed streets and hurrying crowds on the sidewalk seemed overwhelming.

"Right here."

The driver stopped the meter. The small TV screen that Sam hadn't been looking at showed the fare. He added a couple of bucks for the tip and handed it through the opening in the clear divider between back and front.

Sam got out, his gym bag slung over his shoulder. He tipped his Stetson back just a bit on his forehead in case he saw someone he knew.

He walked fast and turned the corner, half expecting to see the happy group that had greeted him on his new phone. There was someone he didn't know in Theo's chair, a young guy. Had to be a relative of Greg's—he had the look.

"Hey there. I'm looking for Mr. Tsianakas," Sam said.

The man got up. "You mean Greg or Theo?"

"Either one."

"Actually, it's my last name too. I'm a third cousin. Don't ask. I'm Steve. Nice to meetcha. And you are?"

"Sam Bennett."

"Right, right." Steve chuckled. "They both mentioned you. Said you were coming back from someplace out west."

"Just got in. You wouldn't happen to know when they'd be back, would you—"

"Sam!"

He turned to see Douglas coming toward him, with Puff in the lead.

"Hi, Doug."

The boy pulled up, out of breath. "That was fun seeing

you on the phone. But we all thought you were going to be back sooner."

"The flight was delayed. Bad weather."

"Yeah, they say it's coming here," Steve said. "Big, bad storm. Heard it's stalled over Pennsylvania right now."

Sam felt sorry for Pennsylvania.

Douglas held the dog's leash and looked back into the trees. His forehead furrowed. "I was going to pick up a tree," he said to Steve, "but I don't see it. Theo put a red tag on it for me."

"Must be there somewhere. Let's go look," Steve said.

Ah. So Douglas Fulton was the mystery buyer of the fir that had been set aside. Sam remembered Theo saying that the kid was buying something special for his mother this year.

He thought of something else: the creepy guy who'd wanted to buy it. Sam had almost had to use the baseball bat to get rid of him. But he hadn't told Theo about the incident. Still, no one on the lot would sell a tree that Theo had marked and set aside.

Douglas and Steve came back.

"It isn't there," the boy told Sam. "Someone must have taken the tag off and bought it."

Steve had a look of concern on his face. "Wasn't me. Haven't sold any trees since I've been here. But there was someone else new filling in yesterday."

Douglas shrugged. His disappointment was clear, but he kept his feelings about it to himself.

"What was so special about that one, Doug?" Sam asked. "There are others just as nice."

"It looked like one we had when I was six and Amanda wasn't born yet. Mom had a photo of it in the family album. Same little crooked branch on top. But perfect."

Sam understood. He didn't ask Douglas any more questions. "Come on," he said. "I'll walk you home."

Douglas's jubilant mood had vanished. He didn't say anything more as they got to the stoop of the building. Sam looked at the window of his first-floor sublet. It reflected the narrow street behind him in old, wavy glass.

Douglas used his key to open the outside door. Sam glanced up to the Fultons' window, which was brightly lit. But there was something on the fire escape that hadn't been there before.

"What's that red box outside your window?" he asked Douglas. "Is that for Christmas?"

"No. It's a big cooler. Our fridge stopped working, so we're keeping milk and eggs outside."

"Isn't the landlord supposed to take care of things like that—" Sam broke off when he saw Douglas's expression. The kid was wise to the ways of the world.

"He says he will, but he hasn't yet. Mom says we just have to make do," Douglas replied flatly.

Sam absorbed the information in silence.

"My mom put her cake samples on the fire escape too." The boy looked at Sam. "You should come up and try some. She's a good baker."

"Well, maybe I will."

"C'mon, Puff." Douglas gave a light tug on the dog's leash. "Time to go upstairs."

Sam fumbled for the key to his apartment door. It wasn't in his pocket. He unzipped his gym bag and looked through it. "See you around," he called when he found it.

"Okay." The boy's voice was distant. He was already halfway to his floor.

Before he went in, Sam took a minute to pick up the advertising circulars that the mailman had left. There was no litter can in the hallway, so he ended up bringing them into the apartment, tossing them on the coffee table because there was nowhere else to put them.

Honking outside distracted him for a few seconds. Sam frowned, remembering the deep hush of the snowy woods he'd left. He was going to have to get used to urban racket again.

He almost slipped on several menus that had been shoved under his door. The NO MENUS sign on the outer door only made the guys who distributed them more ingenious. Sam set down his gym bag. The sublet seemed more cramped than before.

So where was Nicole? He hadn't gotten a call or a text message from her. Sam hung up his denim jacket by the door and bent down to scoop up the scattered menus

There was an unstamped envelope among them. Nicole had written his name on it with a flourish. Sam opened it and pulled out a card with a funny drawing she'd done of her spooky little cat.

Welcome back. So nice to see you on Theo's phone. Am crazy busy—ENJ wants to do a pop-up store in Soho. Call me when you get in, um, not before 11 pm. Will still be at work. Love, Nicole

Sam wondered what a pop-up store was and told himself he'd find out soon enough. Nice note. He liked the sign off. He looked at the clock. It was only seven. He could eat something, relax—the stress of the delayed flight was catching up with him.

He opened the fridge and averted his eyes from the takeout cartons, reaching for a cold beer behind them. Who knew what the leftovers had turned into while he'd been away.

Sam popped the cap and brought the bottle over to the coffee table, setting it down on a circular as he settled into the sofa, which seemed even smaller than before. He got sort of comfortable and reached out for the beer. The ad circular came with it, stuck to the cold, wet glass. He peeled it off, reading the message absently. WHITE SALE! DEEP DISCOUNTS ON ALL APPLIANCES! DON'T WAIT FOR JANUARY!

Hmm.

Maureen Fulton might have gotten the same one. But if the landlord didn't fix or replace her refrigerator, there was the unofficial Friends of the Fultons Committee, which Sam had just founded that very second. He finished the beer and appointed himself chairman, treasurer, and fund-raiser.

He knew exactly where he could pass the hat to buy the family a new one. The gang at the lot would be happy to chip in, and he'd prime the pump with a solid half of the purchase price. But it would be a good idea to go up to the Fultons and borrow a cup of sugar, see if he could measure the space the busted fridge fit into.

Douglas took off his jacket and hung it on the door-knob of their apartment. Then he went down the hall and knocked on Julie's door, handing her Puff's leash when she opened it.

"We had a good walk," he said. Unclipped, the white dog ran to her water bowl and drank thirstily.

"Come on in," Julie said. "Amanda's here. Your mother's talking to the super, so she sent your sister over to look at my Christmas tree. Look who decided to take a nap."

Douglas glanced toward his sister, who was dozing under an afghan, then went to the tree, looking at the ornaments and carefully touching a few. "We don't have ours up yet. Your tree is really nice."

"Thanks. I enjoy decorating it."

He went to the goldfish bowl on Julie's table and looked in. "Hey, fish. You look hungry."

"Herbert J. Schwimmer is always hungry." Julie had named the fish after a kid in her Sunday school.

"Can I feed him?"

"Go right ahead."

Douglas uncapped the fish food jar and sprinkled a little bit over the surface of the water. "Come and get it, Schwimmer."

Maureen was good and mad. But she controlled her temper. Losing it wasn't going to get her anywhere with Norm Krajek, who had showed up but didn't have a clue as to refrigerator repair.

"Isn't there anything you can do?"

Krajek lifted his shoulders in an apologetic shrug. "Ya could call the landlord."

"He won't buy a new one. You know that."

"Can't help ya, Mrs. Fulton."

"Well, then. Thank you for coming," she said stiffly.

"Sorry." Krajek turned to leave and had a hand on the doorknob when her voice stopped him.

"You forgot something." She handed him the can of wood putty and the screwdriver he'd left in the kitchenette.

"Oh. Thanks. Sorry again."

"What did the super want?" Doug asked as he came in.

"He came to look at the fridge. He doesn't think he'll be able to fix it by Christmas."

"What a pain."

"It's temporary. But I'll figure something out." She got busy stacking sample boxes to go into the cooler.

Douglas went into his room and came out with an envelope, casting a glance toward the living room, where a foot-high pink sparkly tree had been placed on the floor. Buster was propped against it.

"Amanda's tree looks nice."

"She's pretty happy with it," his mother replied absently.

Douglas handed her the envelope. "This is what I saved from walking Puff. Maybe we could get a real repairman to fix the fridge."

Maureen stopped what she was doing and looked gratefully at her son. "You, Douglas Fulton, are the best kid ever. But that's your money. You earned it, you keep it."

He watched her work for a while, talking with her about other things. When she turned her back, he went into his room and closed the door. She heard the racket of a video game. The envelope was on the kitchen table. His mother knew he hadn't forgotten it.

There was a knock at the door. Maureen went quickly to it, thinking that Krajek had come back for something else he'd left. She flung it open and saw Sam standing on the doormat holding a measuring cup.

"You're back! So nice to see you. How was the flight?"

"Not a lot of fun. But never mind that. I wanted to know if I, uh, could I borrow a half cup of sugar?"

The idea that this brawny guy had decided to do some Christmas baking—or so she assumed—made her smile.

"Sure. I have some right here on the shelf."

Sam followed her as far as the kitchenette. He eyed her refrigerator. "And a couple of eggs."

"I have a dozen in the—"

"Great," he interrupted her, "I'll get 'em." He opened the fridge and leaned in while he looked over his shoulder at her, sticking his arm in and fumbling around.

"They're not in there." She laughed. She couldn't help it. He just looked so awkward when he straightened. "The fridge is kaput."

"Oh." Sam seemed a little embarrassed. "Stupid of me. The light was on."

"It's the motor or the compressor or something. We're keeping perishables in a cooler on the fire escape. I'll go get the eggs."

"Thanks so much," he said. "Sorry to bother you."

Sam waited until she was lifting the window to slide his arm along the outer side of the refrigerator. He'd already guessed at the interior depth when he'd reached for eggs he knew weren't in it. He stood in front of the dinged white-enamel door, noticing the dull chrome trim and the outdated brand.

The refrigerator was small. The top was level with his nose. He stretched his arm out by the front. Okay. He had an approximate height, inner and outer depth, and the width.

Maureen came back with an egg carton, looking at him a little curiously. Sam covered by grabbing the box of sugar and pouring some into his cup.

"Only two eggs?" she asked, opening the carton.

"That's all I need," he assured her.

"Would you like a box of sample cakes? I've been taking them around to the big stores and gourmet businesses—maybe Doug told you."

"He didn't, no. But I'd love some cakes." He took two eggs from the carton and placed them carefully on top of the sugar in the measuring cup.

Maureen handed him one of the small boxes of samples, and he balanced that on the rim of the cup, holding a hand over the box to keep it from falling off.

"Thanks so much."

"Let me get the door for you. Be careful going down those stairs."

"I will." He grinned at her and said good-bye.

Maureen closed the door with a soft click and shook her head, smiling to herself. For a minute there, it had looked to her like Sam was hugging the busted refrigerator. But he must have only been leaning on it for some reason. She had caught a faint whiff of beer.

But that was his business, not hers. She had a lot of other things to think about.

When Sam got back to his sublet, he had to do some juggling to get the key in the lock. He got in without cracking the eggs and set the cup with them in his refrigerator.

He was hungry. Scrambled eggs with a side of cake sounded pretty good.

An hour later, Nicole called. He'd dozed off.

"Hey. Nice to hear your voice."

"Did I wake you up?"

"Sort of. But I don't care. How are you? I can't wait to see you."

"I could come over right now. The job's done," she said proudly. "The Diamond Moon windows were the biggest draw ever. Finn told me the week-to-date numbers took a huge jump. They're way over even their super-stretch goal."

Sam didn't ask for an explanation of the jargon. He got the idea from the happiness in her voice. "ENJ must love you."

Nicole laughed. "Even better, they pay in a day. This is the freelance gig of my dreams. They want me to work in January too, but I'm free for the rest of the year."

"That's great." He was genuinely happy for her. "Come on over. I need your help with something."

"Be there in thirty minutes."

Sam headed for the shower, wanting to wash away the trip tiredness, and shave. When he was done and dressed again, he heard a taxi pull up outside. The door slammed, and light footsteps came up the stoop.

He buzzed her in before Nicole touched the bell, and stood waiting at the open apartment door.

She pushed the inside door open and ran the last few

steps to him. Sam enfolded her in his arms and walked backward with her clinging to him, murmuring something that sounded like *hi* or *hello* or *how are you* into his clean shirt.

"Still wearing my jacket, huh?"

He heard a mumbled yes. She hung onto him.

He turned around and kicked the door shut. Then he said hello the way he really wanted to. His ardent kisses left Nicole in no doubt of how much he had missed her. Sam threw in some strokes and heated caresses for good measure. Her eyes were closed, and her head tilted back when he lifted his mouth from hers. He nibbled the side of her neck, paying particular attention to the sensitive cord, and finished up with a nip on the earlobe.

"Ooh," she whispered. "Do that again."

"My pleasure."

It was a while before the pleasure stopped. He took the initiative in that department too. Rushing things wasn't what he was all about.

Nicole stepped back when he eased her away from him. She gazed up at him dreamily. "So. Here you are. My Colorado man. I almost don't know what to say."

Sam needed to catch his breath. "Come on. Sit down."

He guided her to the sofa—three short steps—and she sat down in the same corner she'd taken the night he'd cooked steak for her.

"So what was it you needed help with?" she asked, running her fingers through the long, dark hair he'd messed up.

Sam forced himself not to look at her. He found the ad circular and explained about Maureen.

"Let's do it. Playing Santa will be a blast."

Sam chuckled in agreement. "You two know each other by now, right?"

"Yes. I know the whole family. We met at the lot. I went there a few times while you were gone."

"Did you ever get a tree?" he asked.

"No. I really don't have room for one this year with all my art stuff and starting the new project. Unless I put it on the bed-slash-love seat," she laughed.

"Just wondering. Anyway, here's the plan I came up with."

He gave her the basics and they fine-tuned it together. Then they got back to kissing.

Chapter 15

The next day dawned cloudy with a raw wind from the east. Sam could have sworn he smelled snow. But there wasn't so much as a flake.

Douglas's school had gone to half days before Christmas, and he'd persuaded his mother to let him tag around after their downstairs neighbor. They were sitting with Greg in a coffee shop near the lot. Theo had come in to say hi and gone back to the lot, then headed home with his wife, Effie, who'd dropped off the same cousin as yesterday.

Douglas was still working on a plate of hash browns with sausage. The grown guys had eaten their lunch and were finishing their coffee. Greg slapped a hand over the check when a busy waiter dropped it off.

"On me next time," Sam growled.

"Maybe."

Douglas had his mouth full, but he seemed to be listening to the exchange, as if he was studying up on male ritual chest-pounding.

Sam winked at Greg. "I got the kid for the afternoon. Giving his mother a break."

"Right. Is Nicole coming over? Thought you said something like that."

"In a bit. She's going to take Maureen and Amanda to see the best windows of the season. They'll be gone all afternoon."

"That should work."

Douglas looked up from his clean plate, puzzled. "What should work?"

"You'll see." Sam slid to the side. Greg put a twenty and a ten under the saltshaker with the check, and the three left together.

They waited at the corner for the light to change. Out of the corner of his eye, Sam saw a vehicle racing through the yellow. "Watch it, guys!" He pulled Douglas back from the curb in time.

The vehicle—a truck—pulled over half a block down. Douglas stared at it. There was a Christmas tree mounted to the top of the cab.

"Those guys again," Greg said with contempt.

Sam looked hard. The truck was gray, heaped with bagged trees. A folding sign had been stuck next to them. He could only read one word. *FRESHEST.*

There was a trail of dry needles in the street by the curb. It could be the same truck that had clipped the stand and thrown a scare into Theo.

"Sam." Douglas tugged at his sleeve, pointing to the tree tied to the truck's cab. "I think that's my tree. It has the same crooked branch. Look."

Sam exchanged a look with Greg. "Someone bought the Douglas fir that Theo set aside for Doug. I forgot to tell you."

"They must have ripped off the SOLD tag," Douglas insisted to Greg. "Can we go look?"

"If they bought it, it's theirs." Sam tried to reason with him.

Whoever was behind the wheel had rolled down the

window and lit up a cigarette. A grubby hand dangled out the driver's side, holding it.

Sam frowned, trying to think of what to do, looking around. He didn't notice Douglas slip away until the boy was almost at the truck.

Sam took off after him, followed by Greg. When the two men caught up to him, Douglas had clambered onto the side of the truck's cab. They dragged him off.

The rocking got the driver's attention. Sam and Greg had a grip on Douglas, but the man at the wheel got out and came around. The cigarette seemed to be stuck to his lip.

He was the same creep who'd tried to buy Doug's tree from Sam. His eyes narrowed when he saw who was waiting for him. But he brazened it out.

"What the hell's goin' on?" the man asked in a nasty drawl.

"Nothing," Sam said.

"That's my tree on top of his truck," Douglas muttered. "I can see part of the tag where he tore it off."

"It ain't your tree, kid. I bought it. I got the receipt. You crazy? Scram." He took several deep drags and tossed the smoldering butt in the gutter.

"Don't talk to him like that," Sam said. "He's a kid. He made a mistake."

The man cursed and spat. "Get outta here. All of you."

Douglas looked up at the tree again. Sam did too. That time he saw a scrap of red attached to a torn tag. The boy could be right, but that wasn't a good enough reason to start a fight over it.

Greg kept quiet, but Sam could see the anger in his eyes. Douglas stepped forward. "I'll buy it from you," he said to the man.

"Nah. You can't afford a nice tree like that, you little punk."

Sam could smell the hard liquor that was making the creep so bold. Was he so drunk that he didn't realize Sam and Greg could take him?

The man stared at him with cloudy eyes. "You deaf? I said get outta here!"

He lifted his grubby hand, for what reason Sam didn't know, but Sam caught his wrist. Douglas went for the truck again, and Greg collared him.

"What seems to be the problem here?" A cop had pulled up. "Greg? Care to explain?"

"I'll talk to him," Greg said to Sam. "You stay put," he told Doug.

Wide-eyed, staring at the officer on the beat, Douglas obeyed. Sam put an arm around his shoulders. He could feel the boy shaking, but Doug didn't say a word.

Greg leaned into the window of the cop car. The tree seller edged back toward his truck, but a loud command from the cop car stopped him in his tracks.

"Hold it right there."

The officer got out and came over to him. "Do you have a permit to sell on the street?"

"Ah. It's in the toolbox or somewheres like that. Maybe my partner has it."

"Is he in the truck?"

"No."

"Stay there." The officer moved to the driver's side and looked cautiously in the window. He opened the door and removed the keys from the ignition, taking a longer look around the interior of the cab. Then he slammed the door shut and came back around.

"Can I see your license and registration? Use the other door to get the registration."

The man complied, pulling out a beat-up wallet and handing over a license. Then he got the registration out of the glove compartment, his movements jerky, obviously nervous.

The officer stepped back with the license and registration in hand to read the plates, calling them in. The treeseller slumped against the side of the truck. As if he knew what was about to happen, he put his hands on his head.

A response came in over the cop's two-way. "Over and out."

Sam and Greg and Doug watched silently as the officer went back to the man. "I didn't do nothing," he pleaded.

"Your license is expired. The plates are stolen. Your registration is bogus. And you don't have a permit."

The officer reached out and pinched off a handful of needles. "I love that piney smell," he said thoughtfully. Then he crumbled the dry needles with his fingertips and let the fragments blow away. "These aren't fresh," he said. "About the only thing I can't get you on is deceptive advertising. Want to tell me about those outstanding warrants for your arrest?"

The man wouldn't look at him. "I ain't talking to you no more. I got rights."

"Yes, you do." The officer went over them carefully. A second cop car pulled up, top lights flashing. People were beginning to stop and stare.

Douglas stuck close to Sam. "Can we go?" he asked worriedly.

"Not yet. The officer might want to talk to us."

The cop overheard. "In a minute," he said to Greg. "The backup's here." Two more officers got out and started inspecting the truck.

"One more thing," the cop said to the man. "That tree on top is a safety hazard."

"It's nailed to a stand and roped. It comes down real easy."

"That would be my point. Take it off. And give it back to the kid."

The creep found himself surrounded by three of New York's finest. "Can I take my hands off my head?"

"Yeah. Nice and slow."

He undid a couple of knots and dragged the tree off the truck, slamming it down on the sidewalk.

"You guys can go," the first officer told them. "Take that with you. Greg, stop by the precinct later."

"Not a problem." Greg picked up the tree by the crooked branch on the top and set it down in front of Douglas.

The boy was speechless. Sam bent down and hoisted the tree by its trunk, putting it over his shoulder. The stand it had been nailed to would help to keep it there. "Let's go."

"Move along, folks. Nothing to see here," one of the cops said to the scattered crowd. "Move along."

Sam, Greg, and Douglas did too.

"Your mother is going to hear the explanation from us, not you," Sam said to Douglas, who was scurrying to keep up with his long strides.

"She never knew about the tree, though! Can I bring it home now?"

"Later for that," Greg said. "Here comes Nicole."

They were almost in front of the Fultons' building. She saw the tree over Sam's shoulder and walked more quickly. "Who's that for?"

"It's mine!" Douglas said, jumping around. Sam stilled him with a look. "I mean, it's for my mom. It's a surprise. Sam and Greg are going to help me bring it upstairs."

Nicole looked at Sam.

"I'll explain later," he said. "Listen, do you think you could bring Douglas with you?"

She nodded and half kneeled to talk to Douglas, fixing his collar.

"Hey, I was just thinking that it would be a big help if you came with your mom and me to look at Christmas windows, Doug. Getting the stroller on and off the bus is a hassle."

Sam had an idea. "We can keep the tree in my place in the meantime."

The boy wavered. "All right."

Nicole took his hand. "C'mon, let's go get your mom."

Douglas went with her willingly. Greg and Sam waited on the sidewalk outside until they thought it was safe to rush the tree in.

"Where do you want it?" Greg asked, looking around.

"Let's put it on the coffee table."

The spreading branches nearly filled the room.

They waited inside the apartment until they heard the clatter of the stroller and the excited voices of Maureen's two children and her conversation with Nicole.

Sam held up a key when he was sure they were gone. Julie had been told of the surprise and given Sam her key to the Fultons' apartment. "Back to Plan A."

"As in appliance store. They deliver?"

"Of course. They take away the old one too."

The gleaming new refrigerator was eased into the space and leveled by a couple of giants from the Bronx.

One plugged it in and fiddled with a dial inside, then turned to Sam. "It hasta cycle. Tell da lady to give it twenny-four hours to get really cold."

"She probably knows that, but I'll tell her," he said.

"Appreciate the fast delivery, guys." Greg handed each giant a twenty for a tip. "This is for you. And you."

"Hey, t'anks."

"Have a happy hawliday, youse guys. Dat's a nice fridge. Ya got a good deal."

They stuffed the money into their pockets and got busy with the hand truck, strapping the old refrigerator to it and maneuvering it through the apartment door. In another few minutes, Sam looked out the window to watch them load it into the delivery truck. He saw no sign of the two women. Good.

He looked around the apartment for wrapping paper and ribbon. There was a flat pack of folded paper, the kind to wrap little things in, on a side table in the living room, but there was a fat roll of red ribbon next to it. He started to unroll the ribbon, going back to the kitchen.

"You know how to make a fancy bow?" he asked Greg. "No."

Sam cut off a couple of feet with the scissors he found in a drawer and tied it around the refrigerator handle. "Good enough. Now let's go get the tree."

Julie came over and found the tree skirt and a holder at the back of the front closet.

"How long have you known Maureen?" Sam asked as they set up the tree.

"Oh, gosh—since she moved here with Hank, I guess." Julie didn't add anything to that.

Greg was studying the tree. Sam had placed the pink sparkle tree next to it.

"It looks kinda plain," Greg said. "Maybe we should add some decorations."

Julie shook her head. "I know where they are, but I think we should let Maureen and the kids do that."

"Yeah. You're right."

There was a faint commotion from inside the building.

Julie went out and peered down the stairwell, then ran back.

"They're here," she said excitedly. "Hide, guys! Dibs on the closet."

She was small enough to squeeze into it. Sam and Greg stood behind different doors.

The chattering group came up the stairs and barged through the door once Maureen unlocked it.

She saw the tree first. "What—where did that come from?"

"Surprise!" Douglas crowed.

Amanda ran to her pink tree and moved it closer to the big one. "They can be friends!"

Nicole was right behind Maureen, who whirled around and spotted the new refrigerator.

"Oh! But who—"

Sam, Julie, and Greg jumped out. "Surprise! Merry Christmas! It's from all of us and Theo!"

Maureen gasped. Then she started to bawl.

"Don't cry, Mom," Douglas said. "You'll scare Amanda."

Maureen found a chair and sat down with her hand over her mouth. Her son stood next to her and patted her shoulder until she was calmer.

"Thank you," she whispered. "Thank you all."

"Is it okay if we have two trees? I guess I should have asked," Douglas said.

"Yes. Yes, of course. I think we should make that a tradition." She got up. "What am I thinking? I must have a bottle of champagne somewhere. But—it's not cold."

Julie held up the one she'd brought. "This is. Get out the glasses. Chocolate milk for you guys," she said to the children.

Douglas grinned. "There's some in the cooler."

*   *   *

Maureen watched her kids putting some of the ornaments on the big tree. She'd set the fragile ones aside to put on later, just her and Doug, when Amanda went to sleep.

She went through her purse, looking for a pen to write a thank-you note. Her cell phone lit up. She'd missed a call. There was a voice mail message.

She pressed the key to retrieve it and listened.

"Maureen. This is Jon Thomas, from Nash & Thomas. I understand you met Fred Nash. He insisted that I taste your samples, and I have to say I was very impressed."

Her eyes widened.

"So, ah, I was wondering if you would have time to meet with me in January. I'd like to work up some spreadsheets, cost out the recipes, things like that. Get you started, in other words. Let me know."

He gave her the number. She jotted it down.

"That's all. Happy holidays, and stay warm."

Jon Thomas's voice was doing just that. Maureen was flabbergasted. She pressed another key to save his message so she could listen to it again. And again.

He sounded younger than his partner. But not too young. He sounded serious but *nice*. She wondered what he looked like and realized she could probably find that out online.

After both kids were asleep, though.

Maureen snapped out of it. She quickly returned the call. It went to voice mail, but that was to be expected. It was after working hours.

"Hello, Jon. This is Maureen. I got your message. Thanks so much. I'm so glad you like the samples." She hesitated. "I have others you haven't tasted, but they'll keep until January. I just got a new, ah, refrigeration system. Anyway, I'd be happy to come in. Thanks again for your call."

* * *

Chuckling, Sam set the last of several heavy grocery bags on Nicole's counter. "Do we have everything?"

"Sam, there's going to be a blizzard. I like to be prepared."

"It can't shut down the city."

"Oh, yes, it can. Last year was awful. We had three blizzards in a row, and the first one was on Christmas Eve."

Sam unpacked some of the cans, peering at the label on a flat one. "Kippers? What are kippers?"

"They're very high in protein," she said absently, easing a sack of cat chow into a large tin.

"That still doesn't tell me what they are," he laughed. "And we're not at the North Pole, and we don't have to feed sled dogs."

"Oh, hush. You're in my way."

Sam left her to it, mentally adding a bit to the advice he'd given Alex. Never help a woman pack. Or unpack.

He walked over to the cat tower. Whiskeroo was hiding in the carpeted chamber.

"Don't be scared," Sam said, in a friendly, don't-scratch-my-eyes-out voice. "Aren't you looking forward to Christmas?"

A weird feline howl came from inside.

"Guess not."

Sam headed for the sofa and looked at the newspapers Nicole had brought home. The *New York Times* was playing it safe with HEAVY SNOW MAY SET RECORDS THROUGHOUT MUCH OF THE NORTHEAST, over a photo from last year of a stuck bus. The *Daily News* got to the point: HUGE BLIZZARD TARGETS NYC. The *Post* said it all with one giant word in white over black. **WHAMMO!**

The so-called huge storm wasn't here yet.

"Think I'll go out and do a little more shopping," he called.

"Are you crazy?"

Sam got up and put his arms around her. Nicole fought hard for two whole seconds. Then she melted into him. The kiss was the best yet.

"No, I'm not crazy," he finally replied. "I'm from Colorado, that's all, and I don't get all excited about snowstorms. Although I am looking forward to putting a snowball down your back."

Nicole was flushed and smiling. "If you have to go, then go now."

"If you insist." He reached for his jacket and put on his Stetson. Nicole threw the apartment keys at him. "See you."

Sam ran down the stairs, eager to be outside. The air was heavy with cold, with a hint of electricity. He did smell snow. There were a few flakes whirling around.

Just in case, he decided to take a taxi. The present he'd picked out for Nicole was waiting and gift-wrapped. He hadn't trusted her not to peek, and she wouldn't have any trouble guessing what might be inside.

Sam whistled and a yellow cab appeared. He got in and told the driver where to go. "This is going to be a round-trip with two stops," he told the driver.

There weren't that many people on the streets, but some determined shoppers were still out. They pulled over at an address on 57th Street that offered exactly what Sam wanted. He'd figured out the size from things she already owned.

Sam strode in, waving to the salesman. "Thanks for holding this for me," he said.

"I was thinking of closing," the man replied. "It's going to be a big storm."

He gestured toward a small television on the counter.

Sam paid for the wrapped gift, not really listening to the weather hype. "Thanks again."

The salesman let him out, then started turning off the store lights. The snow was falling, and it wasn't just a few flakes.

Sam paused before he got into the taxi. The city lights made every flake sparkle, and the tops of the tall buildings were beginning to disappear.

"Go back a couple more blocks," he said. "Fifty-Seventh and Fifth."

The driver got him there.

Sam had made this purchase in advance too. He dashed through the doors and headed for the distinguished elderly man who'd helped him select Nicole's other present.

"Do you need to look at it again, sir? We are closing early."

"I trust you."

The elderly man put a pale blue box with a hand-tied white silk bow into a matching shopping bag and handed it to Sam. He felt a little silly carrying such a dainty thing, and tucked it into his jacket.

He skidded on the sidewalk on his way to the waiting taxi. The wipers were whooshing the snow away with some difficulty.

"That's it. Back to where I started, please."

The cab stopped in front of Nicole's building. Sam paid the fare and added a fat tip, then got out. He stomped through several inches of snow that had accumulated on the stoop but paused to look up at the vast, silent snow-storm that had descended on the city.

The old neighborhood looked like a fantasyland, iced with deep snow. Christmas lights shone blurrily through apartment windows here and there. There was no one in sight.

Sam let himself into Nicole's apartment and put the big box down.

"Glad you're back," she said.

"You could be right about the storm," he admitted, taking off his Stetson.

"What's in the big box?"

"Wouldn't you like to know. Wait until Christmas."

Nicole took his hat and brushed off the snow in the kitchen sink. He slipped the shopping bag out of his jacket and put it on a high shelf when she wasn't looking. She turned around to take his jacket when he shrugged out of it, brushing it over the bathtub and hanging it up on the rod.

Sam went to the window. He heard a sound he knew: the raging wind was driving the snow hard. "Damn. I can't see the buildings across the street."

"Told you."

"This could be fun."

Nicole shrugged. "You know, I just realized we could use another dozen eggs. Could you run out?"

Sam shook his head. "Think I'm going to stay right here, if that's okay with you."

Nicole came to look out the window, and he moved her in front of him, putting his arms around her waist and dropping a kiss on her hair.

"Beautiful, isn't it?" she said in a soft voice.

"It is. You are too," he whispered.

The street was plowed out by the following night, Christmas Eve. Nicole had restrained herself from peeking in the big box and she hadn't found the small shopping bag— he'd moved that from the shelf to a better hiding place.

Sam was the restless one.

"Quit moving that box around," she told him.

"Just trying to find the right place for it."

"Put it under that." She gestured toward the huge paper tree she'd cut out and hung on the wall. There hadn't been room for a real one from the lot, not with sketches for future projects taking up every inch of available space. The paper tree was adorned with photos of everything they'd done in New York pinned to it and some from Colorado that his sister Annie had e-mailed.

"All right. If you insist."

"Sam. Do you want me to open it now?"

He grinned at her. "Yeah. Something to do. I guess I have cabin fever. Or do they call it apartment fever in New York?"

Nicole sailed by him and picked up the box, shaking it. There was a soft sort of noise from inside. "It's lighter than I thought," she said.

"You mean you never touched it?"

"Nope."

"Go ahead and open it. I can't stand the suspense."

She made him wait. "Nice paper. I could use this for something." She peeled it off carefully, looking at the shop logo on the box. "That's not a store I know." She opened it and parted the tissue paper.

"A Stetson!" Nicole put it on her head, laughing with joy. "I love it! How did you know my size?"

"You have other hats," he said.

She tipped the brim back and got up to kiss him.

"You looked so damn cute in mine, I had to get you one that fit. You can wear it when you come visit me in Colorado."

"Yes! When exactly?"

Her arms were around him. She nuzzled the side of his neck. It took him a little while to answer.

"Ah—after New Year's. And by the way, we are going to whoop it up in Times Square, right?"

"Absolutely. My first time."

"How about that," Sam started to say. He was interrupted by a flurry of kisses from Nicole that took his breath away.

"Whew. Wow. Okay," he said. "While I'm on a roll . . . I do have another present for you."

Nicole was still giddy. She didn't take off the hat. "Okay." Her eyes were brighter than he'd ever seen them.

Sam brought out the little shopping bag, but he covered the logo with his hand. "I hope you don't mind. It's kind of small."

"Don't be silly."

He pulled out the pale blue box with the white ribbon. Nicole drew in a breath.

Sam went down on one knee before he handed her the box. "I know it's too soon. This is just my way of saying, um, thank you for the best damn Christmas a man ever had, and, um, I love you, and we can probably figure out the rest in about a year."

She squeaked.

"Here. You have to undo the bow," he said.

She did.

The velvet box opened without a sound. A pretty little marquise diamond on a plain band shone forth, nestled in white silk.

Nicole gasped. Sam took the ring out of the box and slipped it on her left hand. "Looks good. What do you think?"

She threw her arms around him. Sam stood up without letting her go. He whirled her around. "Be mine, city girl. What do you say?"

"Yes!"